POKÉMON™

ORIGAMI

FOLD YOUR OWN ALOLA REGION POKÉMON

PIKACHU PRESS™

Publisher: Heather Dalgleish
Art Director: Chris Franc
Design Manager: Kevin Lalli
Cover Designer & Background Illustrator: Mike Cressy
Editor: Wolfgang Baur
Merchandise Development Manager: Eoin Sanders
Merchandise Development: Valérie Bourdon
Project Manager: Emily Luty

IVY PRESS
Origami Designers: Janessa Munt (Pikachu, Rowlet, Litten, Popplio, Mimikyu, Togedemaru, Alolan Exeggutor, and Rotom Dex) and Wensdy Whitehead (Pikipek and Alolan Vulpix)
Text and step illustrations: David Mitchell
Design: JC Lanaway
Photographer: Neal Grundy
Art Director: James Lawrence
Editorial Director: Tom Kitch

The Pokémon Company INTERNATIONAL

PUBLISHED BY
The Pokémon Company International
10400 NE 4th Street, Suite 2800
Bellevue, WA 98004 USA

3rd Floor Building 10, Chiswick Park,
566 Chiswick High Road
London, W4 5XS United Kingdom

Visit us on the web at www.pokemon.com

PRODUCED BY
Ivy Press
An imprint of The Quarto Group
The Old Brewery, 6 Blundell Street
London N7 9BH, United Kingdom
T (0)20 7700 6700 F (0)20 7700 8066
www.QuartoKnows.com

ISBN: 978-1-604-38197-9

Printed in Dongguan, China
First printing, September 2017.

17 18 19 20 21 6 5 4 3 2 1

How this book works

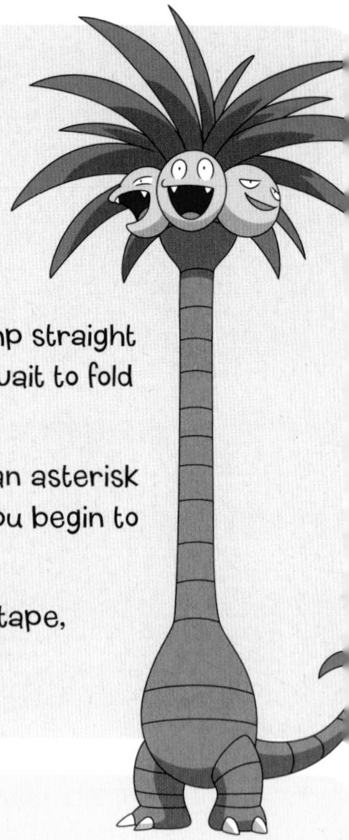

The paper templates you should use to fold the characters are on pages 49 to 80. Because this is a book for ordinary people, not Origami Masters with five hands and extra long fingers, the designs have been kept as simple as possible by sometimes using two or more sheets of paper.

The easiest characters to fold are the projects at the beginning of the book. You can jump straight into folding Alolan Exeggutor, if you want, but it might be better to first fold Rowlet and wait to fold Alolan Exeggutor until you have gained some experience and skill.

Each project tells you which template you should use to make the character. There is an asterisk on the back of each template that tells you which way up the paper should be when you begin to fold. Then it's just a matter of following the folding instructions.

Occasionally, you will need to make cuts or use tape or glue when you see the scissor, tape, or glue symbols (see Key to Symbols below)

How to understand the folding instructions

Origami folding instructions show you in illustrations, and tell you in words, how to fold the paper, step by step, to create your Pokémon characters. Here's how it works:

Let's begin with a simple sequence of three steps and written explanations that show you how to make just one simple fold.

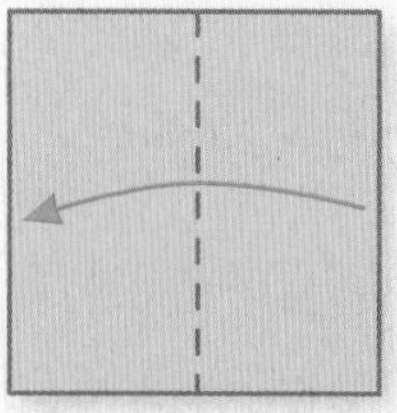

1 Fold in half sideways.

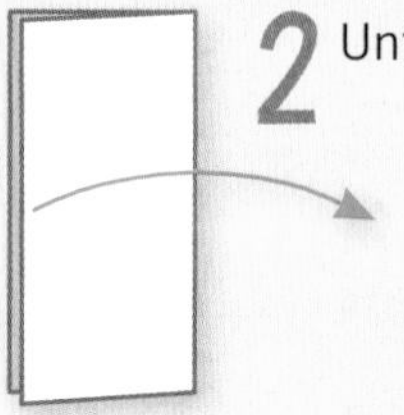

2 Unfold.

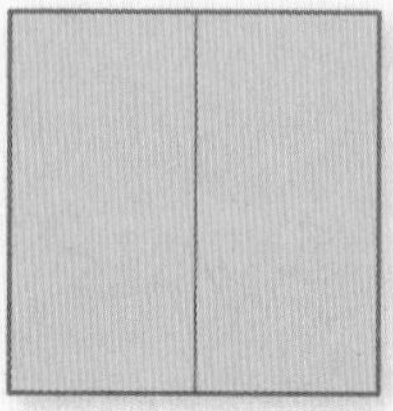

3 Finished.

Here are the things you need to know to follow the origami diagrams:

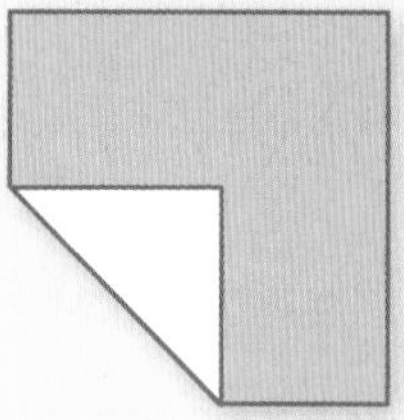

The edges of the paper are shown as solid lines. The front of the paper is shown shaded and the back of the paper is shown white. It's important to check before and after every fold that your paper looks the same as the illustrations.

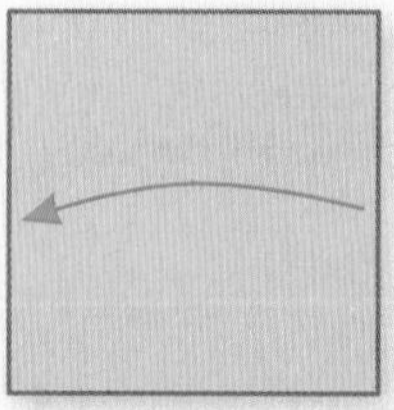

Step 1 is a folding instruction made up of two parts: a movement arrow and a fold line. The movement arrow tells you which part of the paper moves, which direction it moves in, and where it ends up. In this case, the movement arrow tells you to pick up the right edge of the paper and fold it across to the left in front until it lies on top of the left edge. The two edges of the paper are the location points for this fold, that is, the points (usually edges, corners, or creases) that you use to help you make the fold accurately.

Key to symbols

This push arrow symbol tells you that you need to turn a corner or a point inside out.

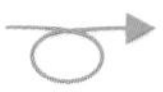
This symbol tells you to turn the paper over, usually sideways.

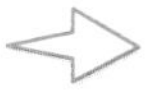
This symbol tells you that the next diagram has been drawn on a larger scale.

A circle is used to highlight particular areas mentioned in the instruction.

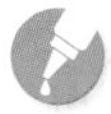
You will need to use glue where you see this symbol.

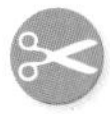
You will need to use scissors where you see this symbol.

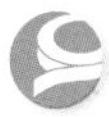
You will need to use adhesive tape where you see this symbol.

When you have made a fold, you will need to flatten it to make a crease. The fold line shows you where this crease will form. It's always a good idea to flatten the paper completely, press it down firmly with the soft part of a finger, then run a nail along the edge to make your crease really sharp. Once you have flattened a fold to create a sharp crease, you will have created a line of permanent weakness in the paper.

Step 2 shows you what the result of making the first fold will look like. Sometimes edges that lie exactly on top of each other as the result of a fold are shown slightly offset on the "after" diagram so that you can see they are there. Sometimes this isn't necessary and only the front edge is shown. Try not to let this confuse you.

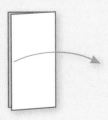

Sometimes a movement arrow is used without a fold line to mean open out using the crease you have already made. Every illustration in a folding sequence (apart from the first and the last) is both an "after" picture for the step before and a "before" picture for the step after. So step 2 shows you the result of following the folding instruction in step 1, but also gives you another instruction that leads to step 3.

In the third illustration, the crease you made in step 1 is shown as a thin line. The trick to following folding instructions is to always look one step ahead so that you know what the result of making a fold should look like before you begin to make it.

Here are a few more things you need to know about the folding instructions and how they work.

This version of the movement arrow means fold, crease firmly, then unfold. This illustration is a combination of instructions 1 and 2 and is a kind of shorthand used to save space in the book.

A dashed and dotted fold line with a dotted movement arrow means that the fold should be made away from you behind the paper. So this folding instruction means fold the right edge backward behind the paper onto the back of the left edge, then flatten to a crease.

An illustration of this kind tells you to swivel the white triangular flap to the back by reversing the direction of the existing crease. The crease acts like a hinge when you do this.

Sometimes the two different types of fold line are used together to show you how a combination of creases made in different directions through the paper (some backward, some forward) can be used to collapse the paper into a different shape.

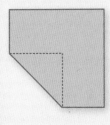

Dotted lines are also occasionally used to show hidden edges or fold lines, imaginary lines that are used to help locate a fold or lines to cut along. Sometimes they are also used to show where the paper will end up after you have made a fold. This illustration shows what the result of following the folding instruction above would look like.

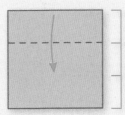

This type of symbol shows that the edge of the paper should be imagined as divided into a number of equal sections to help you locate a fold. In this case, you would fold the top edge downward to make a crease one-third of the way down the paper. It is normally OK for this division to be approximate instead of accurate.

Pikachu

Pikachu is small but tough-and doesn't give up! Give Pikachu your all when folding this popular Pokémon, and you'll see a familiar face come together with lightning speed.

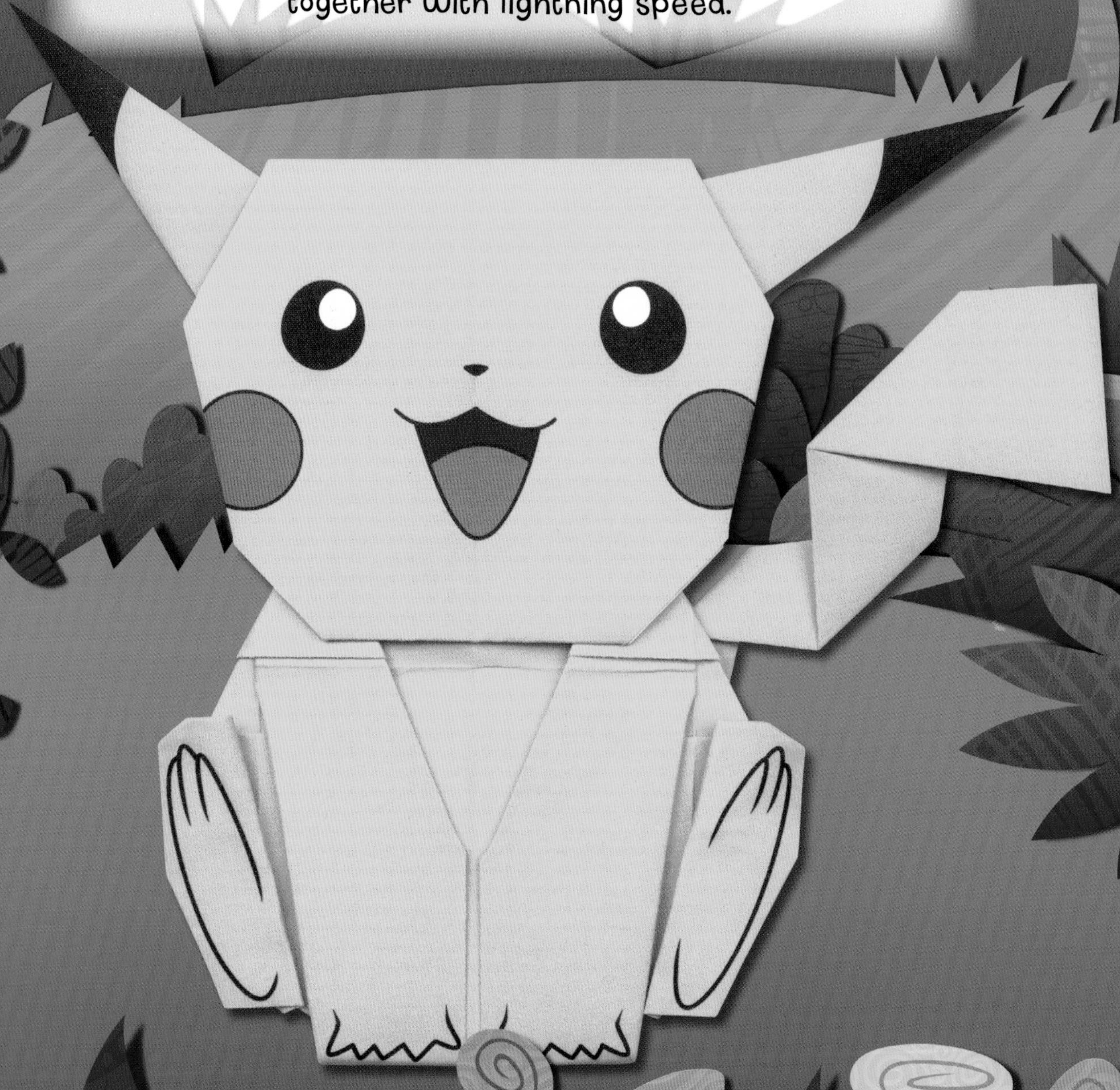

TYPE: Electric **HEIGHT:** 1'04"/0.4 m **WEIGHT:** 13.2 lbs./6.0 kg

How To Make
Pikachu

Pikachu is folded from four pieces of paper: one large square, one small square, and two small triangles. The large square becomes his body while the small square and the two triangles become his face, ears, and tail. You can find the templates on pages 49 and 51. Cut out all the pieces carefully.

Folding the body

Make sure you start folding with the large square template arranged so that the asterisk is at the top.

1 Fold in half sideways, then unfold.

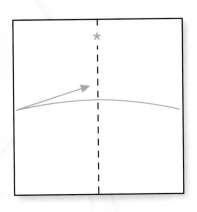

2 Fold the left and right edges into the center.

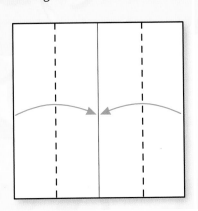

3 Fold the top edge down to lie along the two small black lines printed on the template.

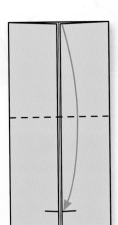

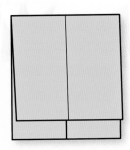

4 Turn over sideways.

5 Fold the right and left edges into the center.

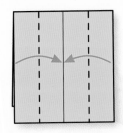

6 Open out the front layers and squeeze the top of each flap, symmetrically, to look like step 7.

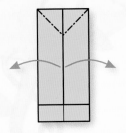

7 Turn over sideways.

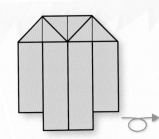

8 Fold the bottom edge of the front layer up to the top, then unfold.

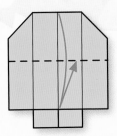

9 Turn over sideways.

10 Fold the front layers out using the existing creases.

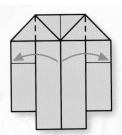

11 Fold both the top left and right corners of the front layer diagonally toward the middle, making sure that the creases start from the points marked with circles and that the result looks like step 12.

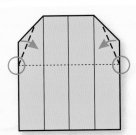

12 Fold both the right and left edges of the front layers in, using the existing creases.

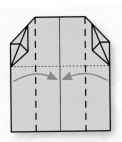

13 Fold the bottom edge of the front layers up, finishing as shown in step 14.

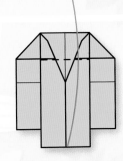

14 Fold the new bottom edge up to butt against the bottom edge of the front layers, then unfold.

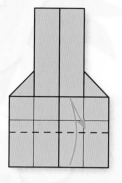

15 Fold the bottom edge up using the crease made in step 8.

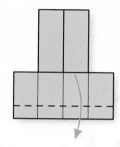

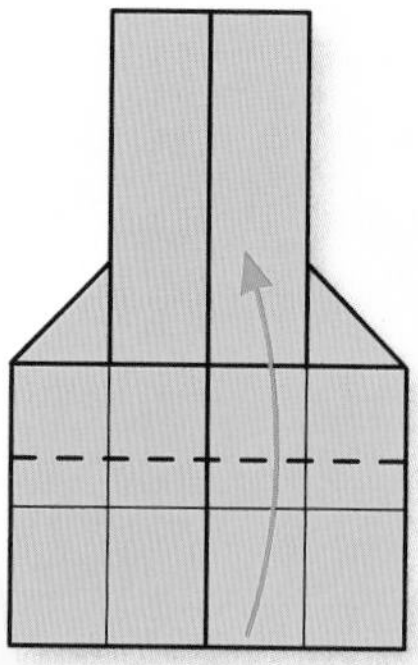

16 Fold the top edge of the front layers down using the second crease made in step 14.

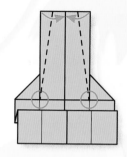

17 Fold both top corners into the center, making sure that the bottom of your creases start from the points marked with circles.

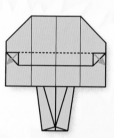

18 Fold the top edge down using the existing crease.

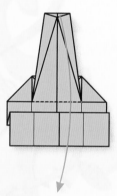

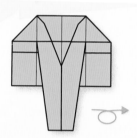

19 Turn over sideways.

20 Fold the bottom corners of the front layers diagonally in using the hidden edge of paper underneath (marked by a dotted line) as a guide to help you locate the folds.

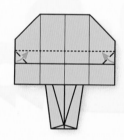

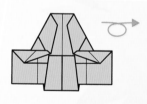

21 Open out the folds made in step 20.

22 Fold the sloping right edge in as shown and squash to look like step 23. The points marked with circles show you how to locate the fold. Repeat for the left side.

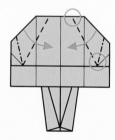

23 Fold the bottom edge up so that the new bottom edge is just below the level of the toes printed on the front.

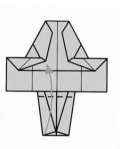

24 Turn over sideways.

25 Fold both outside edges in as shown, using the points marked with circles to locate the top of the folds. The new creases should lie parallel to the outside edges of the front layers.

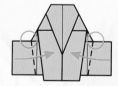

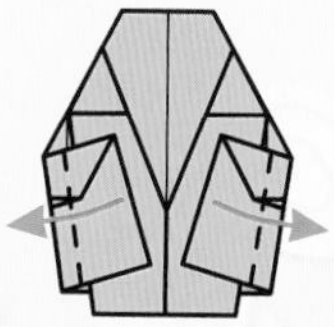

26 Fold the inside edges of the front layers out again to create the feet.

27 Turn over sideways.

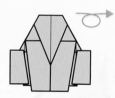

28 Fold both bottom corners of the middle layers (marked with circles) in as far as they will go to look like step 29.

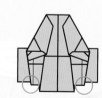

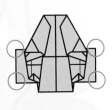

29 Make four tiny folds to round off the corners of the feet.

30 Turn over sideways.

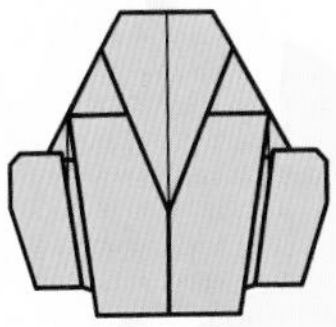

31 Pikachu's body and feet are finished.

Folding the face

Make sure you start folding with the small square template arranged so that the asterisk is at the top.

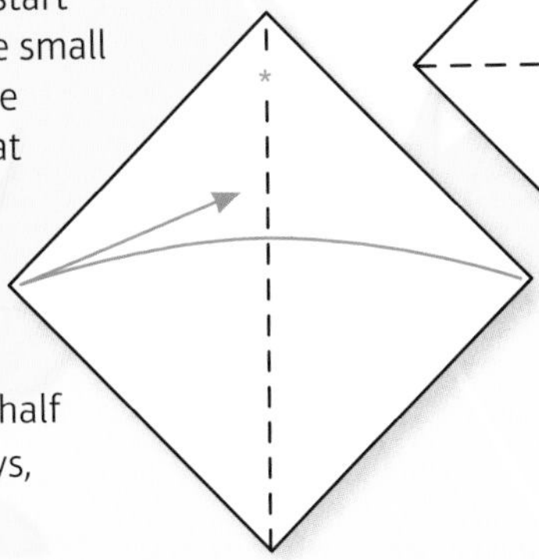

32 Fold in half sideways, then unfold.

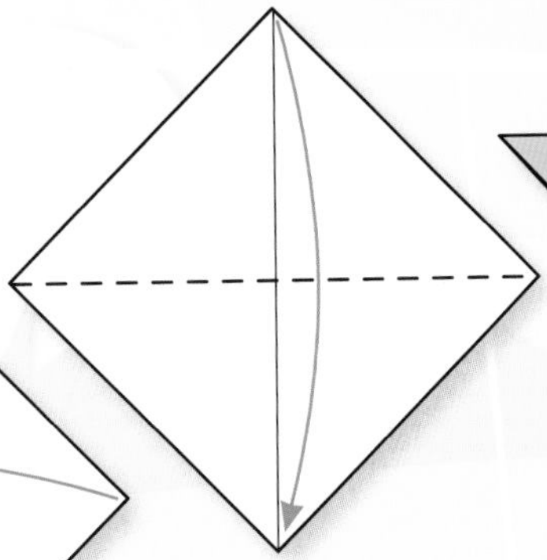

33 Fold in half down.

34 Fold the bottom corner of just the front layer up to the top, then unfold.

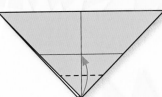

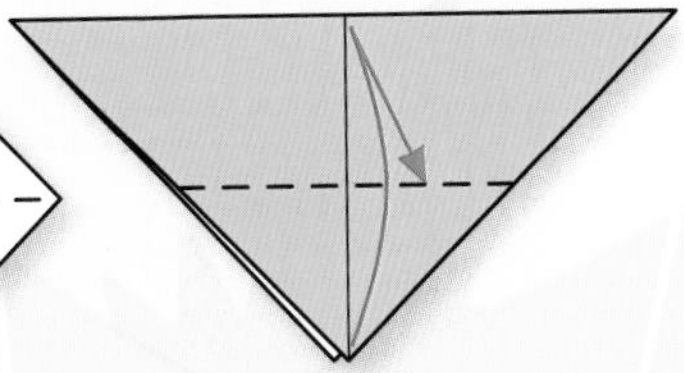

35 Fold the bottom corner of both layers up to the point where the creases intersect.

36 Fold both top corners in to the vertical crease just below the top corner of the front layer.

37 Fold both the left and right corners in as shown, making sure you fold the same amount of paper in at the same angle on both sides.

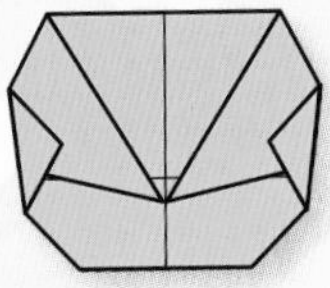

38 Turn over sideways.

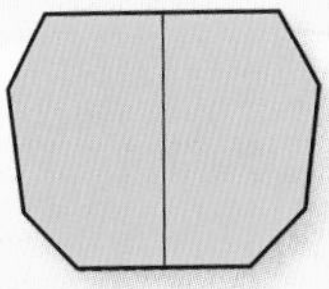

39 Pikachu's face is finished.

Folding the ears

Make sure you start folding with the correct triangular template arranged plain side up.

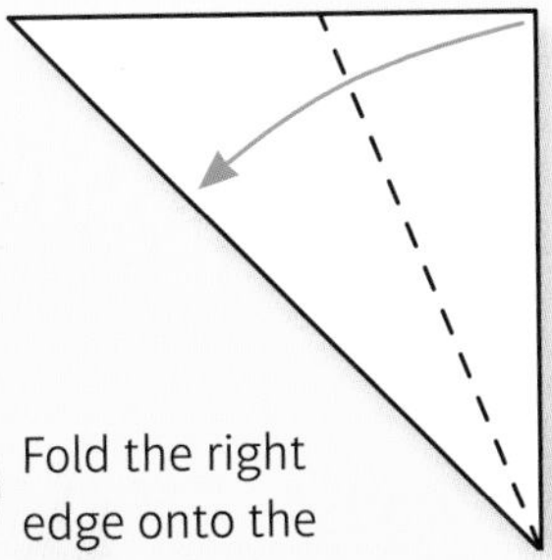

40 Fold the right edge onto the sloping left edge.

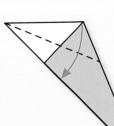

41 Fold the top edge onto the sloping left edge.

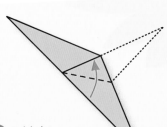

42 Fold the bottom half of the sloping left edge in to butt against the bottom edge of the front layers. The dotted line shows where the bottom point should end up.

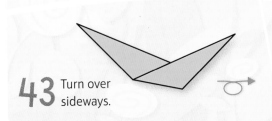

43 Turn over sideways.

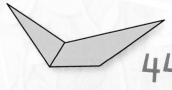

44 Pikachu's ears are finished.

Folding the tail

Make sure you start folding with the correct triangular template arranged plain side up.

45 Fold the sloping left top edge onto the bottom edge.

46 Fold the sloping top edge onto the bottom edge.

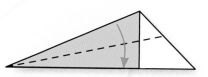

47 Fold the right point in and tuck it underneath the other layers.

48 Fold the left point up to the position marked by the dotted line.

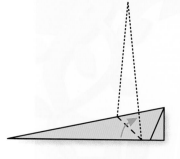

49 Fold the top point down to the position marked by the dotted line.

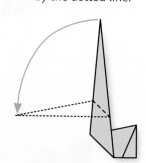

50 Fold the left point up to the position marked by the dotted line.

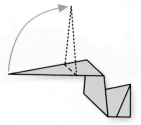

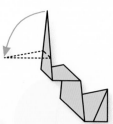

51 Fold the top point down to the position marked by the dotted line.

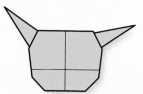

52 Pikachu's tail is finished.

Assembling Pikachu

53 Apply glue to the area shown shaded gray here on Pikachu's ears.

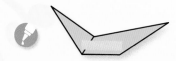

54 Put the face on top of the ears and press together in this position.

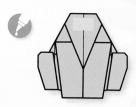

55 Apply glue to the area shown shaded gray here on Pikachu's body.

56 Put the face on top of the body and press together in this position. Wait until the glue has dried, then turn over sideways.

57 Attach the tail to the body with a small piece of adhesive tape as shown. Turn over sideways again.

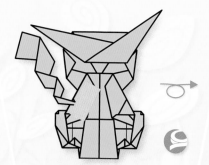

58 Pikachu is finished.

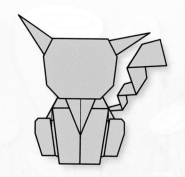

8

Rowlet

Rowlet likes to rest in the sun during the day and sneak up on foes at night. Give this one a flurry of folds, and get Rowlet ready for action.

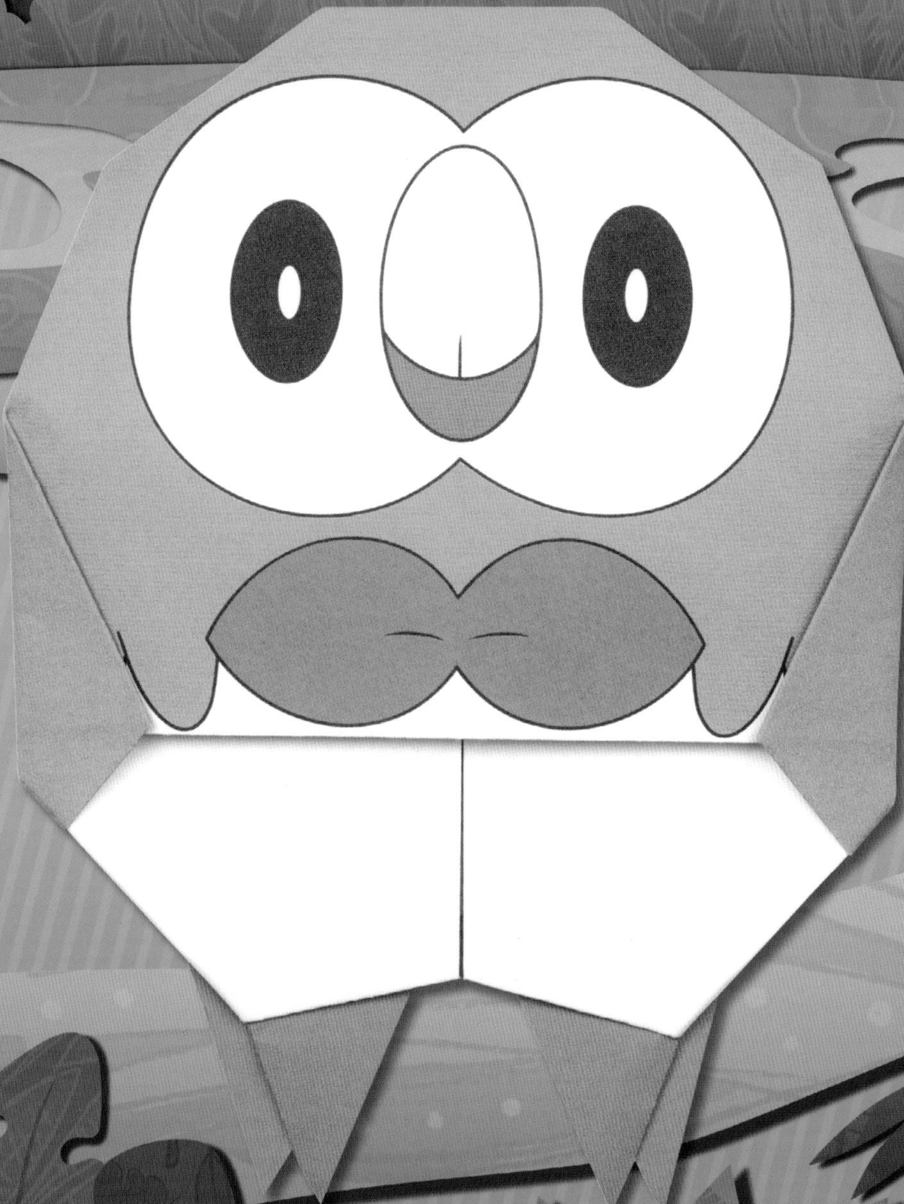

TYPE: Grass-Flying **HEIGHT:** 1'00"/0.3 m **WEIGHT:** 3.3 lbs./1.5 kg

How To Make
Rowlet

Rowlet is folded from a single square of paper. You can find the template on page 53. Cut the template out carefully.

Folding Rowlet

Make sure you start folding with the template arranged so that the asterisk is at the top.

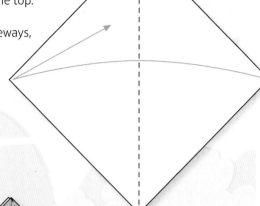

1 Fold in half sideways, then unfold.

2 Fold in half up.

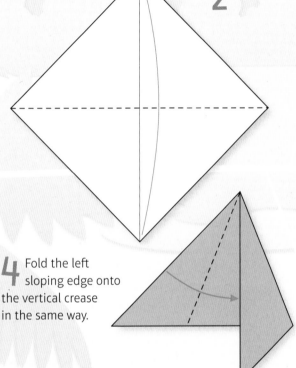

3 Fold the right sloping edge onto the vertical crease.

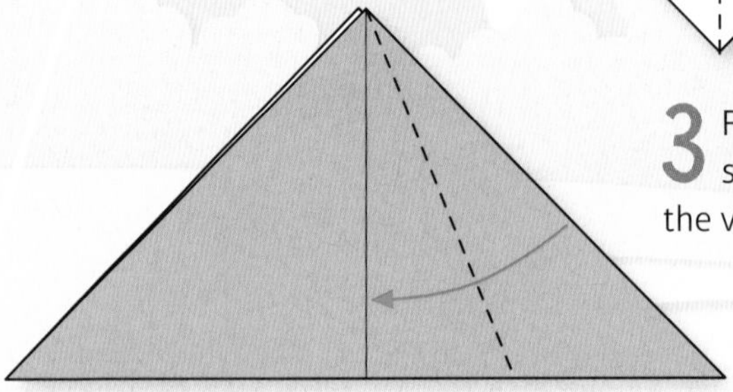

4 Fold the left sloping edge onto the vertical crease in the same way.

5 The dotted line marks the hidden edge of the back layers. You can see where this edge is if you hold the paper up to the light. Fold the top corner down to the center of this hidden edge.

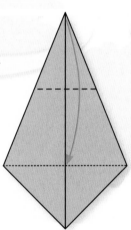

6 Fold both top corners in as shown. Try to make the folds look as much like step 7 as possible.

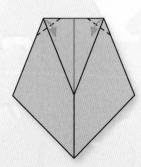

7 Fold both the bottom points up along the white lines so that the inside edges of the new front flaps are parallel to the existing edges just above them.

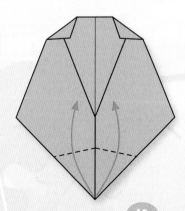

8 Fold both new front flaps down along the edge of the orange feet, again making sure that the folds are made parallel to the hidden edge of paper just above them, which is marked here with a dashed line.

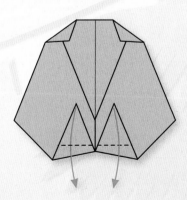

9 Turn over sideways.

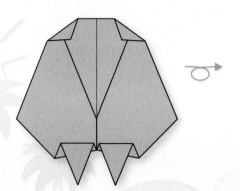

10 Fold both the right and left corners in so the edges are between the feathers on Rowlet's chest and the points rest on the fold line.

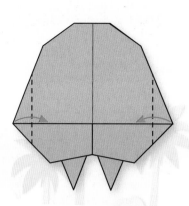

11 Turn over sideways again.

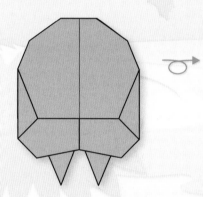

12 Fold both the outside bottom corners diagonally in as shown.

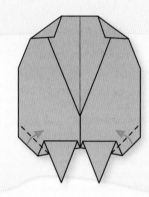

13 Open up the inside edge of the bottom right point and slide the tip of a small pair of scissors in between the layers. Make two small cuts along the top and bottom right edges. The thick black lines show the length the cuts should be.

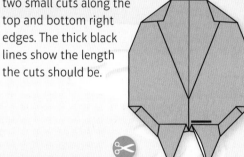

14 Part of the front layer has been released by these cuts. Fold it across to the right as shown.

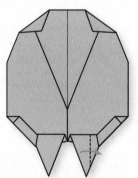

15 Check that the corner of the new front layer does not protrude beyond the layers beneath it. Repeat steps 13 and 14 on the bottom left point in exactly the same way.

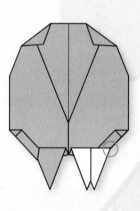

16 Turn over sideways.

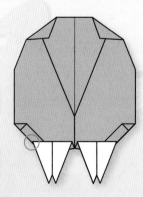

17 Rowlet is finished.

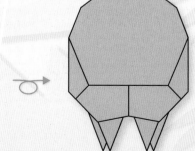

Togedemaru

Togedemaru has it all: round shape, fluffy fur, and electric Pokémon powers, so Trainers love it. How do you fold an origami so neatly round? Let's find out!

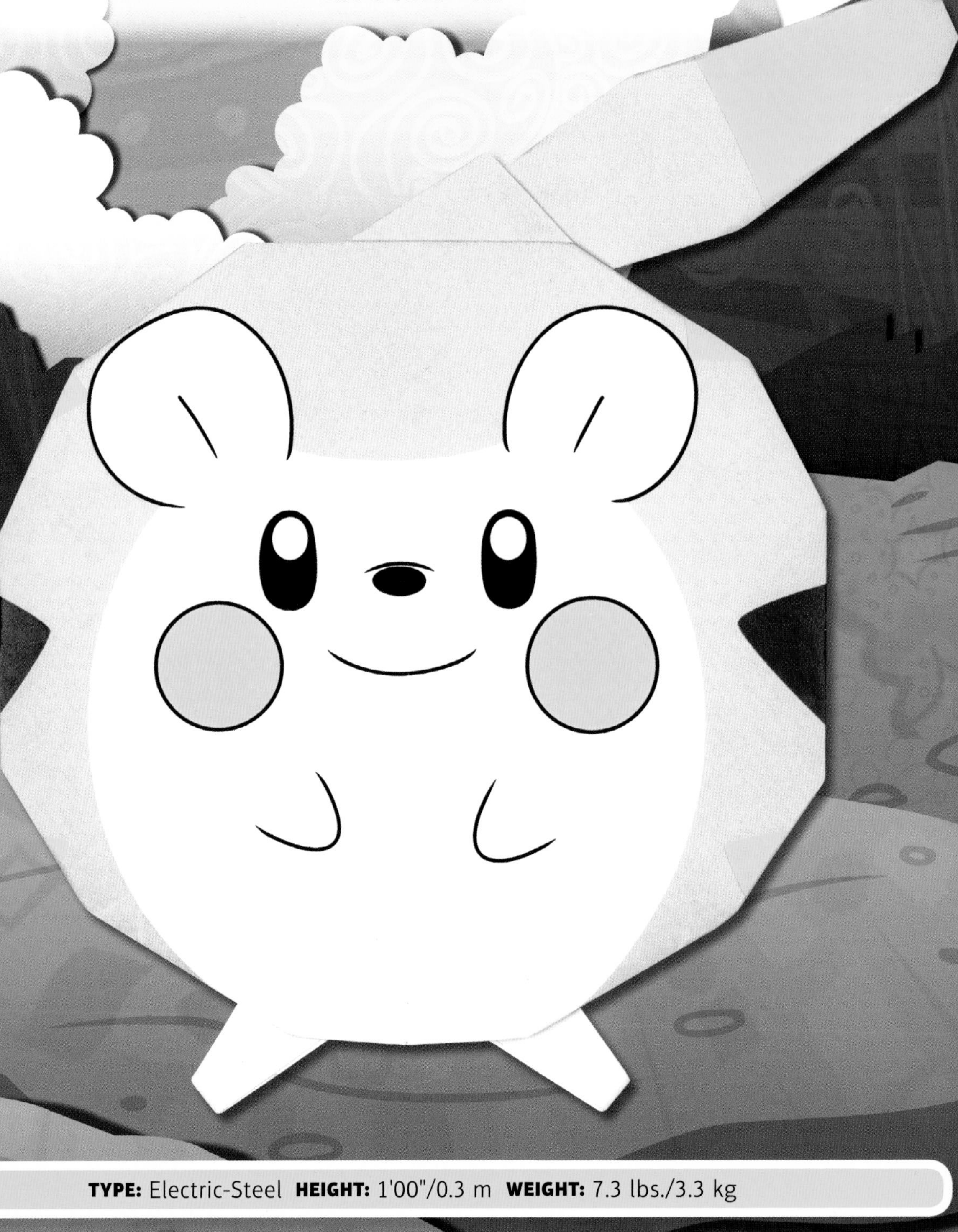

TYPE: Electric-Steel **HEIGHT:** 1'00"/0.3 m **WEIGHT:** 7.3 lbs./3.3 kg

How To Make Togedemaru

Togedemaru is folded from two pieces of paper: one large square, which becomes the body, and a small rectangle which becomes the antenna. You can find the templates on pages 55 and 77. Cut out all the pieces carefully.

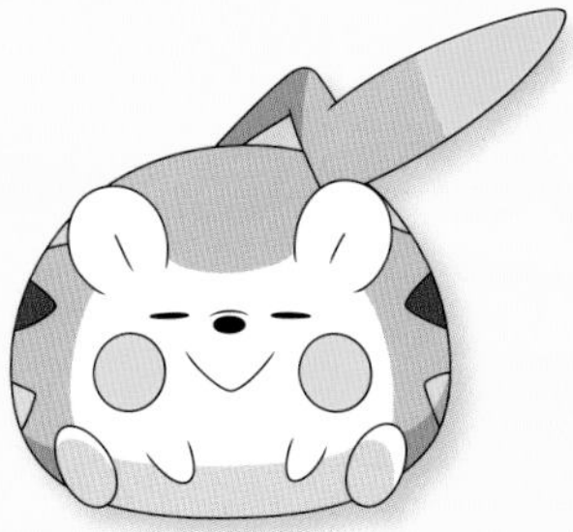

Folding the body

Make sure you start folding with the large square template arranged so that the asterisk is at the top.

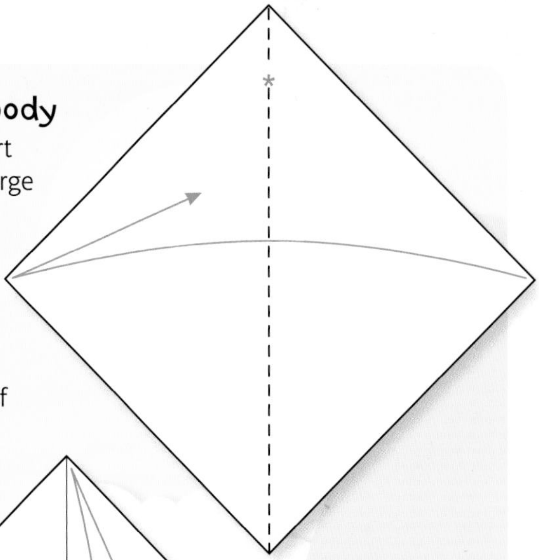

1 Fold in half sideways, then unfold.

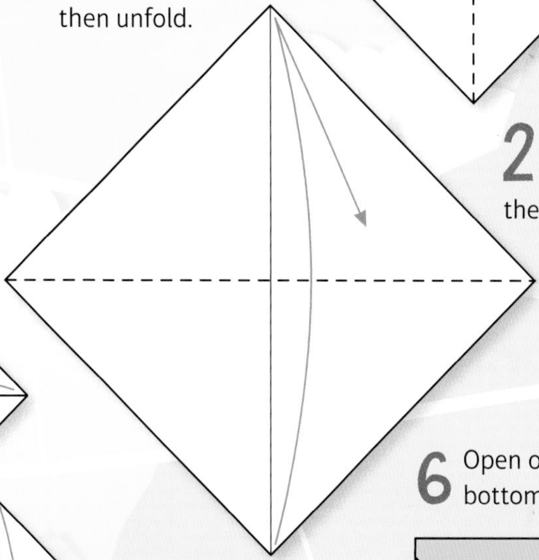

2 Fold in half down, then unfold.

3 Fold both the right and left corners into the center.

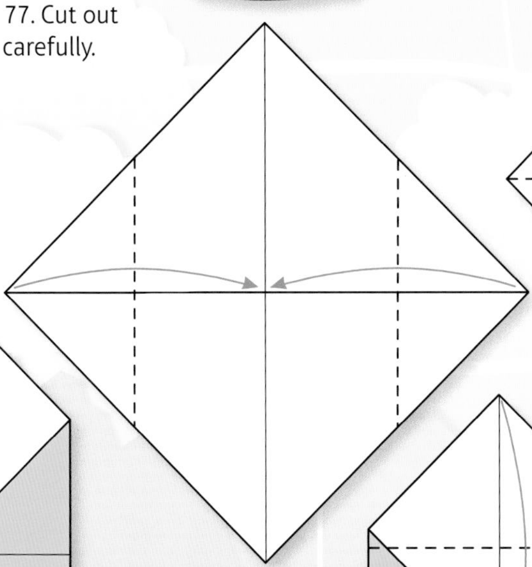

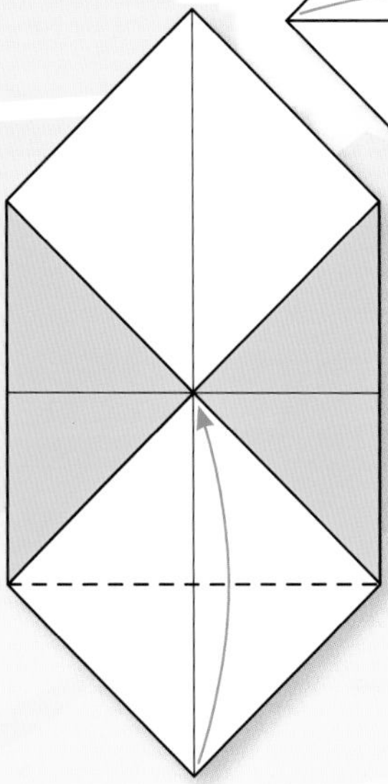

4 Fold the bottom corner to the center as well.

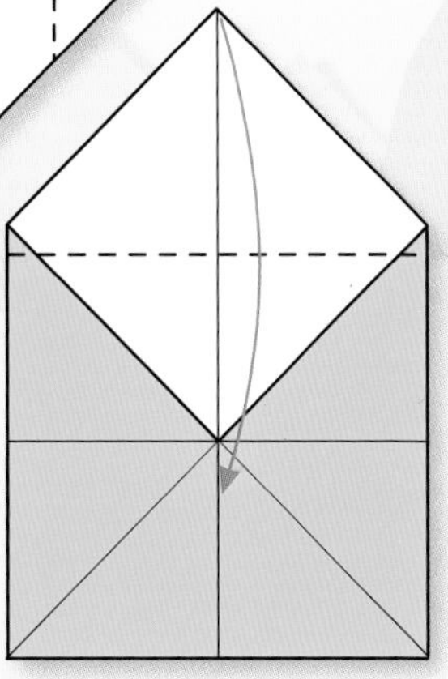

5 Fold the top corner down along the white line so that it ends just below the center of the paper.

6 Open out the bottom flap.

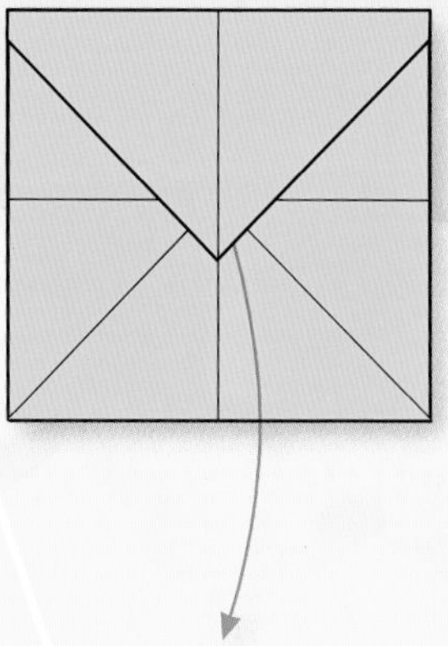

7 Cut along the crease marked with the thick black line, then fold the right-hand half of the bottom flap up using the existing crease.

8 Fold the new front flap in half diagonally as shown.

9 Fold both layers of the bottom front flap in half diagonally down as shown, then unfold.

10 Turn the top point of the front flap inside out in between the other layers by reversing the direction of the crease you made in step 9.

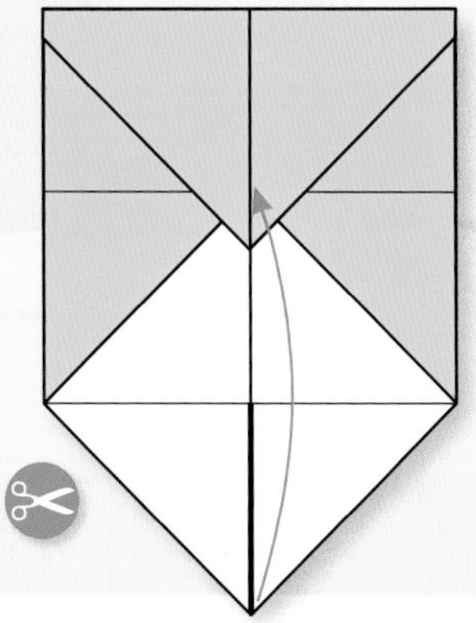

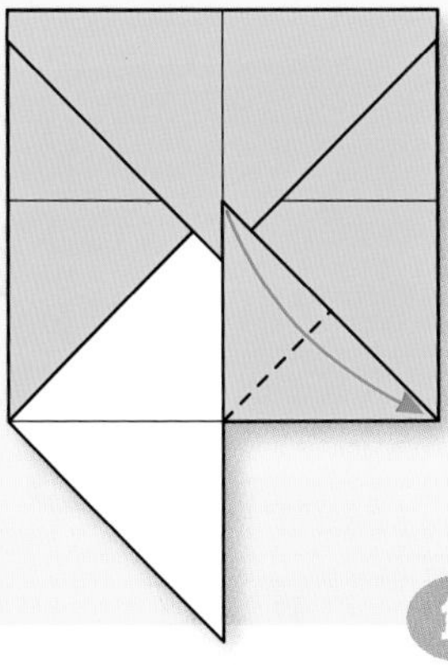

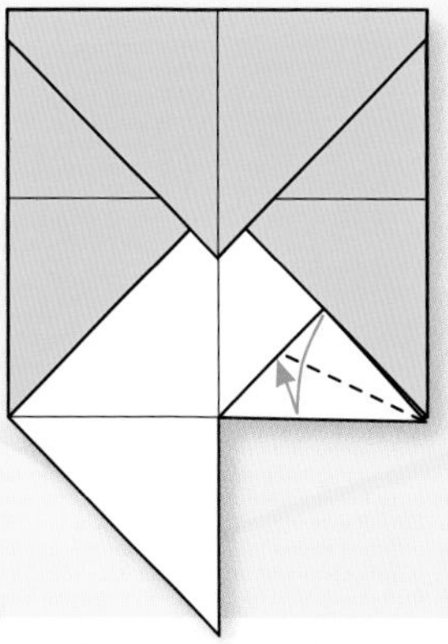

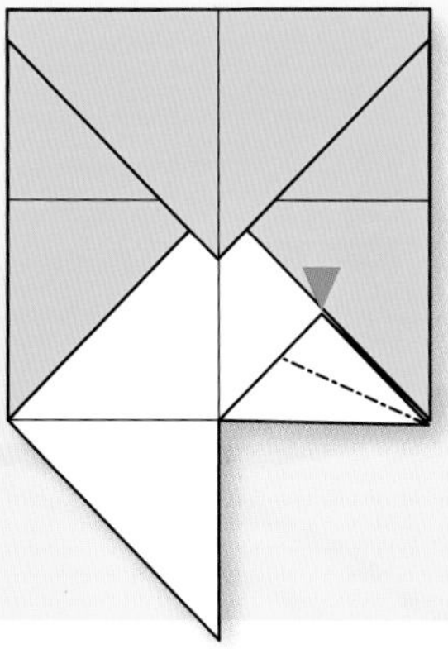

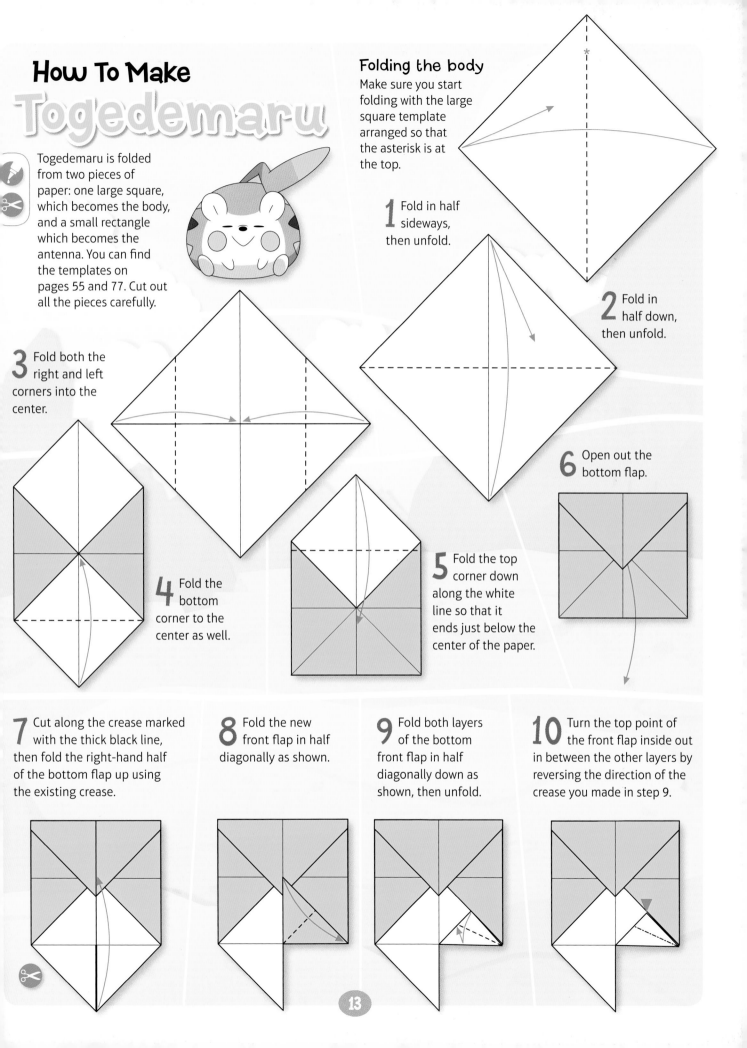

11 Fold the new front flap across to the left, along the dashed line as shown.

12 Fold the right edge in as shown to align with the center crease of the front flap. Make sure the top and bottom edges of the moving part of the paper line up with the edges under them after the fold has been made.

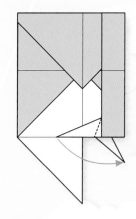

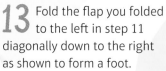

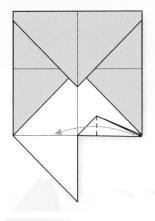

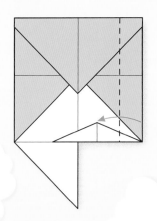

13 Fold the flap you folded to the left in step 11 diagonally down to the right as shown to form a foot.

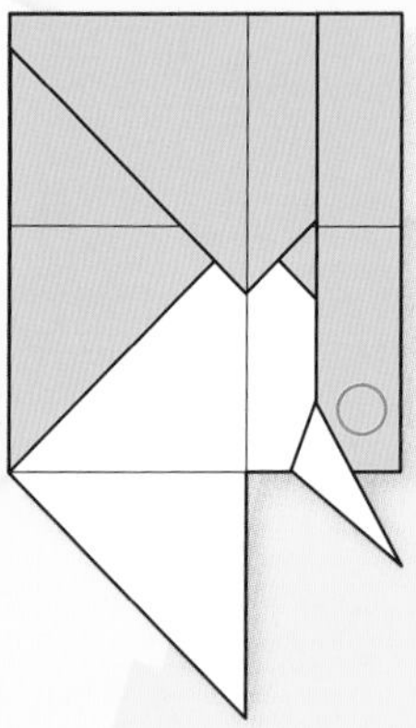

14 Bring the flap marked with a circle to the front.

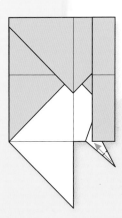

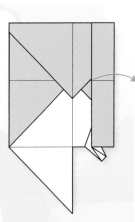

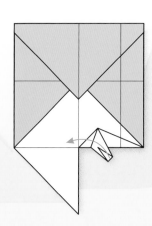

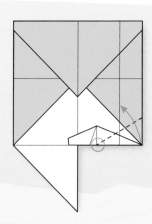

15 Fold the tip of the foot in so that it touches the corner of the front layer.

16 Open out the front flap.

17 Fold the leg across to the left using the existing crease.

18 Fold the bottom right corner onto the crease made in step 12, making sure the crease starts from the point marked with a circle.

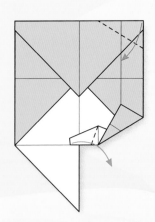

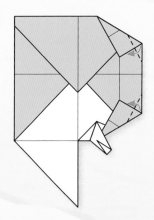

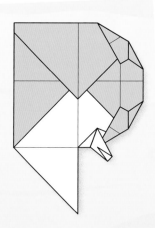

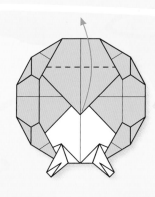

19 Fold the top right corner in a similar way. Also return the foot to its previous position.

20 Make these two small folds to round off the edges of the body.

21 Repeat steps 7 through 20 on the left-hand half of the paper, matching the right side.

22 Fold the bottom point of the center flap up, and tuck it underneath the front layers as far as it will go.

23 This is what the result should look like. Unfold the top corner folds made in steps 19 and 20.

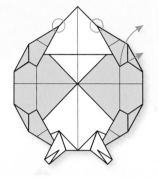

24 Fold the top corner diagonally down so that it lies on the hidden edge of paper marked with a dotted line. Your new crease should begin from the point marked with a circle.

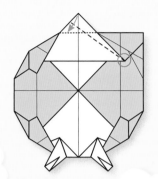

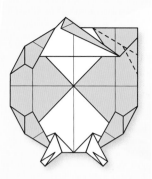

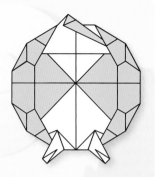

25 Remake the folds you previously made in steps 20 and 21.

26 Togedemaru's body is finished.

Folding the antenna

Arrange the template so that the asterisk is at the bottom.

27 Fold the top right corner in. The top of the crease should be at the top edge about one-third of the way to the left. The bottom of the crease should start at the bottom right corner.

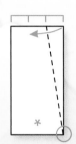

28 Fold the top left corner in a similar way.

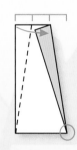

29 Open out the folds made in steps 27 and 28.

30 Fold the bottom corners in the same way as you did the top corners.

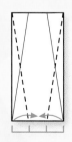

31 Fold the top corners in again using the existing creases.

32 Make two tiny folds to round off the top corners.

33 Turn over sideways.

34 The antenna is finished. Apply glue to the area shaded blue, then turn over and attach to the body as shown in step 35.

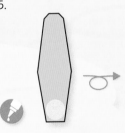

Assembling Togedemaru

35 Attach the antenna to the body in this position. Turn over sideways.

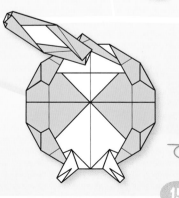

36 Togedemaru is finished.

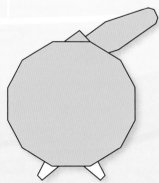

Popplio

Popplio has that wonderful way of blowing water balloons from its nose, and it works hard and practices every day to control them. Give your folding a good workout, and you'll be rewarded with a beautiful, playful Popplio origami.

TYPE: Water **HEIGHT:** 1'04"/0.4 m **WEIGHT:** 16.5 lbs./7.5 kg

How To Make
Popplio

Popplio is folded from two pieces of paper. The larger piece becomes the head and body while the smaller piece becomes the ears. You can find the templates on page 57. Cut out both pieces carefully.

Folding the head and body

Make sure you start folding with the template arranged so that the asterisk is at the top. Start with the colored side face up.

1 Fold in half from top to bottom, then unfold.

2 Fold the top edge onto the crease made in step 1, then unfold.

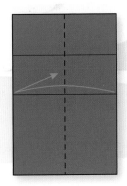

3 Fold in half sideways, then unfold.

4 Turn over sideways.

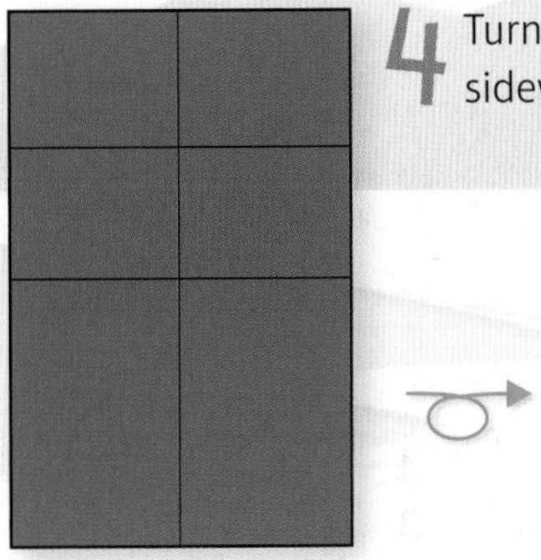

5 Fold both the right and left edges onto the vertical center crease.

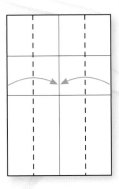

6 Fold both bottom corners in as shown.

7 Fold the bottom point up as shown.

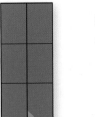

8 Open out all the folds completely without turning over.

9 Fold the bottom edge up using the crease you made in step 7.

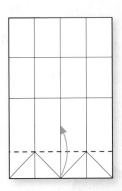

10 Make fold A followed by fold B using the existing creases, and then flatten the paper to look like step 11.

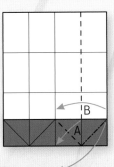

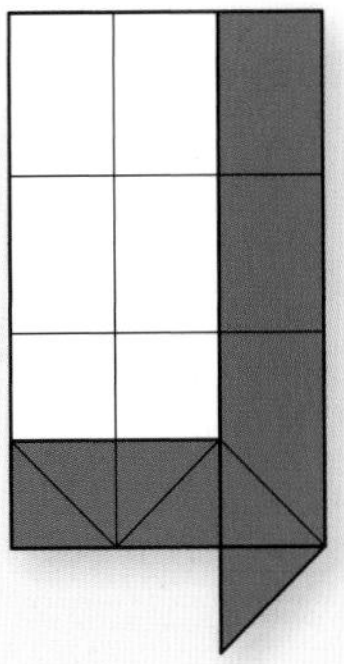

11 Repeat step 10 on the left half of the paper. The result should look like step 12.

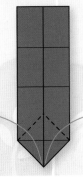

12 Fold both bottom points out as shown using the existing creases.

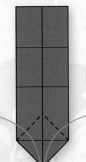

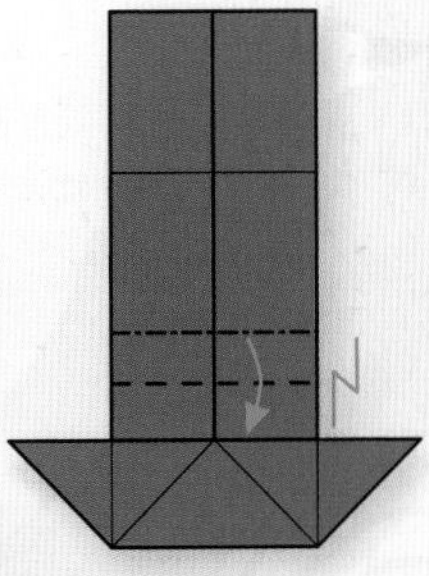

13 Make a zigzag pleat by folding the existing crease (marked by a dotted and dashed line) onto the top edge of the front layers.

14 Make a second zigzag pleat by folding the existing crease (marked by a dotted and dashed line) down so that it lies along the hidden edge of paper below it (marked by the dotted line).

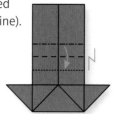

15 This is what the result should look like. The next step is drawn on a larger scale.

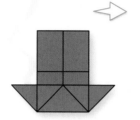

16 Fold the top edge of the right point onto the sloping crease to create the right leg.

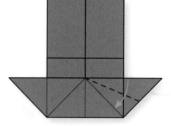

17 Fold the right leg diagonally down into its final position using the existing crease.

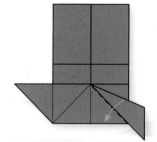

18 Fold the corner of the top zigzag pleat in as shown. The dotted line marks the hidden edge of the top of the zigzag pleat. You can use this to help you make this fold accurately.

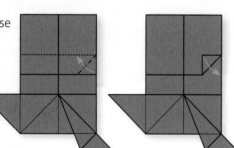

19 Unfold.

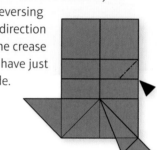

20 Turn the corner of the pleat inside out in between the other layers by reversing the direction of the crease you have just made.

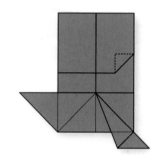

21 Repeat steps 16 through 20 on the left half of the paper.

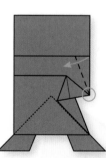

22 Your paper should now look like this. Turn over sideways.

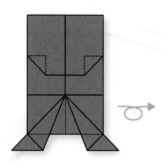

23 The dotted line marks the hidden edges of the legs. Fold the right edge of the bottom zigzag pleat onto the nearest of these hidden edges and squash the paper to look like step 24. This is a difficult move and you will probably need patience to get it right.

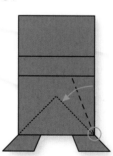

24 Now fold the top right corner of the top zigzag pleat in diagonally in a similar way and squash to look like step 25.

25 Fold the top right corner in diagonally as well. The dotted line shows you how to locate this fold.

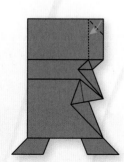

26 Repeat steps 23 through 25 on the left half of the paper.

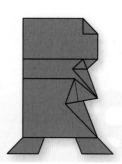

27 Cut two tiny slits in the bottom front edge in the positions marked by the thick black lines.

28 Fold the paper released by the cuts in diagonally to create the outline of Popplio's belly. Also make two tiny folds to blunt the points of the feet.

29 Popplio's head and body are finished.

Folding the ears
Make sure you start folding with the template arranged plain side up.

30 Fold in half down.

31 Fold in half sideways.

32 Fold just the front layer in half sideways.

33 Turn over sideways.

34 Fold just the front layer in half sideways.

35 Open out as shown.

36 Make a zigzag pleat as shown. Step 37 shows what the result should look like.

37 Fold both ends of the strip diagonally in to create the ears. The creases must begin at the points marked with circles. Adjust the angle of the folds so that the result looks like step 38.

38 Turn over sideways.

39 Make four tiny folds to round the corners of the ears so that the result looks like step 40.

40 Popplio's ears are finished.

Assembling Popplio

41 Place the ears in position so that there is no gap between the ear and the head at the left-hand side. Hold the ears firmly in place with your left hand at the point marked with a circle. There will now be a slight gap between the other ear and the head at the right-hand side. With your right hand, push the paper inward until this gap disappears, and flatten the ears in their new position.

42 Both ears should now touch the head as shown.

43 Remove the ears and apply glue to the area shown shaded in gray here.

44 Glue the ears onto the body. Turn over sideways.

45 Popplio is finished.

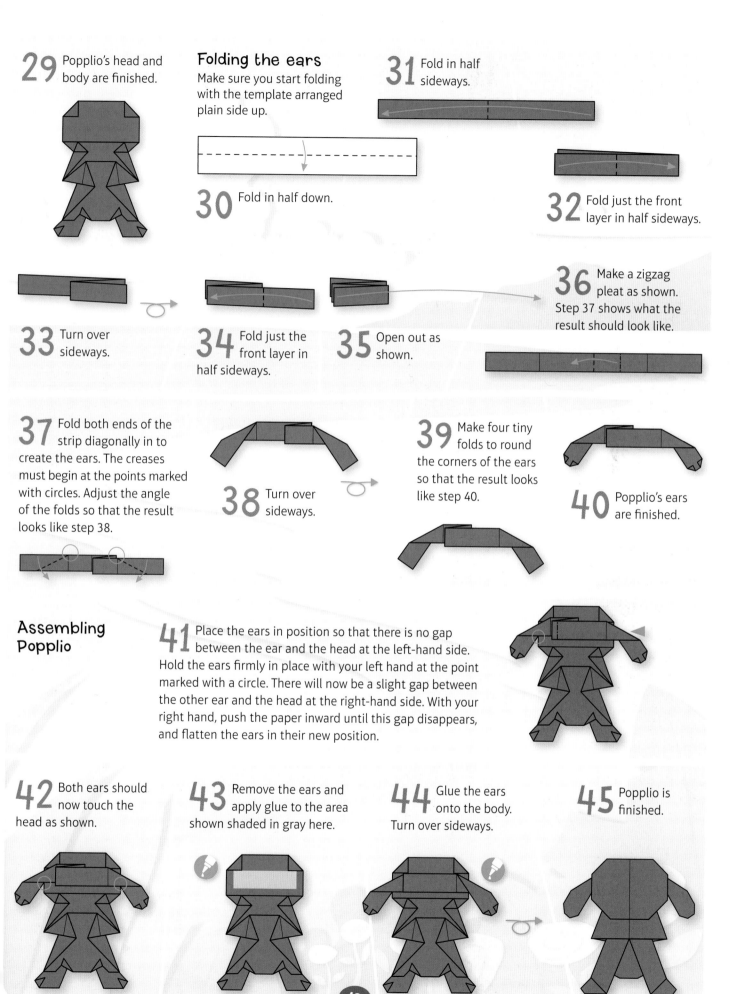

Mimikyu

Mimikyu must look pretty scary, because it's always hiding under an old rag and imitating Pikachu to try to make friends. It's a fun, slightly off-kilter kind of origami, too, with just the right tilt at the top.

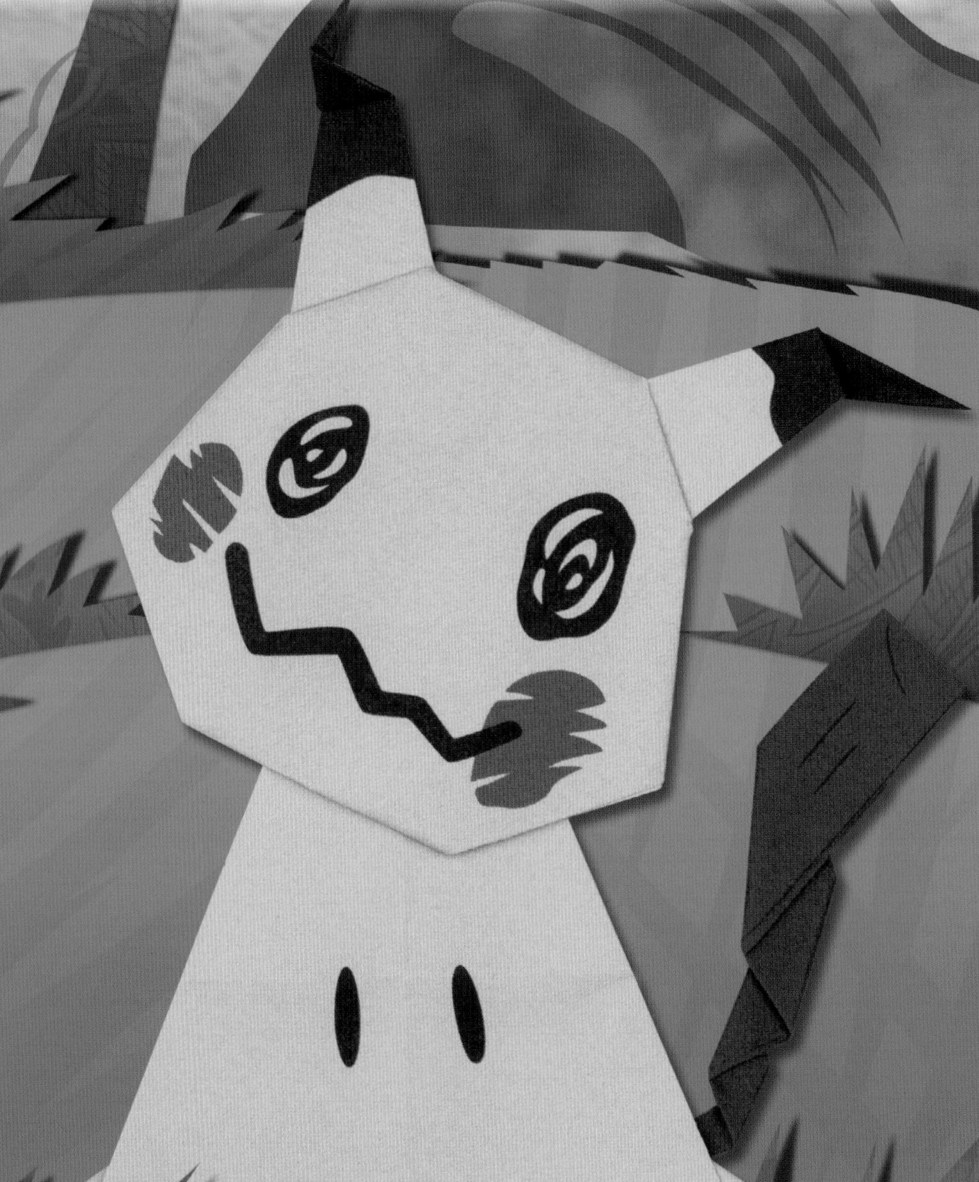

TYPE: Ghost-Fairy **HEIGHT:** 0'08"/0.2 m **WEIGHT:** 1.5 lbs./0.7 kg

How To Make Mimikyu

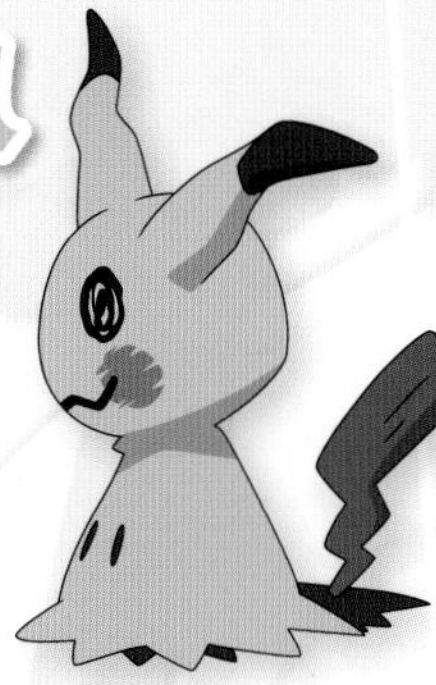

Mimikyu is folded from two squares. One of these becomes the rag face and ears, the other the body and tail. You can find the templates on page 59. Cut out all the pieces carefully.

Folding the body

Make sure you start folding with the body template arranged so that the asterisk is at the top. Start with the colored side face up.

1 Fold in half sideways, then unfold. Turn over sideways.

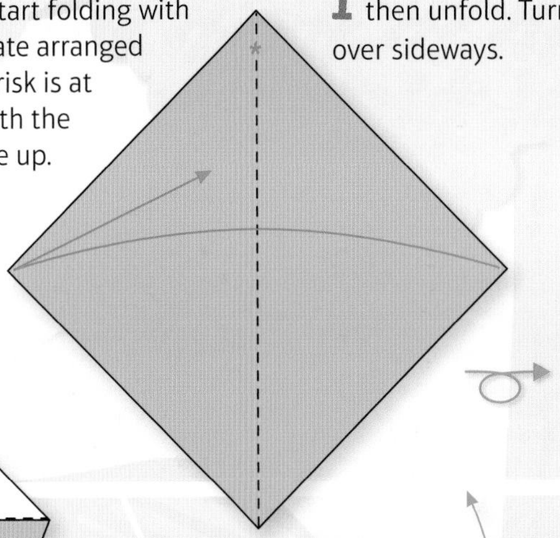

2 Fold both the lower sloping edges onto the vertical center crease.

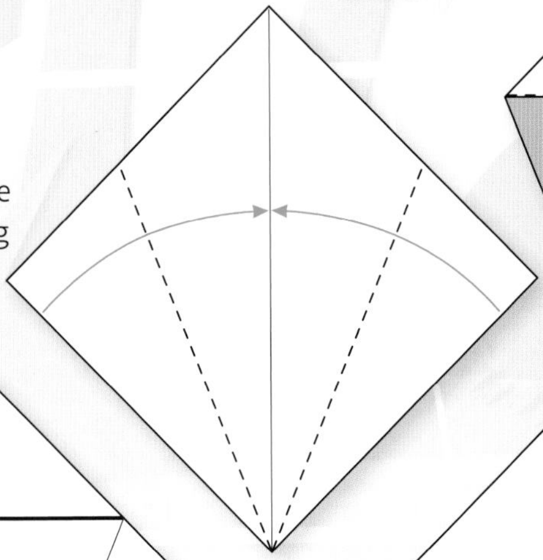

3 Fold the top corner down along the line of the top of the front layers.

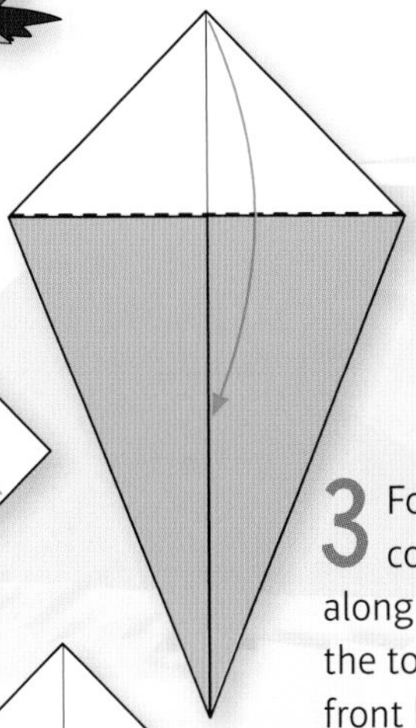

4 Open out completely.

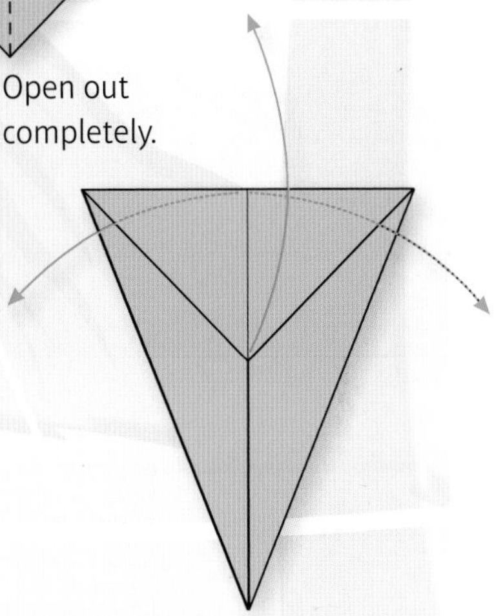

5 Cut along the crease marked with a thick black line to separate the paper into two parts.

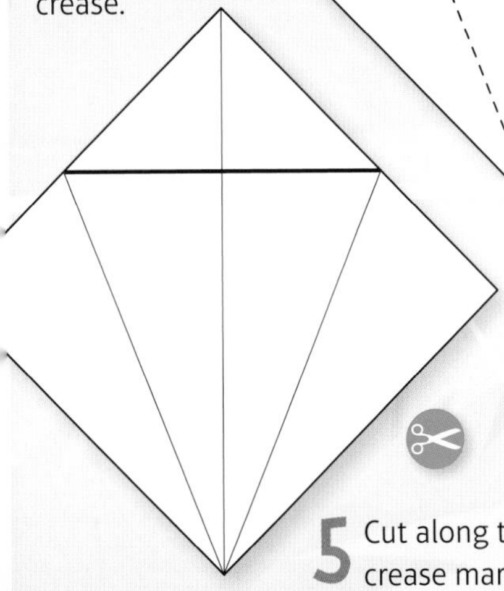

6 Set the top part aside. This will be used to fold the tail. Remake the folds made in step 2.

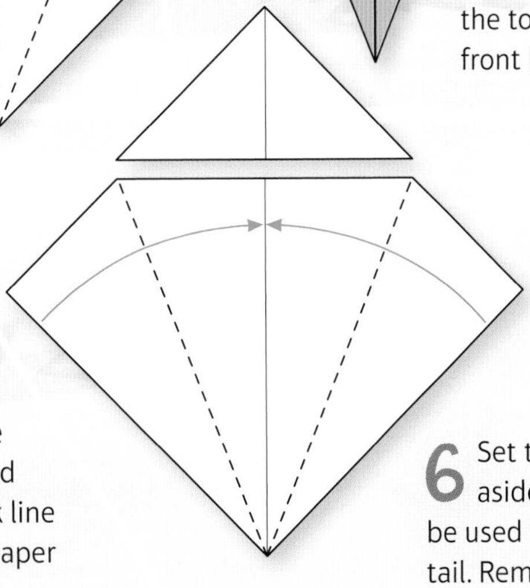

7 Fold in half up, then unfold.

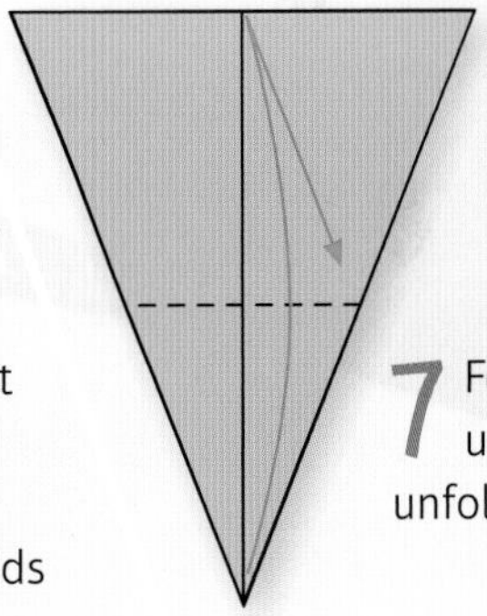

8 Fold the top edge down along the crease made in step 7.

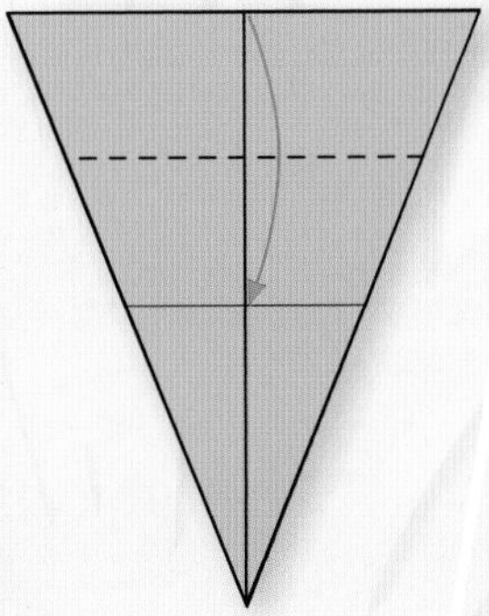

9 Fold the bottom edge of the front layers up to lie along the top edge.

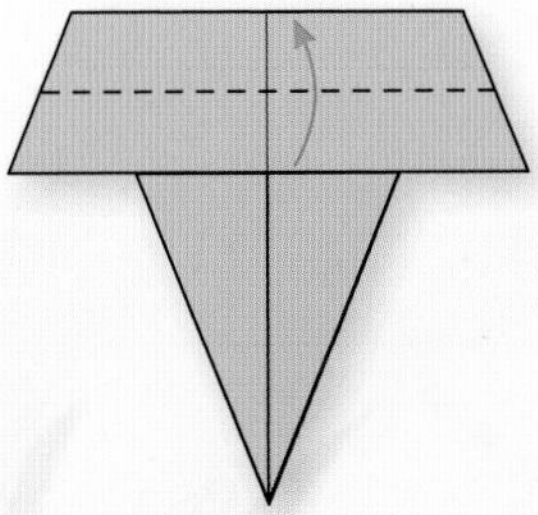

10 Fold both outside edges of the front layers onto the top edge as shown.

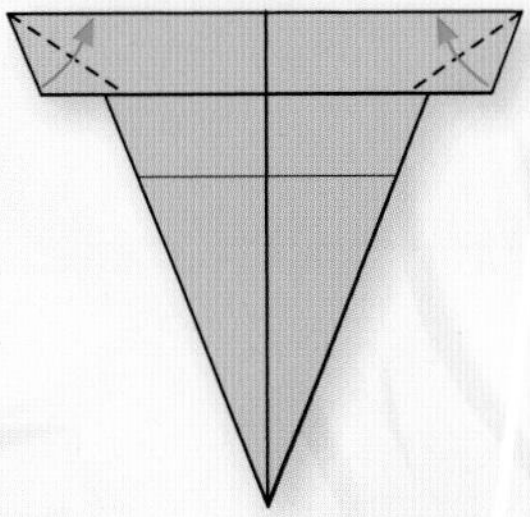

11 Turn over bottom to top.

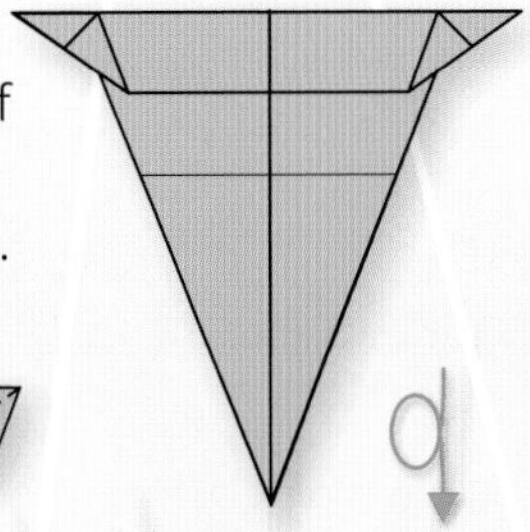

12 Mimikyu's body is finished.

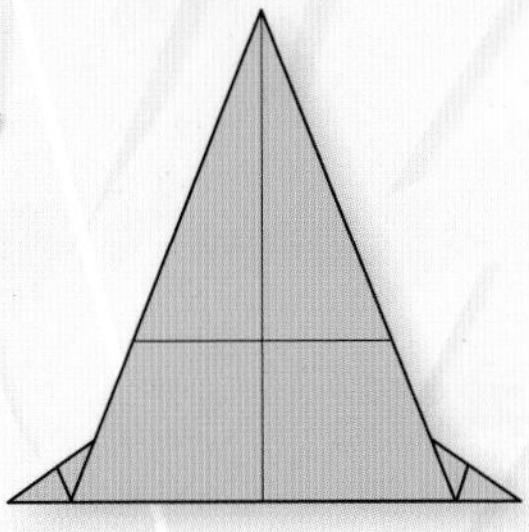

Folding the tail

Arrange the triangle you cut off the body template in step 5 so that the plain side is facing toward you.

13 Fold the left point onto the top corner, then unfold.

14 Fold the top corner onto the crease made in step 13, making sure the right point remains sharp.

15 Fold the bottom edge onto the right sloping edge.

16 Turn over sideways.

17 Fold the right point in as shown.

18 Fold the bottom corner up as shown.

19 Fold the left point up to the position marked by the dotted line.

20 Fold the top point down to the position marked by the dotted line.

21 Make two more similar folds so that the result looks like step 22.

22 Turn over top to bottom.

23 Mimikyu's tail is finished.

Folding the rag face and ears

Make sure you start folding with the template arranged so that the asterisk is at the top.

24 Fold in half down.

25 Fold both top outside points onto the bottom corner.

26 Fold both lower sloping edges into the center.

27 Fold the top corner down as shown.

28 Open out the folds made in step 26.

29 Fold both front bottom points diagonally up, making sure the creases are located as shown.

30 Open out completely.

31 Cut along the creases marked with thick black lines.

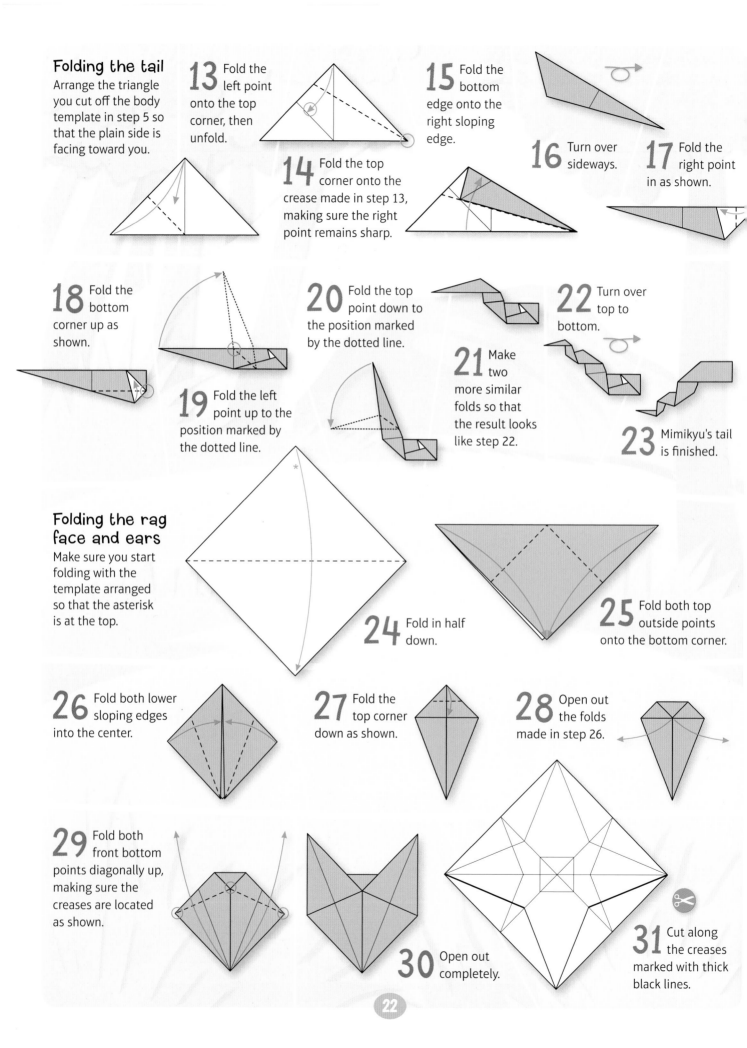

32 Fold in half down using the existing crease.

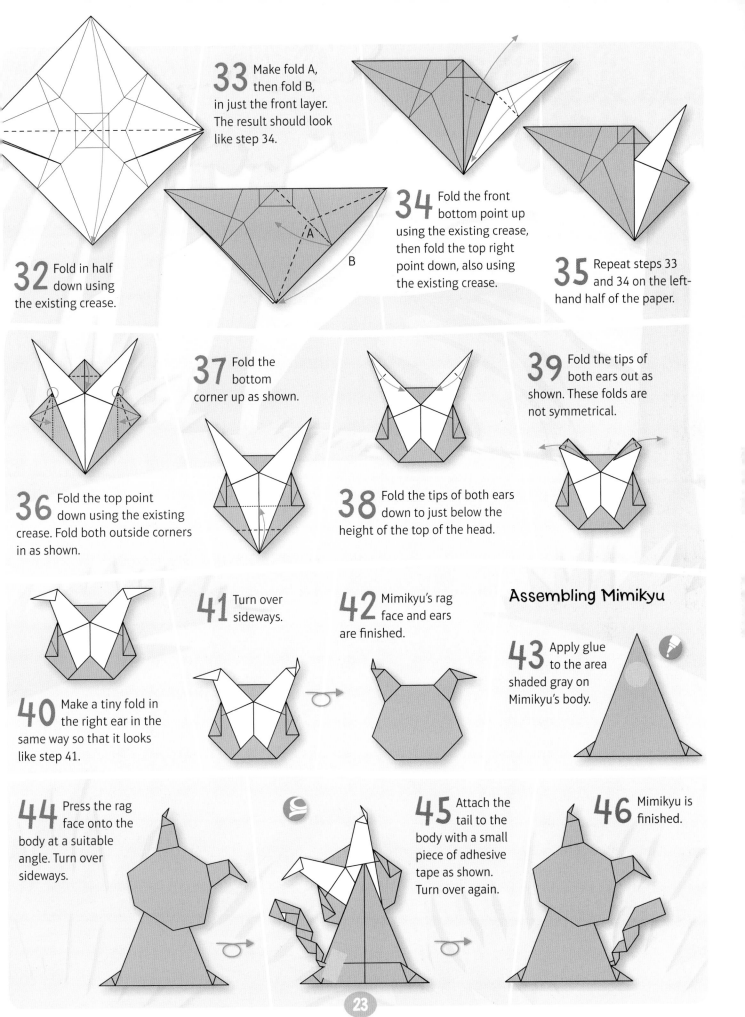

33 Make fold A, then fold B, in just the front layer. The result should look like step 34.

A
B

34 Fold the front bottom point up using the existing crease, then fold the top right point down, also using the existing crease.

35 Repeat steps 33 and 34 on the left-hand half of the paper.

36 Fold the top point down using the existing crease. Fold both outside corners in as shown.

37 Fold the bottom corner up as shown.

38 Fold the tips of both ears down to just below the height of the top of the head.

39 Fold the tips of both ears out as shown. These folds are not symmetrical.

40 Make a tiny fold in the right ear in the same way so that it looks like step 41.

41 Turn over sideways.

42 Mimikyu's rag face and ears are finished.

Assembling Mimikyu

43 Apply glue to the area shaded gray on Mimikyu's body.

44 Press the rag face onto the body at a suitable angle. Turn over sideways.

45 Attach the tail to the body with a small piece of adhesive tape as shown. Turn over again.

46 Mimikyu is finished.

Rotom Dex

The Rotom Dex is just what it sounds like: a Pokédex inhabited by Rotom, a Pokémon with the power to animate various appliances. It's a great Trainer tool, and also a wonderful shape for origami!

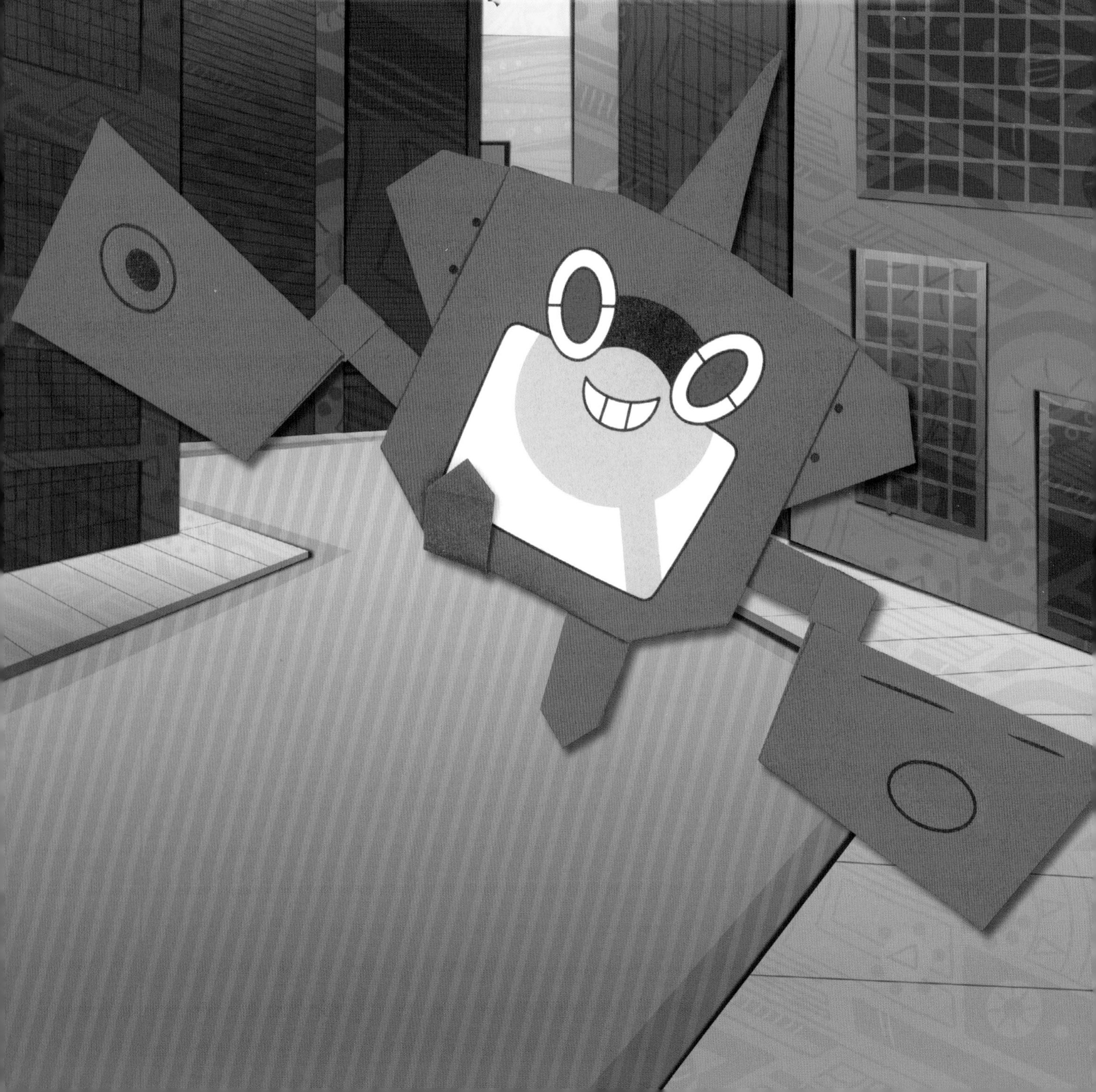

How To Make Rotom Dex

Rotom Dex is folded from four templates. You can find these on page 61. Cut out all the pieces carefully.

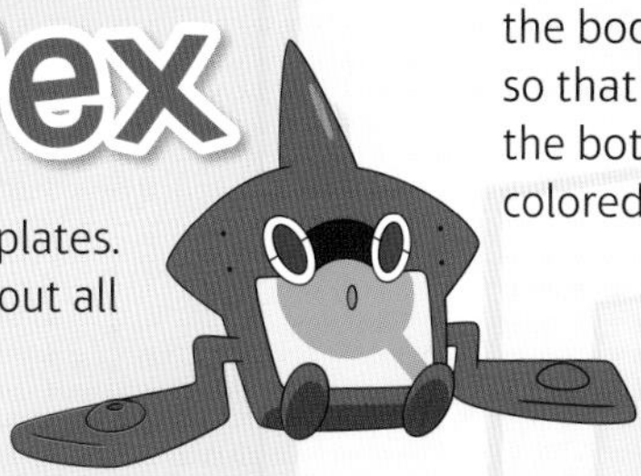

Folding the body

Make sure you start folding with the body template arranged so that the asterisk is at the bottom. Start with the colored side face up.

1 Fold in half sideways, then unfold. Turn over sideways.

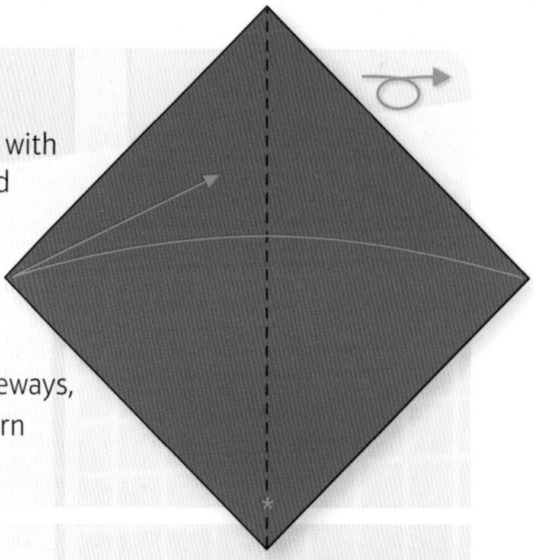

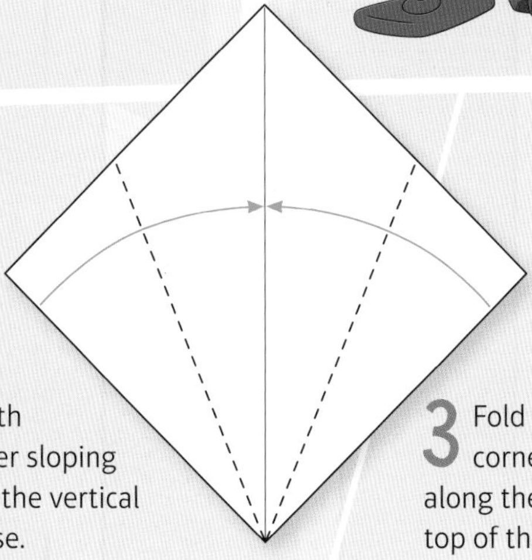

2 Fold both the lower sloping edges onto the vertical center crease.

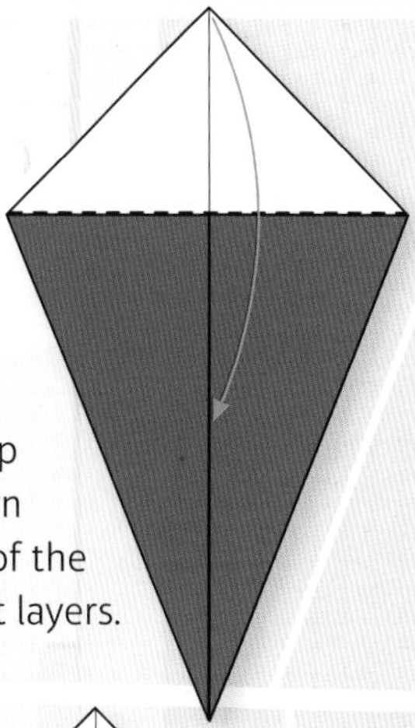

3 Fold the top corner down along the line of the top of the front layers.

4 Fold the top edge down, then unfold, making sure that the new crease is formed at the level of the bottom corner of the front layer.

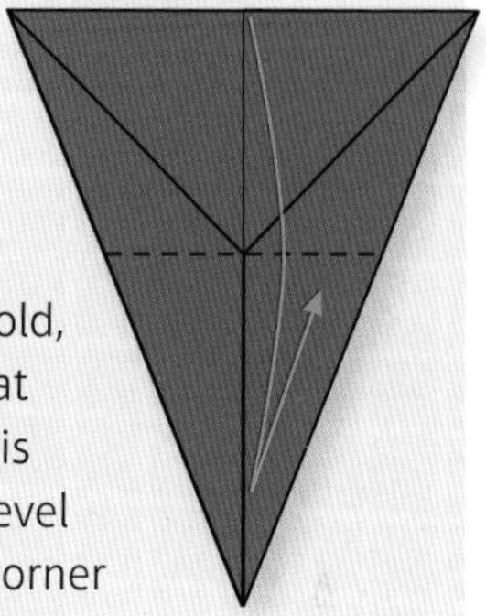

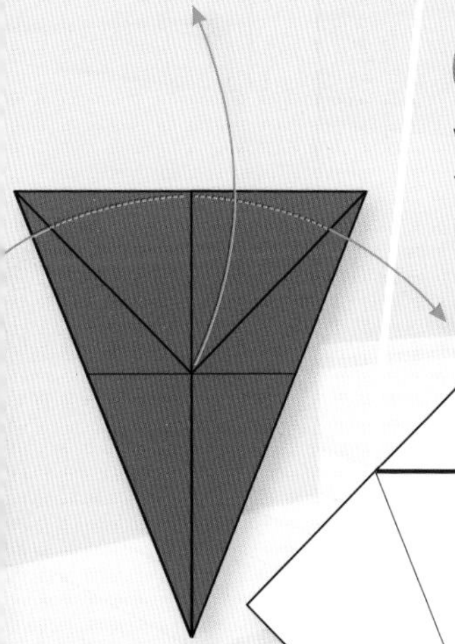

5 Open out completely.

6 Cut along the crease marked with a thick black line to separate the paper into two parts.

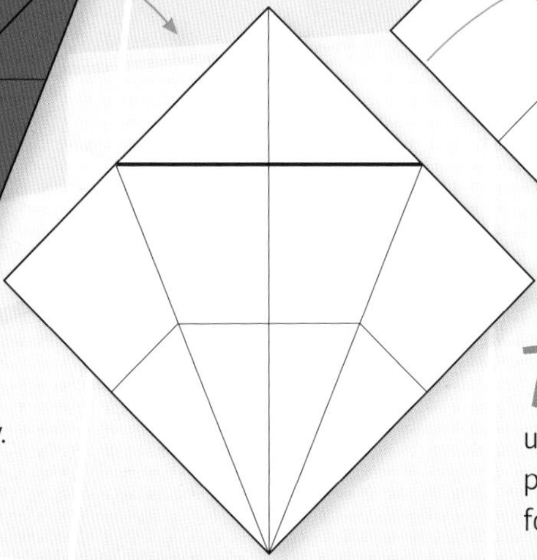

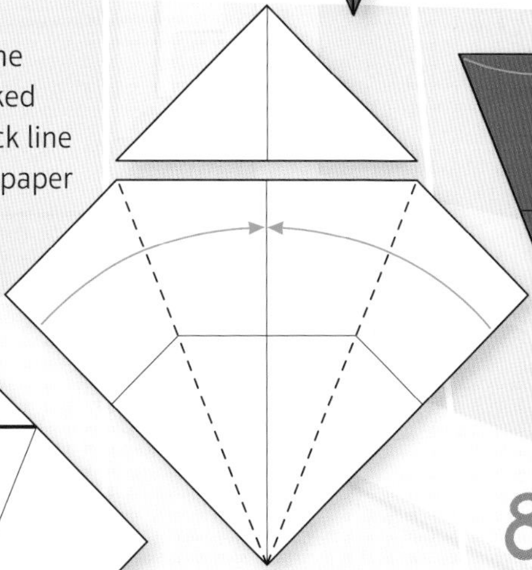

7 Set the top part aside. This will be used to fold the head point cover. Remake the folds made in step 2.

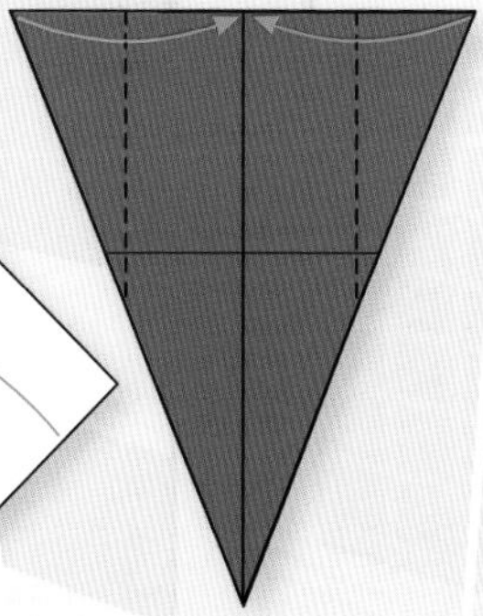

8 Fold both the top corners into the center of the top edge.

9 Fold both front flaps out diagonally so that the black dots are next to the body.

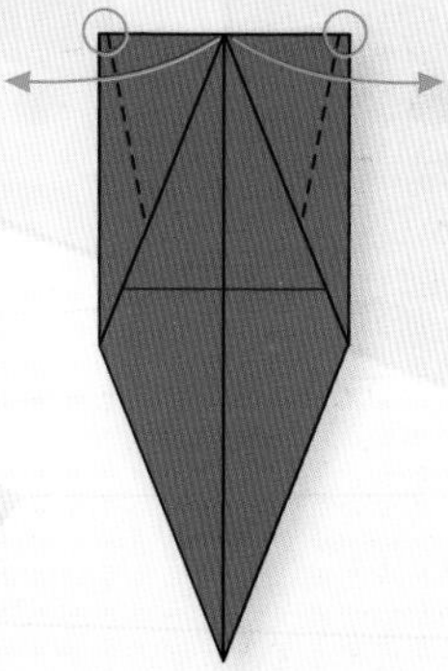

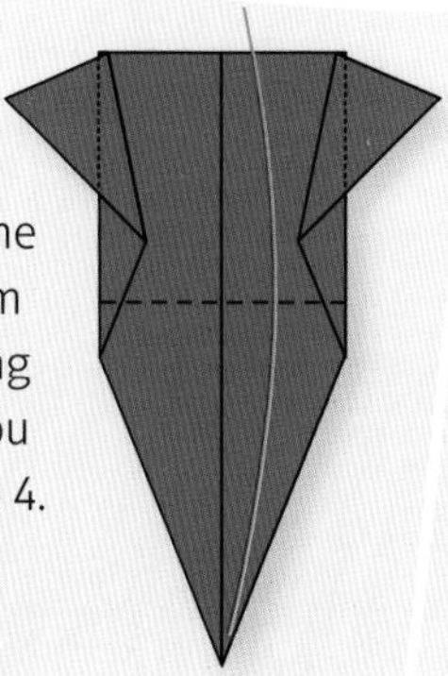

10 Fold the bottom point up using the crease you made in step 4.

11 Make four tiny folds to shape the top of the body to match step 12.

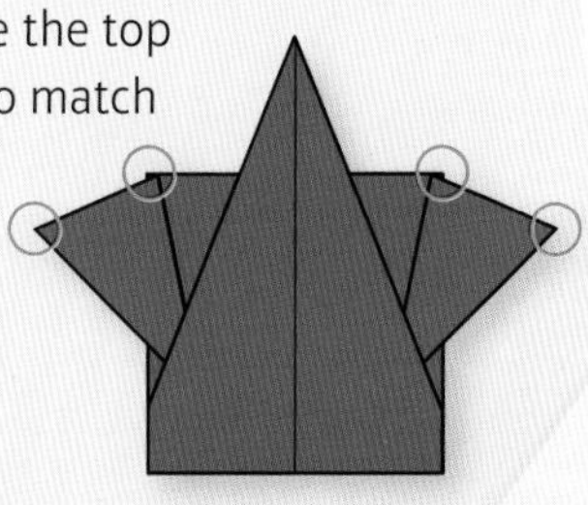

12 Fold the right sloping edge of the front layers onto the vertical center crease and flatten the paper to look like step 13. Make the same fold on the left half of the paper.

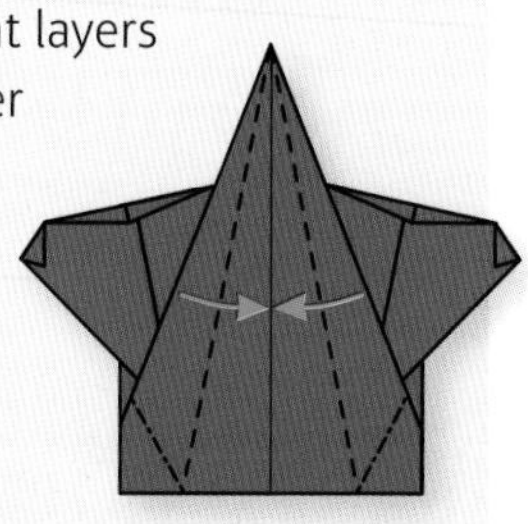

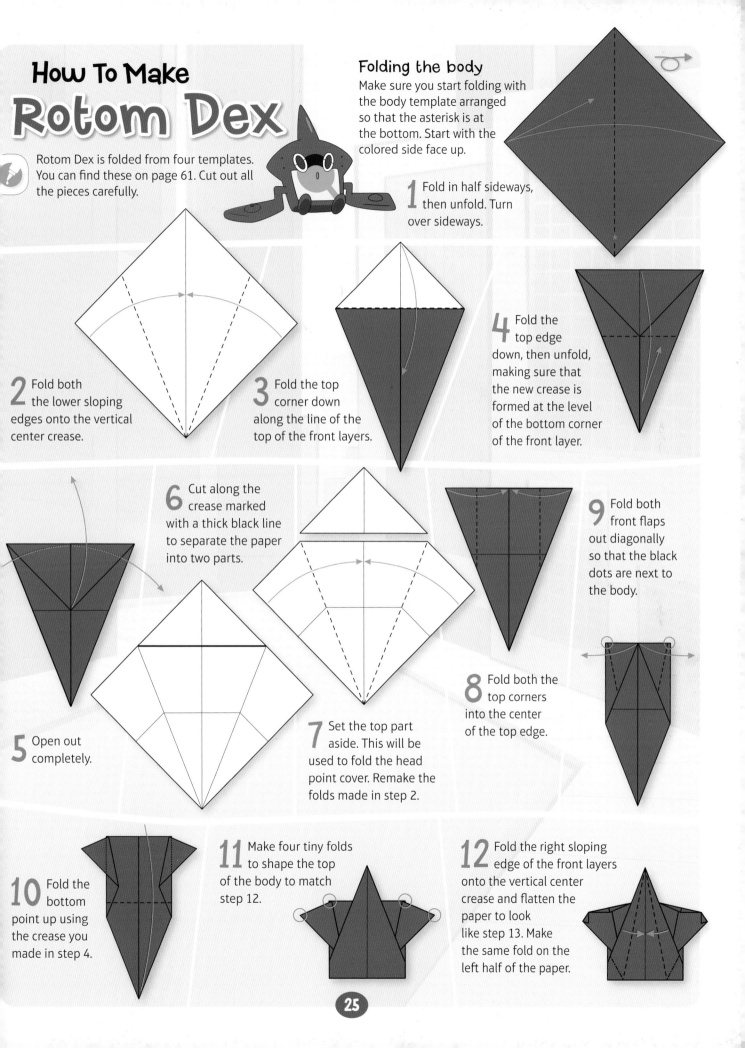

13 The body is not yet finished. It needs to be fitted with a cover for the head point to clean up the finished appearance.

Folding the head point cover
The head point cover is folded from the triangle you cut off the large square in step 6. Arrange this triangle so that the colored side is facing away from you.

14 Fold both sloping edges onto the vertical center crease.

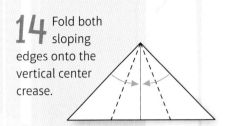

15 Fold both the new sloping edges into the center as well.

16 Slide the head point up inside the head point cover as far as it will go.

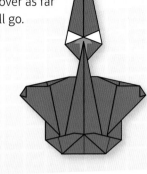

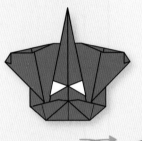

18 Rotom Dex's body is finished.

17 The result should look like this. Turn over sideways.

Folding the feet
Make sure you start folding with the template arranged so that the asterisk is at the top.

19 Fold both the left and right edges onto the bottom end.

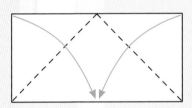

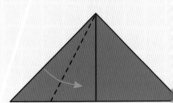

20 Fold the left sloping edge in as shown. The result should look like step 21.

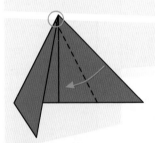

21 Fold the right sloping edge in in a similar way so that the result looks like step 22.

22 Fold the left corner onto the inner edge of the front layer.

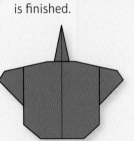

23 Make a tiny fold to shape the bottom of the left foot.

24 Turn over sideways.

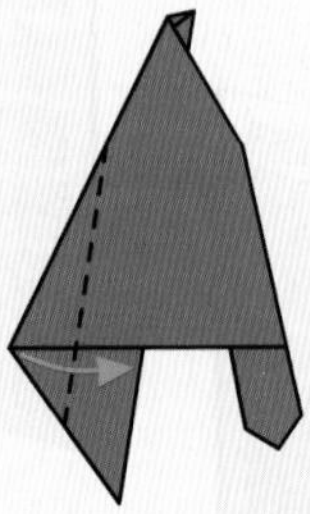

25 Fold the left corner onto the inner edge of the back layer.

26 Make a tiny fold to shape the bottom of the other foot

27 Turn over sideways.

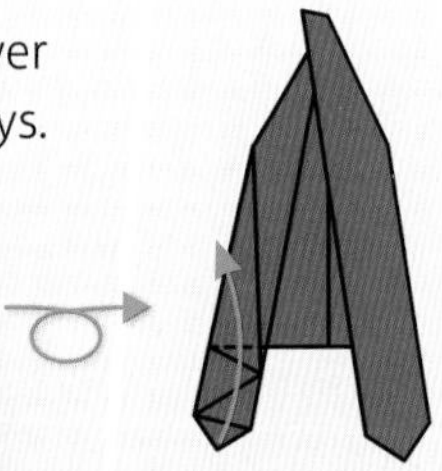

28 Fold the left foot up as shown.

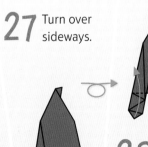

29 Rotom Dex's feet are finished.

Folding the arms
There are two templates, marked "left arm" and "right arm." Fold the right arm first. Make sure you start folding with the template arranged so that the asterisk is at the top.

30 Fold the left edge onto the bottom edge, then unfold.

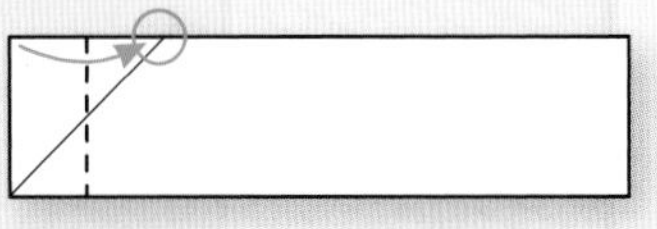

31 Fold the left edge in as shown.

32 Fold the front flap in half sideways, then unfold.

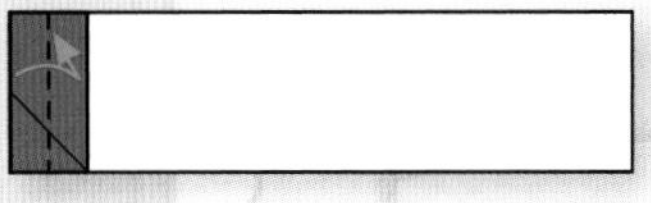

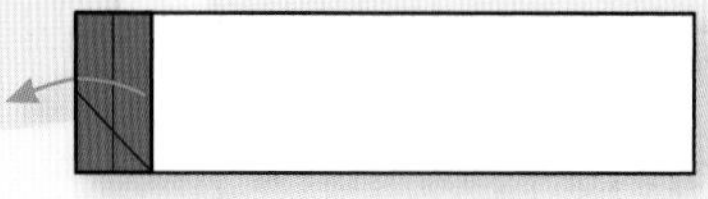

33 Open out the fold made in step 31.

34 Fold the right edge onto the nearest vertical crease.

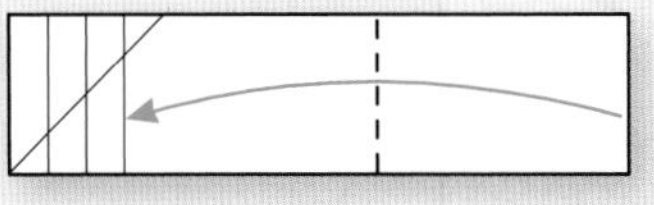

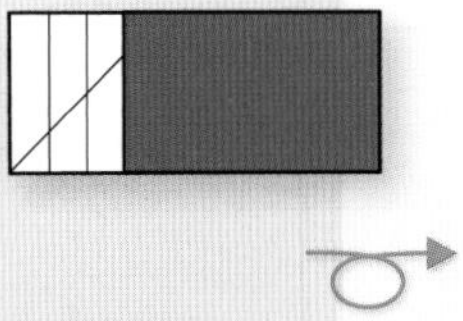

35 Turn over sideways.

36 Fold the top edge of only the front layer onto the left edge.

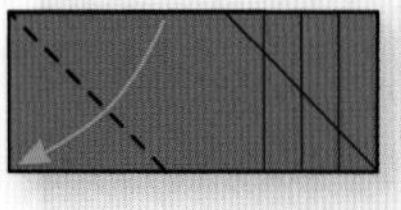

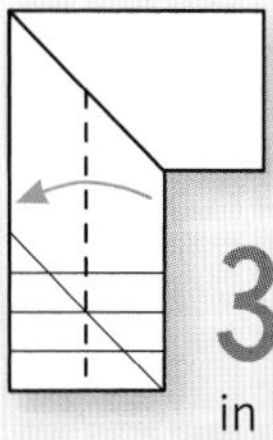

37 Fold the front layers in half sideways.

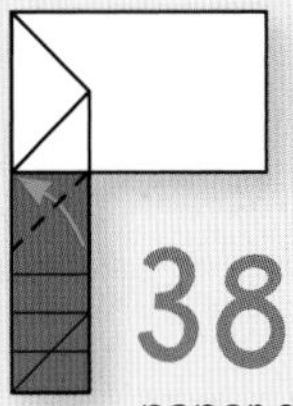

38 Fold the bottom part of the paper diagonally up and to the left as shown.

39 Fold the right edge of the front layers across to the left. Also fold the top right corner in as shown.

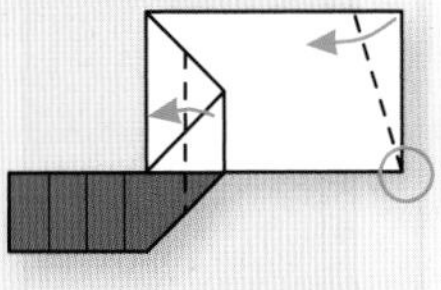

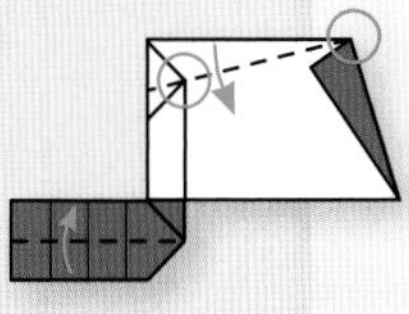

40 Fold the bottom edge up as shown. Also fold the top left corner in as shown.

41 Turn over sideways.

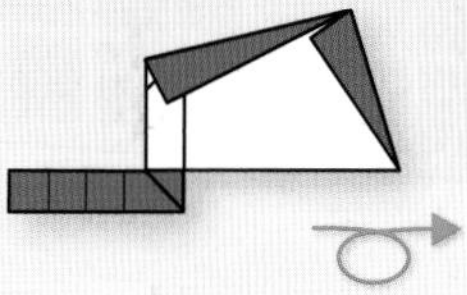

42 The right arm is finished. Fold the left arm from the other template by making the same sequence of folds but reversing them in mirror image (shown below), left to right and right to left.

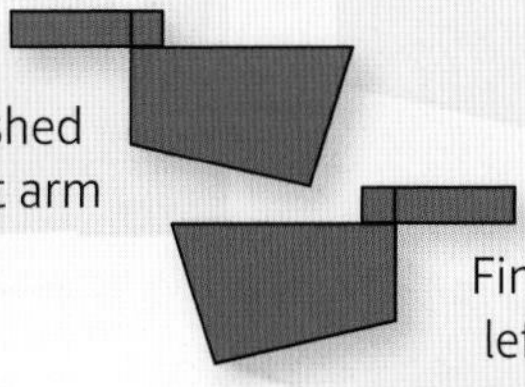
Finished right arm
Finished left arm

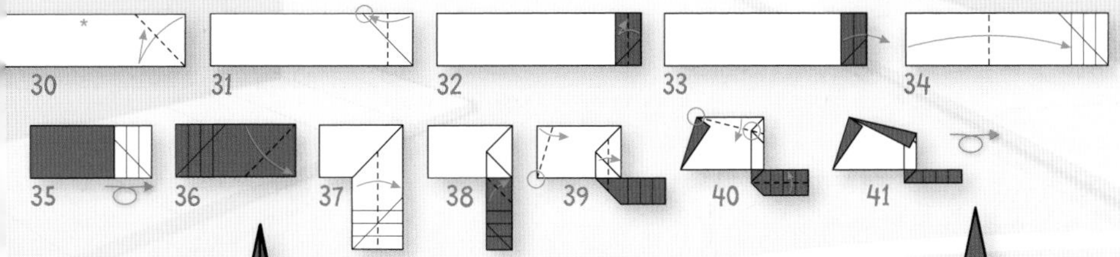
30
31
32
33
34
35
36
37
38
39
40
41

Assembling Rotom Dex

43 Apply glue to the parts of the arms shown shaded gray here, then turn them over sideways.

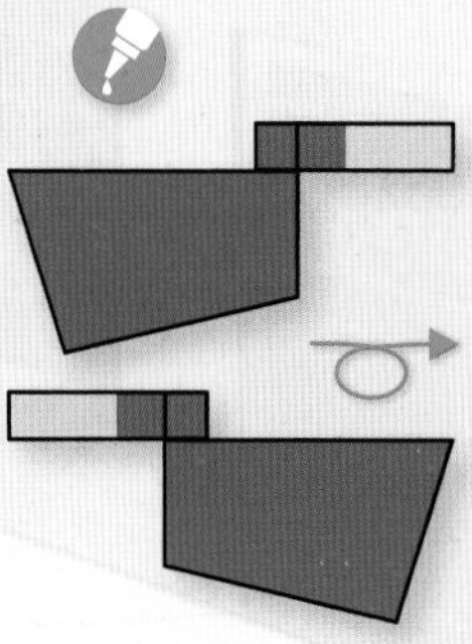

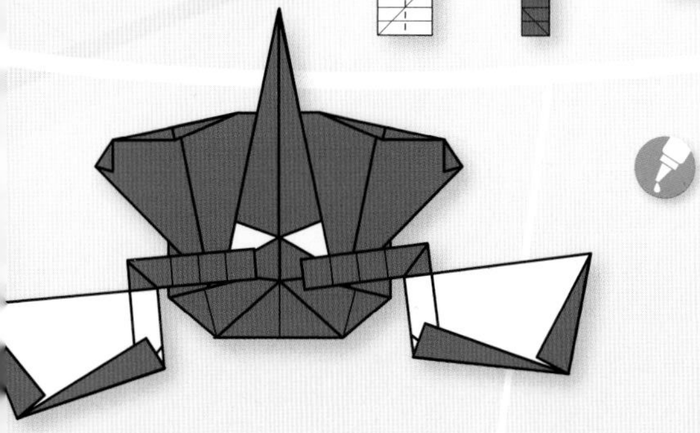

44 Attach the arms to the back of the body as shown. Press firmly in place and let the glue dry. Turn over sideways again.

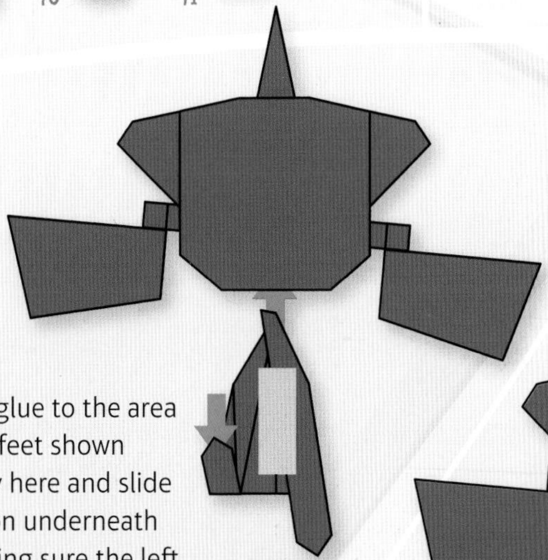

45 Apply glue to the area of the feet shown shaded in gray here and slide up into position underneath the body, making sure the left foot stays in front.

46 Rotom Dex is finished.

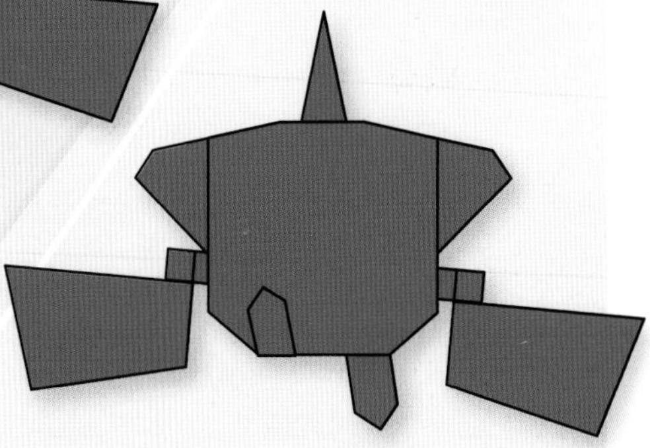

Litten

Litten's stripes and tail give it color and style, and it has that feline stare down. It's a hot Fire-type Pokémon, and the Litten folds are a good place to start an origami journey. Give it a shot, and see Litten take shape with purrfect folds.

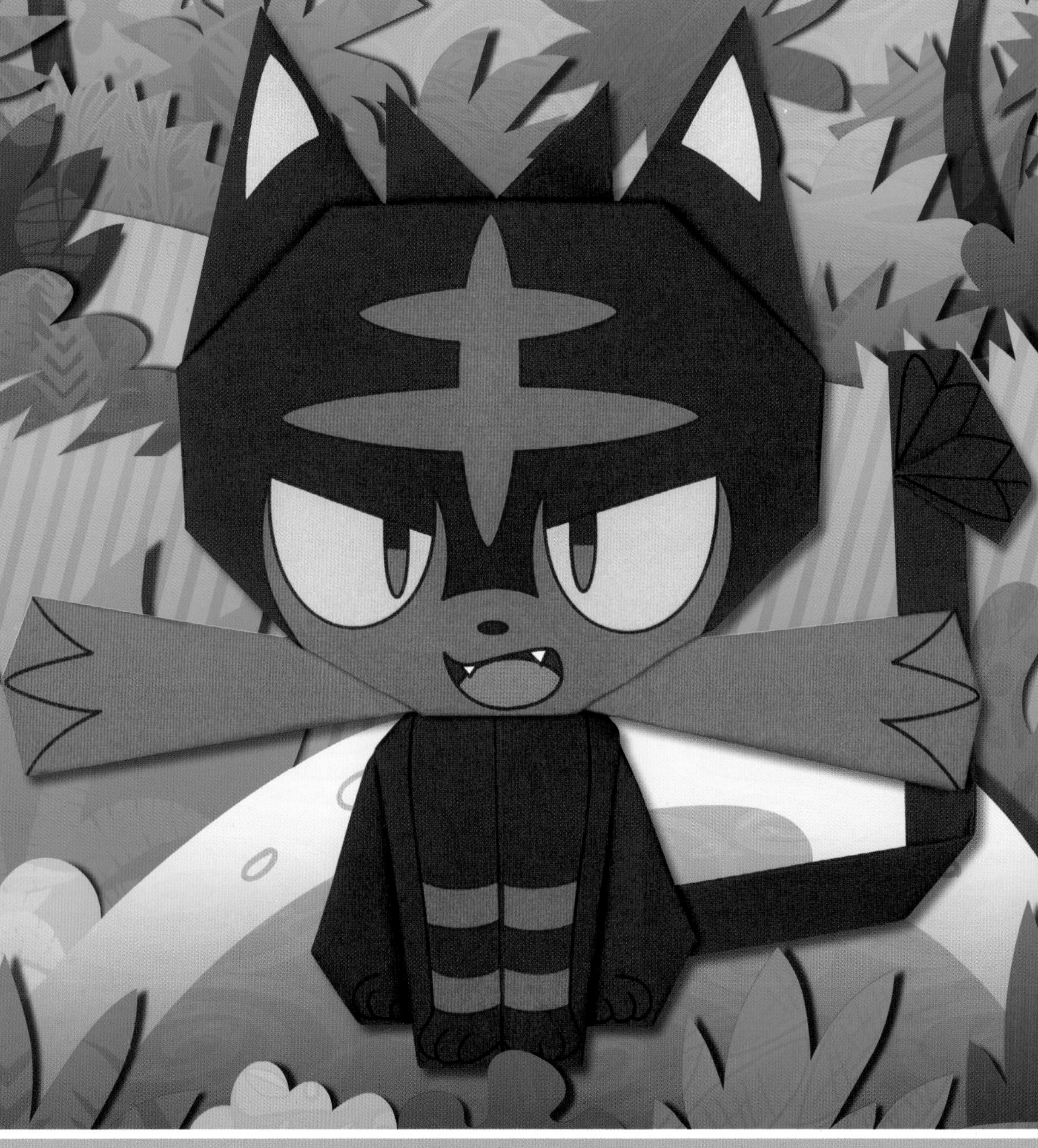

TYPE: Fire **HEIGHT:** 1'04"/0.4 m **WEIGHT:** 9.5 lbs./4.3 kg

How To Make
Litten

Litten is folded from one large square and three rectangles. You can find the templates on pages 63 and 77. Cut out all the pieces carefully.

Folding the head

Make sure you start folding with the template arranged so that the asterisk is at the top.

1 Fold in half sideways, then unfold.

2 Fold the top right sloping edge onto the vertical center crease, then unfold.

3 Fold in half down.

4 Fold both the top corners diagonally down to the bottom corner.

5 Fold the top corner down as shown.

6 Cut along the thick black line through the top flap to separate the inner ears.

7 Fold the inner ears up, making sure that the result looks like step 8.

8 Fold the bottom right front layer up, making sure the result looks like step 9. Note how the new crease crosses the existing crease at a slight angle.

9 Adjust the angle of the fold made in step 8 so that the inner and outer ears are arranged exactly as shown. Create the left outer ear in the same way.

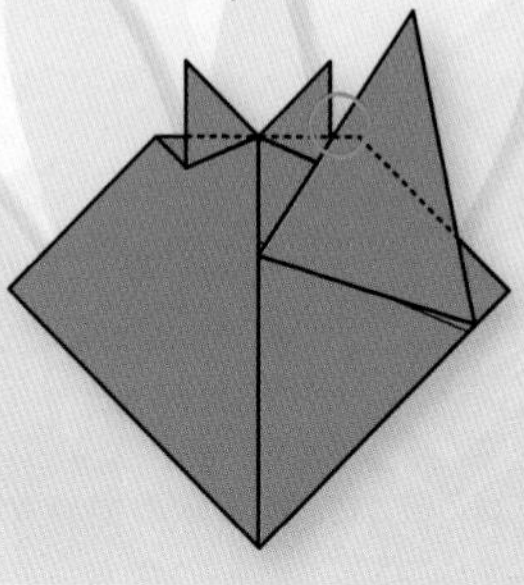

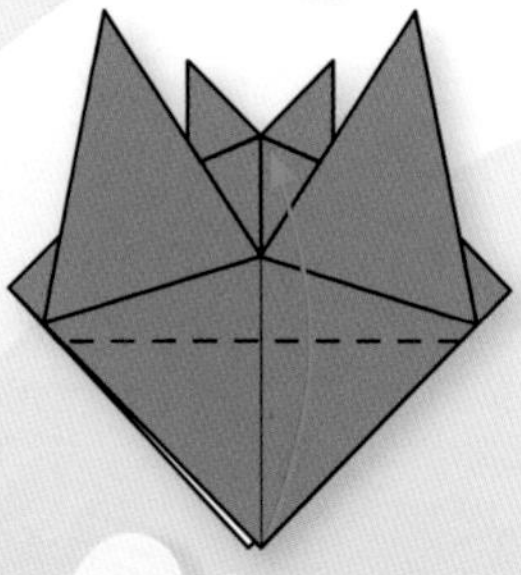

10 Fold the front layer of the bottom point upward as shown.

11 Fold in both outside corners. The points marked with circles show you how to locate these folds. Also fold the bottom corner upward at the bottom of Litten's mouth.

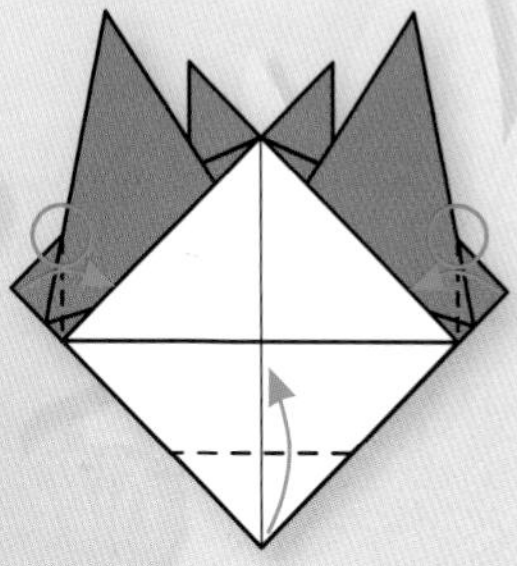

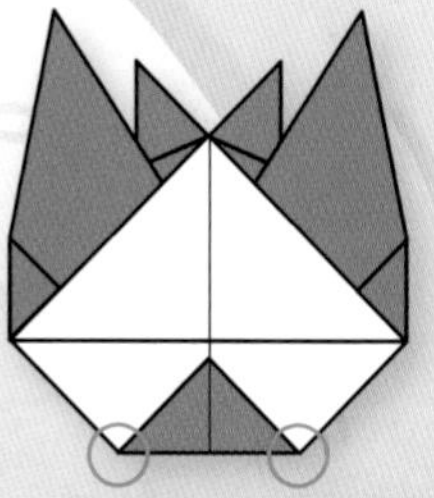

12 Make two tiny folds to shape the bottom of the head so that the result looks like step 13.

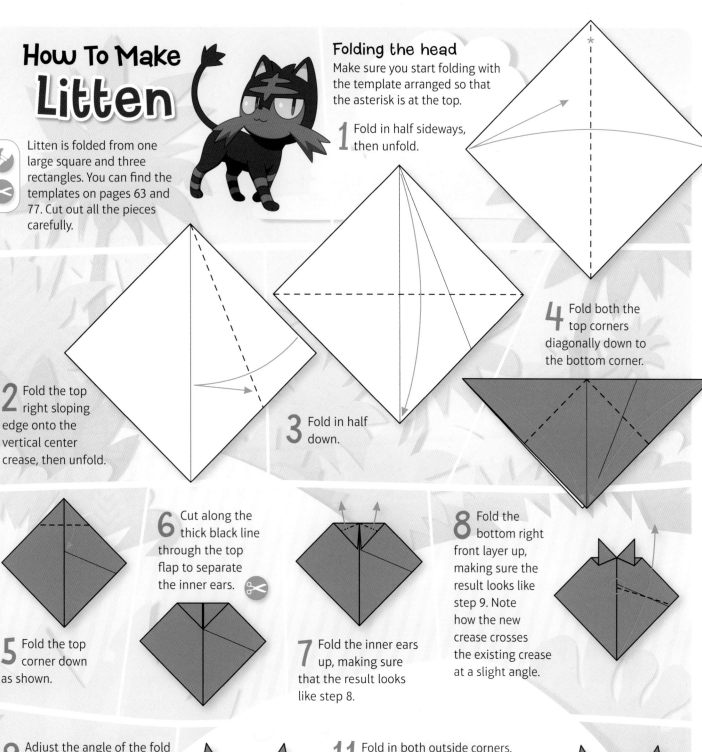

13 Turn over sideways.

14 Litten's face is finished.

Folding the body

Make sure you start folding with the body template arranged so that the asterisk is at the top.

15 Fold in half sideways, then unfold.

16 Fold both outside edges into the center, then unfold them.

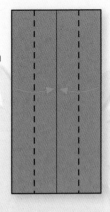

17 Fold the top edge down to just above the bottom edge. Step 18 shows what the result should look like.

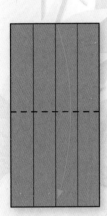

18 Turn over sideways.

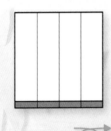

19 Fold the outside edges of the front layer in using the existing creases, then flatten the triangles at top to look like step 20.

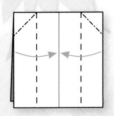

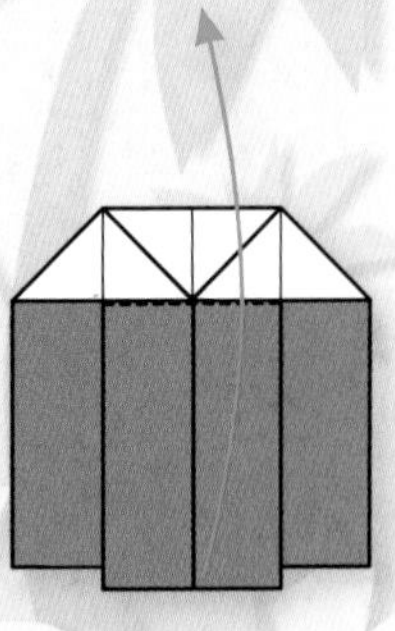

20 Fold the bottom front edge up as shown.

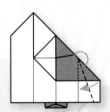

21 Fold both top corners in to lie on the vertical crease.

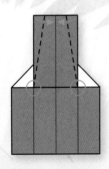

22 Fold the top edge down using the existing crease.

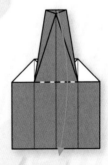

23 Turn over sideways.

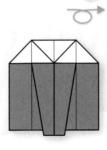

24 Fold the top edge onto the left-hand vertical crease.

25 Fold the right edge in so that the result looks like step 26

26 Fold the bottom right corner in again so that the result looks like step 27.

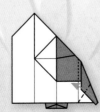

27 Repeat folds 24, 25, and 26 on the left half of the paper.

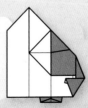

28 Turn over sideways.

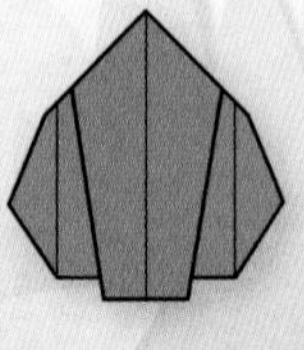

29 Litten's body is finished.

Folding the whiskers

Make sure you start folding with the template arranged so that the asterisk is at the top.

30 Fold in half up.

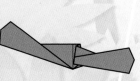

31 Fold in half sideways, then unfold.

32 Make four tiny folds to shape the ends of the whiskers. You will need to look at the other side to get shape them correctly.

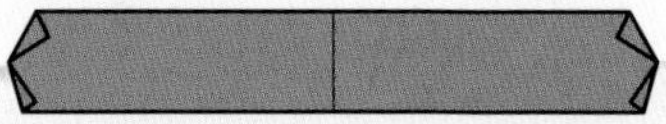

33 Fold both ends up diagonally as shown.

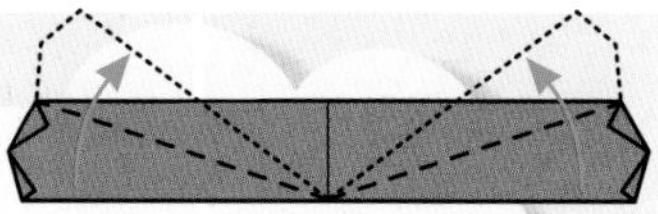

34 Pleat the right half of the paper by making two folds, aligning it with the center crease, so that the result looks like step 35.

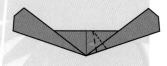

35 Repeat step 34 on the other half of the paper.

36 Fold the bottom corner up.

37 Litten's whiskers are finished.

Folding the tail

Make sure you start folding with the template arranged so that the asterisk is at the top and the tail pattern faces you.

38 Fold in half down, then unfold.

39 Fold both the top and bottom edges into the center.

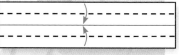

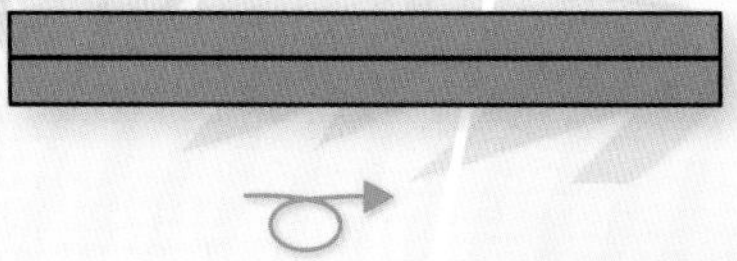

40 Turn over sideways.

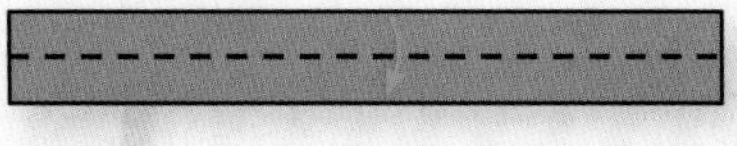

41 Fold in half down.

42 The next steps just show the right-hand end of the paper.

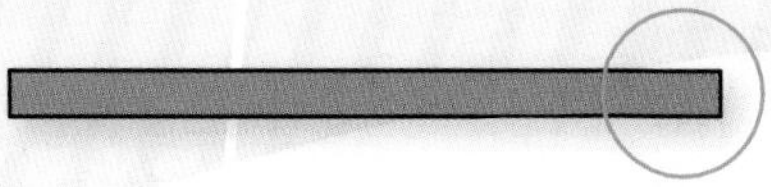

43 Fold the top right corner of the front and middle layers down diagonally as shown. Lay your paper on this illustration to make sure you are making the fold at the correct angle.

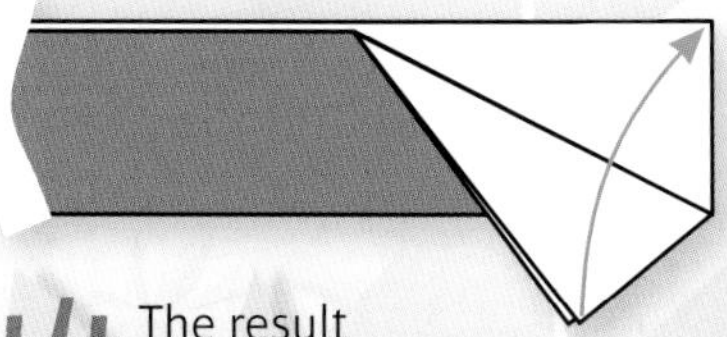

44 The result should look as shown. Undo the fold.

45 Make this fold in just the front layer of the paper, once again laying your paper on this illustration to make sure you are making the fold at the correct angle, then flatten the paper to look like step 46.

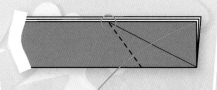

46 The result should look as shown.

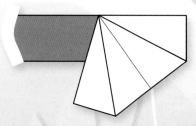

47 Litten's tail is finished.

Assembling Litten

48 Turn the whiskers over sideways.

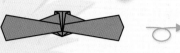

49 Apply glue to the back of the neck, and slide the neck up inside the whiskers.

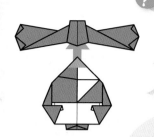

50 Apply glue to the back of the head in the area shown shaded gray here, and attach the whiskers in the way shown.

51 Apply glue to the area of the tail shown shaded gray, and slide the tail up inside the pocket at the back of the body as far as it will go.

52 Fold the tail up so that the result looks like step 53.

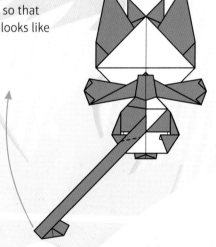

53 Fold the tail up again so that the result looks like step 54.

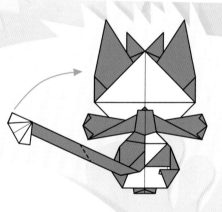

54 Turn over sideways.

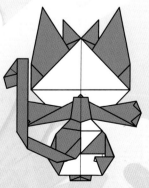

55 Litten is finished.

Alolan Vulpix

Alolan Vulpix have six tails that can create a spray of ice crystals—a great way to cool down when it gets too hot on the islands! Six tails also make the Alolan Vulpix a wonderful type of origami—check it out!

TYPE: Ice **HEIGHT:** 2'00"/0.6 m **WEIGHT:** 21.8 lbs./9.9 kg

How To Make Alolan Vulpix

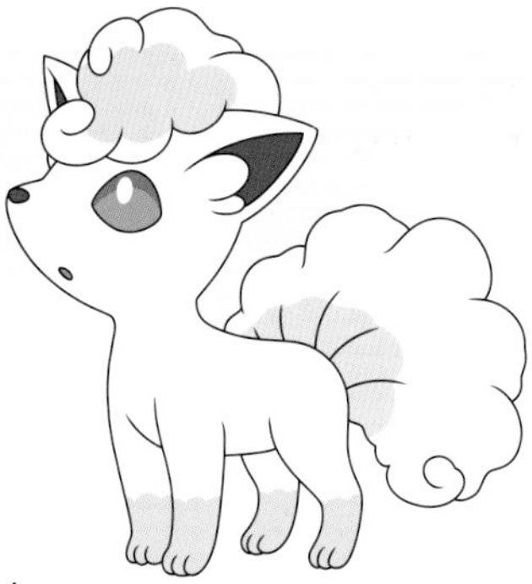

Alolan Vulpix is folded from two large squares and one small square. You can find the templates on pages 65, 67, and 77. Cut out all the pieces carefully.

Folding the tuft and the tails

Make sure you start folding with the body template arranged so that the asterisk is at the top.

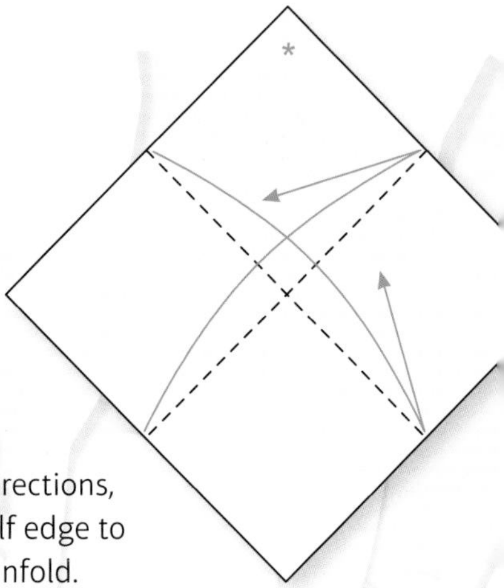

1 In both directions, fold in half edge to edge, then unfold.

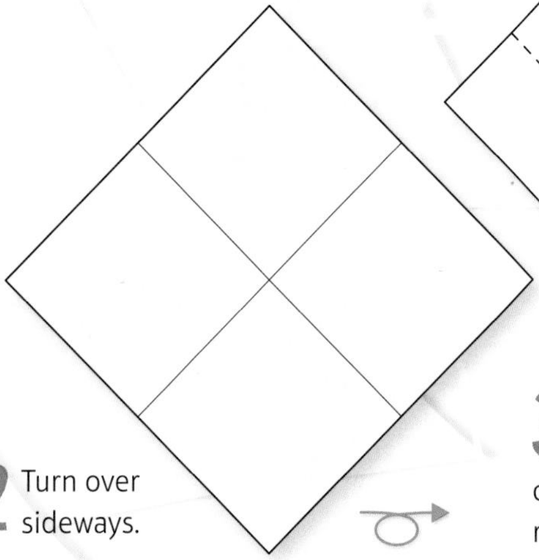

2 Turn over sideways.

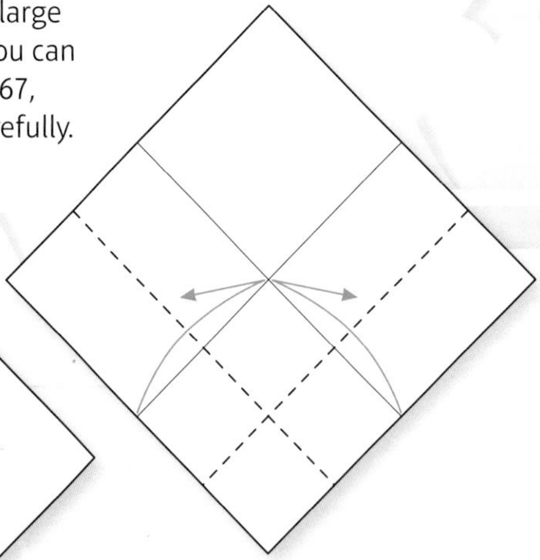

3 Fold the left lower sloping edge onto the diagonal center crease, then unfold. Repeat on the right side of the paper.

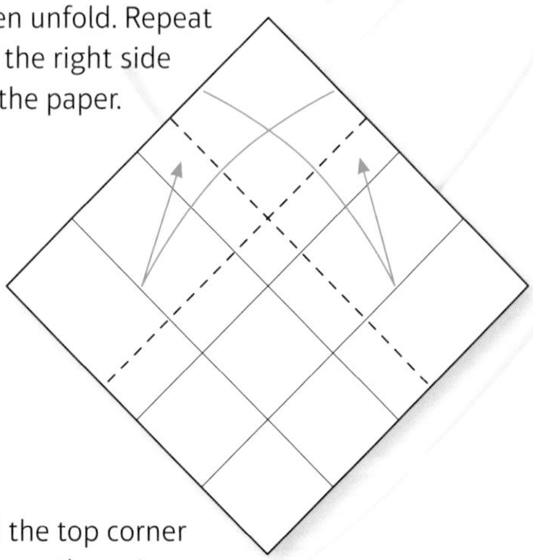

4 Fold the left top sloping edge onto the crease made in step 3, then unfold. Repeat on the right side of the paper.

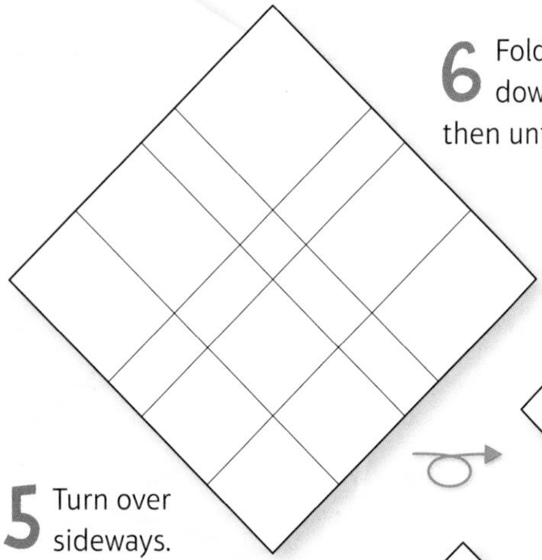

5 Turn over sideways.

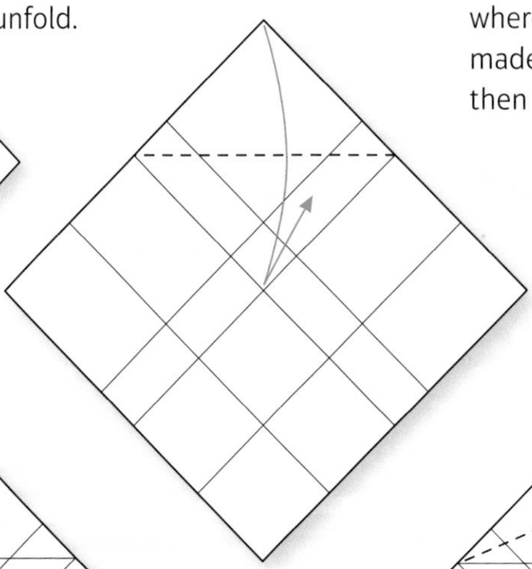

6 Fold the top corner down to the center, then unfold.

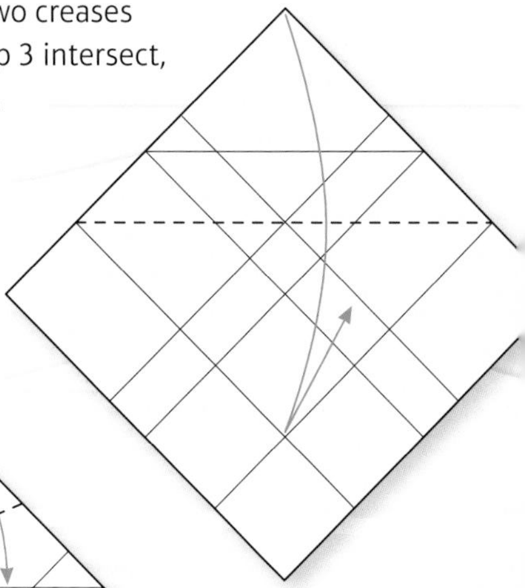

7 Fold the top corner down to the point where the two creases made in step 3 intersect, then unfold.

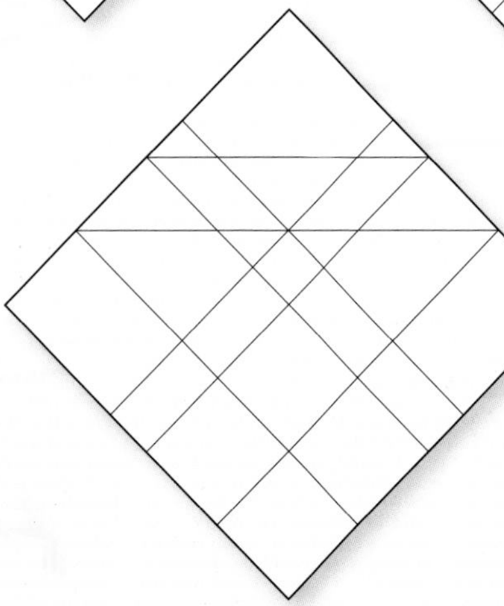

8 Turn over sideways.

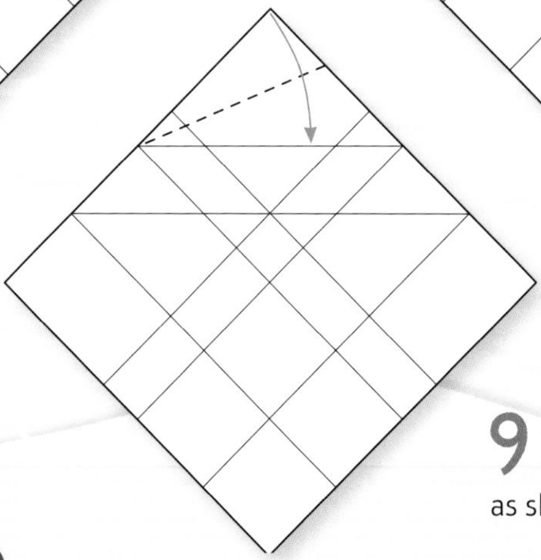

9 Fold the top corner down diagonally as shown.

10 Fold the new top corner down diagonally in a similar way.

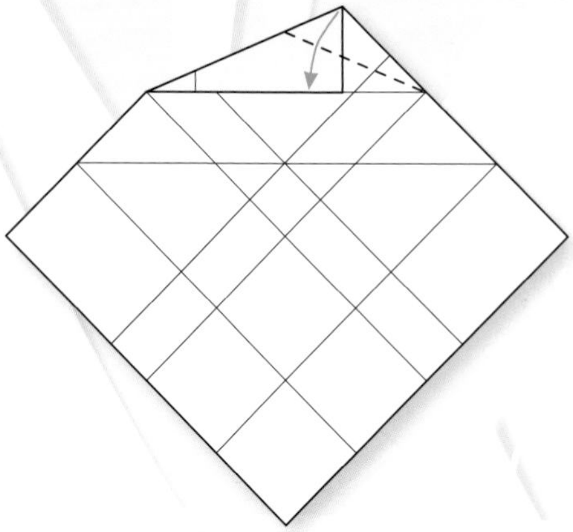

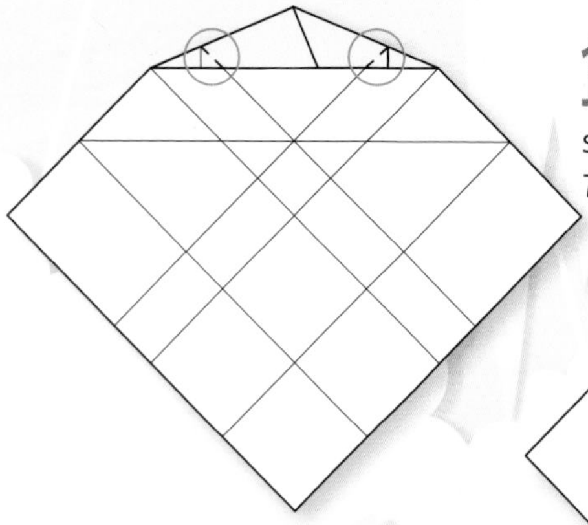

11 Remake the top part of the creases made in step 4 through all the layers.

12 Use the creases made in steps 4 and 7 to collapse the paper into the shape shown in step 13, pushing the step 7 creases down and toward the center.

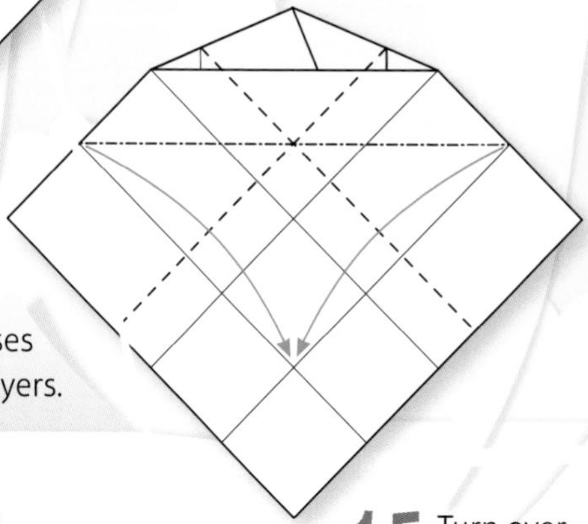

13 Fold the bottom corner of the front flap up using the existing crease and flatten the paper to look like step 14. Make sure the bottom of the new creases begin from the point marked with a circle.

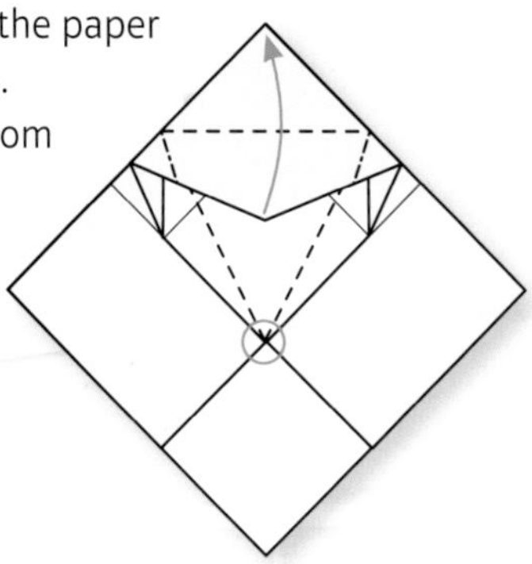

14 Fold the top part of the front layers out and using the existing creases lower the flap and flatten the paper to look like step 15.

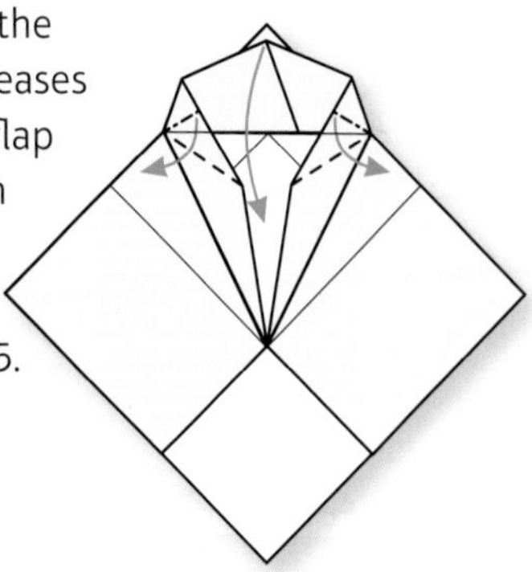

15 Turn over sideways.

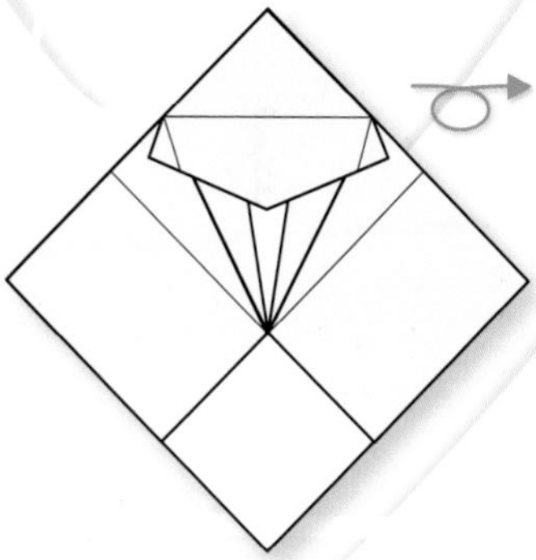

16 Fold both top sloping edges in as shown and flatten the top corner to look like step 18. Step 17 shows how this is achieved.

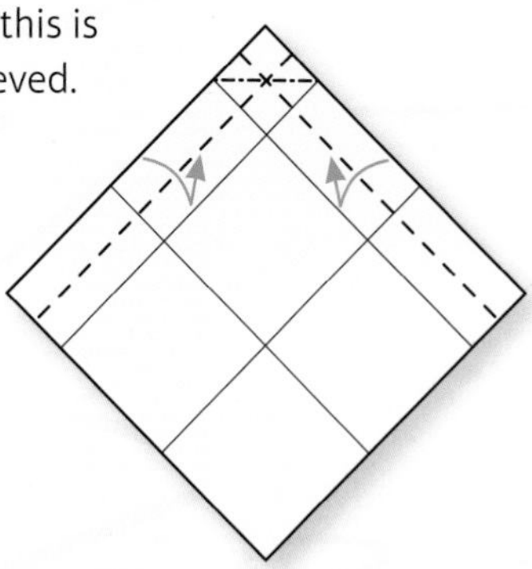

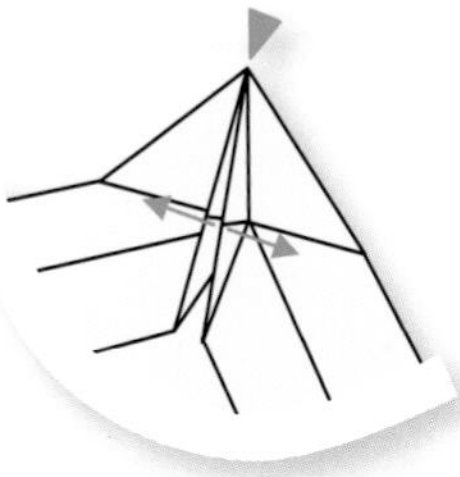

17 Separate the two small rectangular flaps of the top layer, then flatten the top corner.

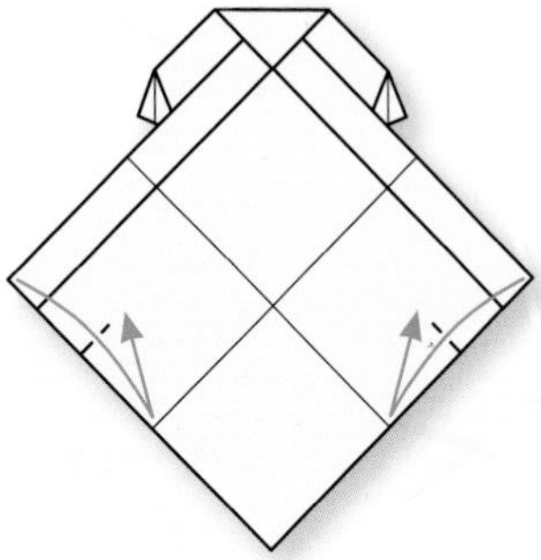

18 Make two tiny creases to help you locate the next few folds.

19 Fold the bottom corner up, using the creases you made in step 18 to locate the fold. Make this fold through all the layers.

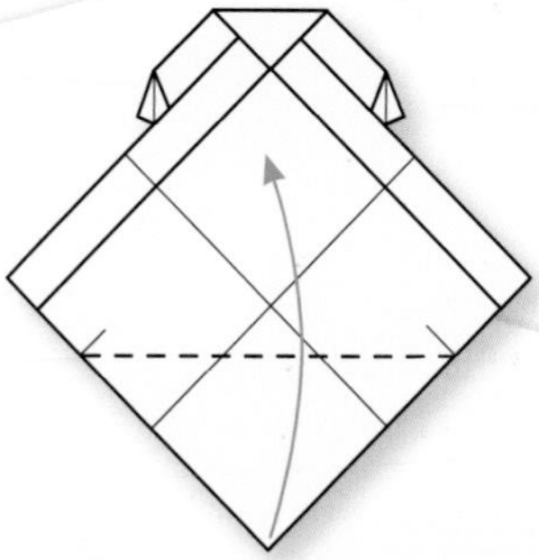

20 Fold both outside corners in at the edge of the tails.

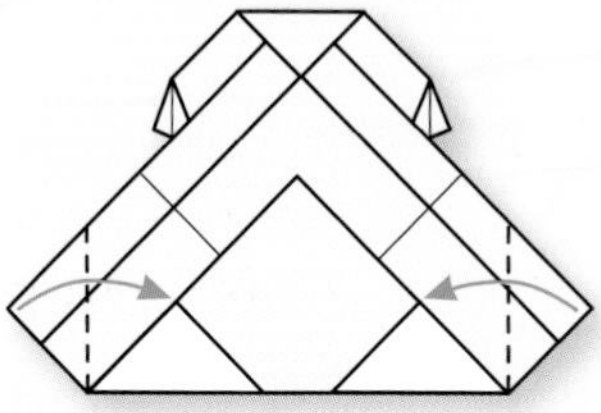

21 Fold both bottom corners in. Step 22 shows what the result should look like.

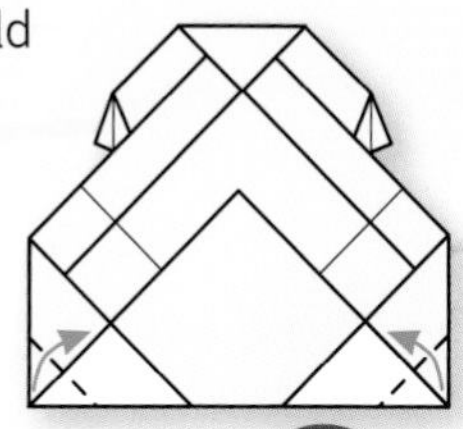

22 Turn over sideways.

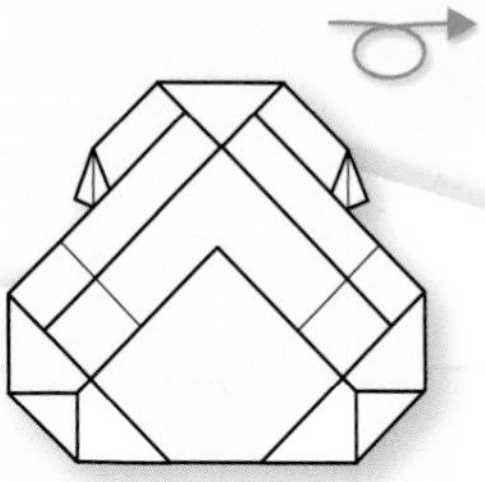

23 Alolan Vulpix's tuft and tails are finished.

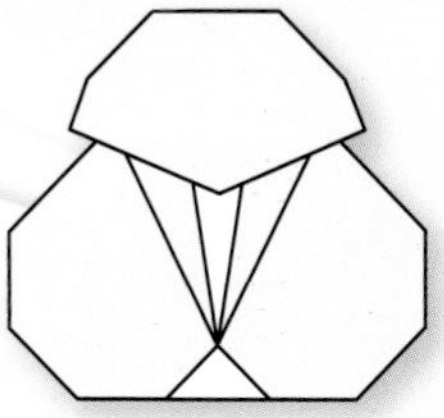

Folding the legs

Make sure you start folding with the body template arranged so that the asterisk is at the top.

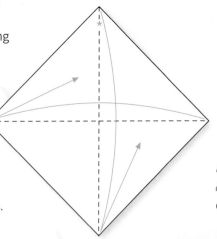

24 Fold in half diagonally, then unfold, in both directions.

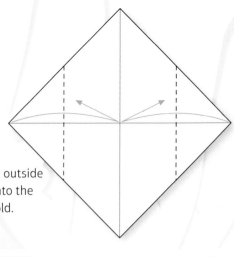

25 Fold both outside corners into the center, then unfold.

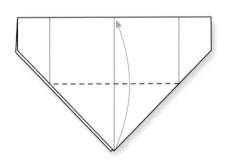

26 Fold both outside corners in as shown to the folds made in step 25.

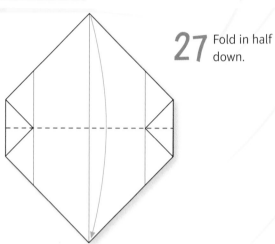

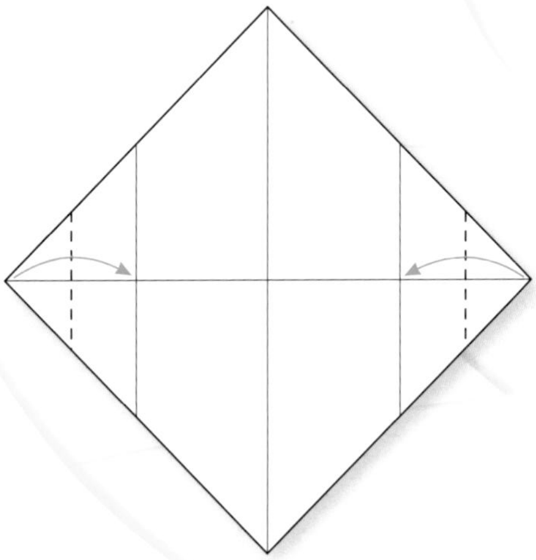

27 Fold in half down.

28 Fold the bottom corner up to the center of the top edge. Make this fold in both layers.

29 Fold both top corners diagonally down along the line of the edges of the front layers.

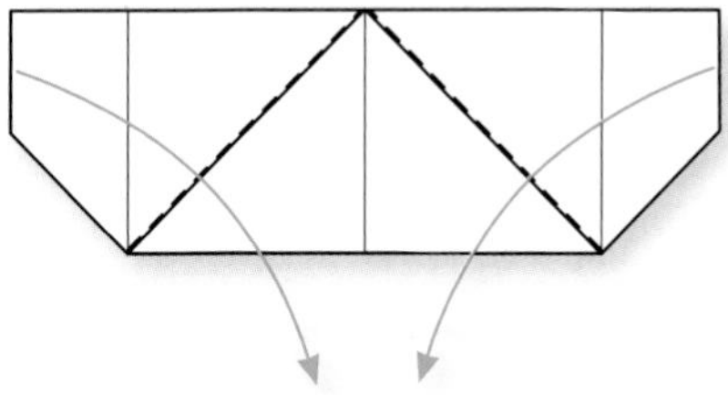

30 Turn over sideways.

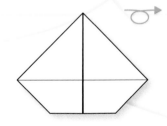

31 Fold the right corner in as shown. Let a slight gap open up between the back layers at the bottom as you do this.

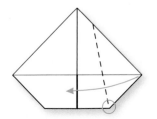

32 Repeat on the left-hand side and encourage the gap to open wider.

33 Undo the last two folds.

34 Fold both outside corners in as shown, just short of the creases made in steps 32 and 33.

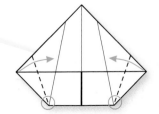

35 Remake folds 32 and 33.

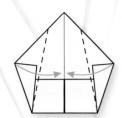

36 Fold both bottom corners in to shape the legs. You will be able to feel where the top of these creases should begin.

37 Turn over sideways.

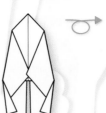

38 Alolan Vulpix's legs are finished.

Folding the face

Make sure you start folding with the template arranged so that the asterisk is at the top.

39 Fold in half sideways, then unfold.

*

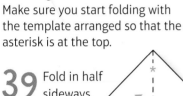

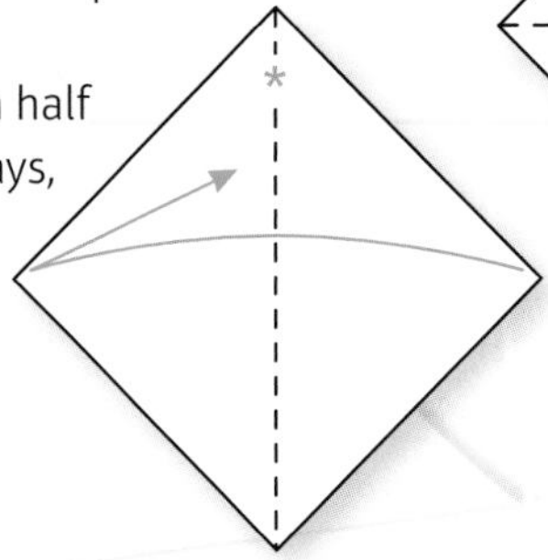

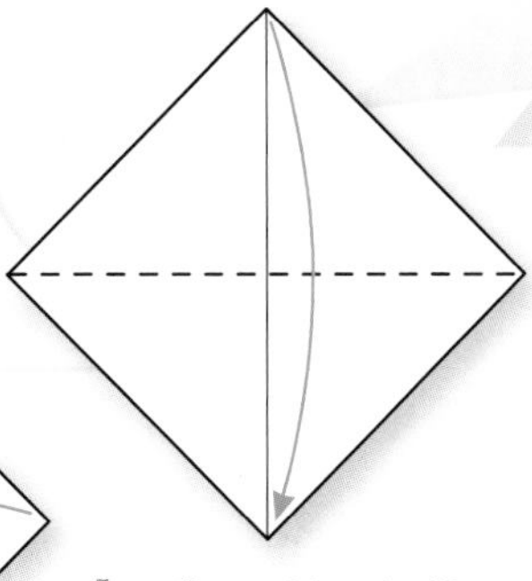

40 Fold in half down.

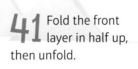

41 Fold the front layer in half up, then unfold.

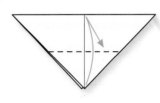

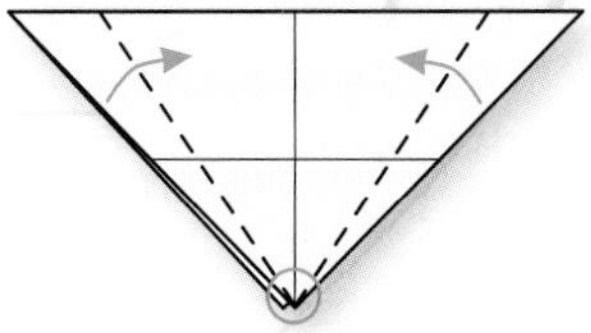

42 Fold both sloping edges in diagonally near the edge of the ears.

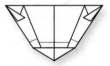

43 Fold both top points down as shown, then make another small fold on each side so that the result looks like step 44.

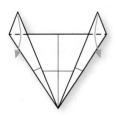

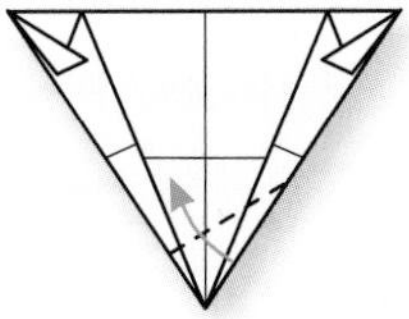

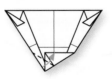

45 Fold the new bottom point diagonally up toward the right in a similar way.

44 Fold the bottom point diagonally up to the left so that the result looks like step 45.

46 Alolan Vulpix's face is finished.

Assembling Alolan Vulpix

47 Apply glue to the back of the legs, then turn over sideways.

48 The top of the legs goes underneath the tuft so that the top of the paper is just concealed.

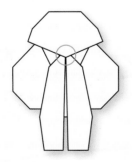

49 Apply glue to the back of the face, then turn over sideways.

50 Slide the face up into place underneath the tuft.

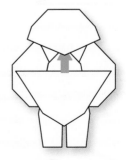

51 Alolan Vulpix is finished.

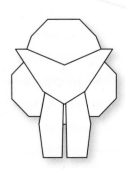

Pikipek

Pikipek uses that super beak to drill into trees and create hidden places to store berries and other items. Its beak gives it a distinctive origami profile, too!

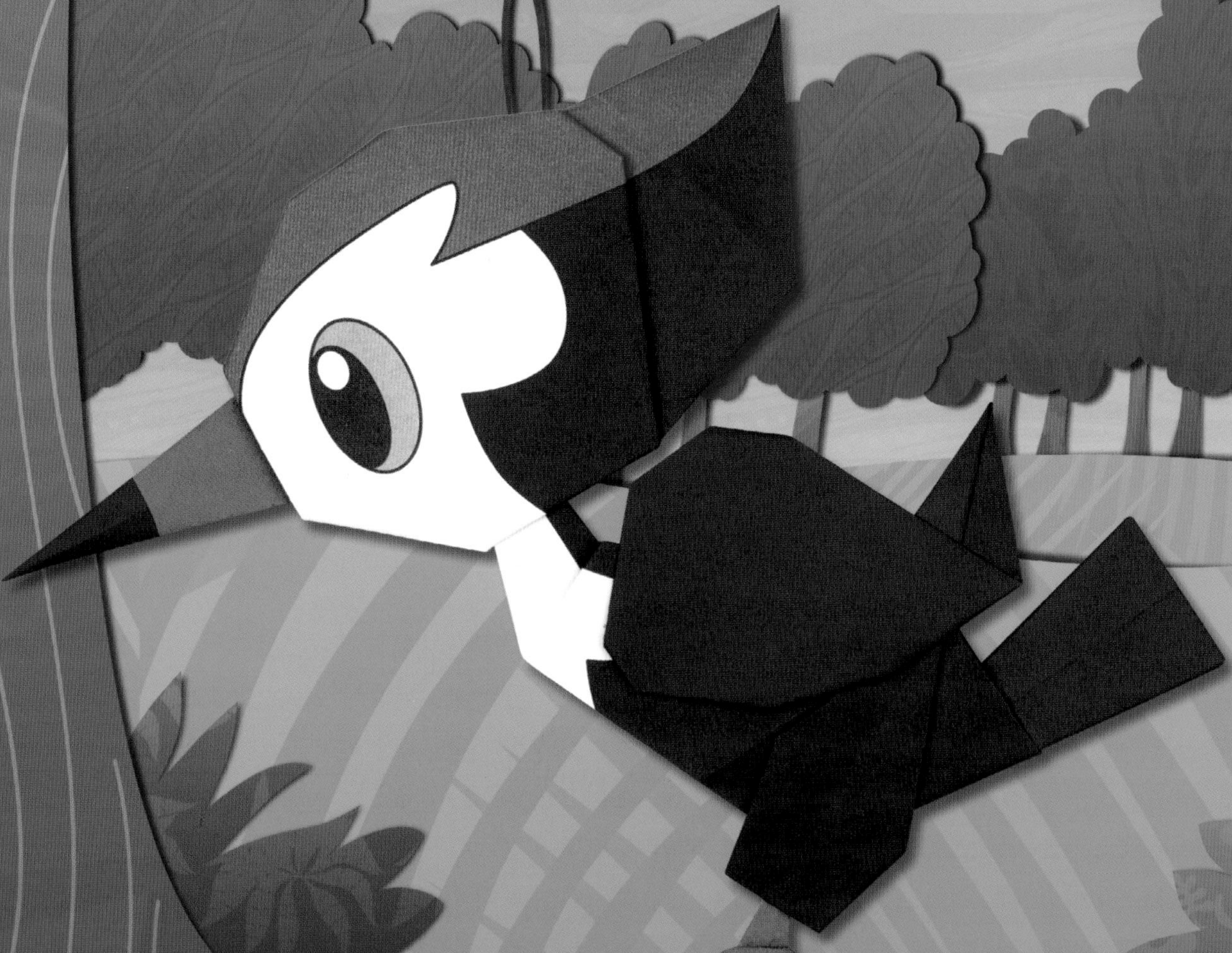

TYPE: Normal-Flying **HEIGHT:** 1'00"/0.3 m **WEIGHT:** 2.6 lbs./1.2 kg

How To Make
Pikipek

Pikipek is folded from four pieces of paper. The head and body are folded from full-size squares, the wing from a quarter-size square, and the foot from an eighth-size square. You can find the templates on pages 69 and 79. Cut out all the pieces carefully.

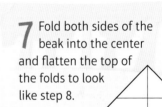

Folding the head
Make sure you start folding with the template arranged so that the asterisk is at the top.

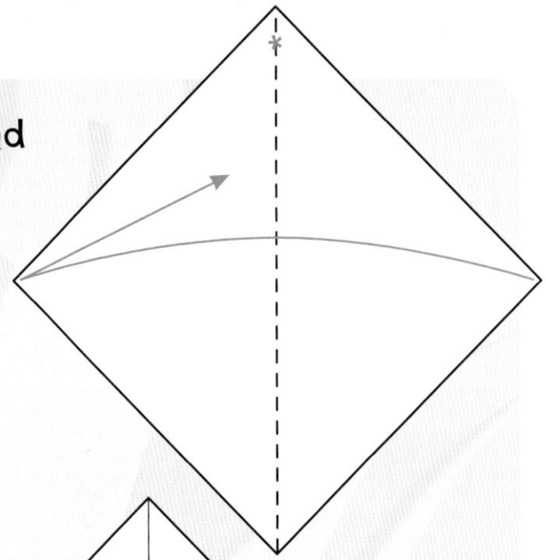

1 Fold in half sideways, then unfold.

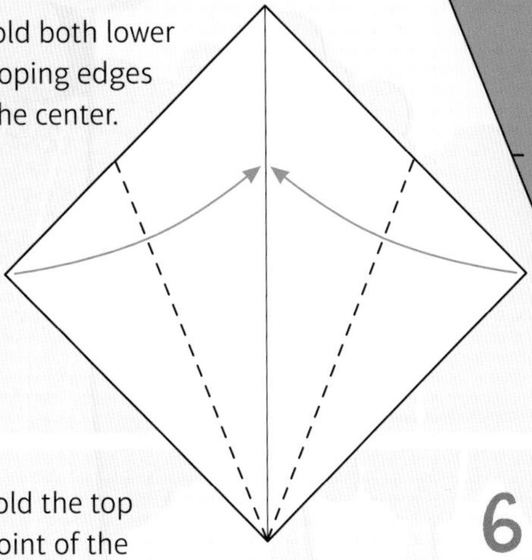

2 Fold both lower sloping edges into the center.

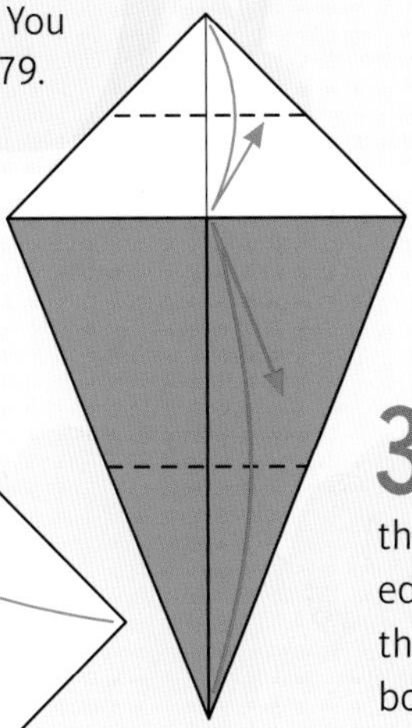

3 Fold the top corner down to the center of the top edge of the front layers, then unfold. Fold the bottom corner up to the same point, then unfold.

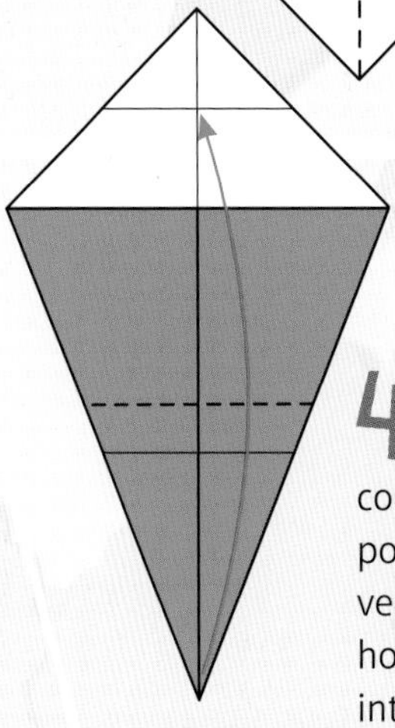

4 Fold the bottom corner up to the point where the vertical and top horizontal creases intersect.

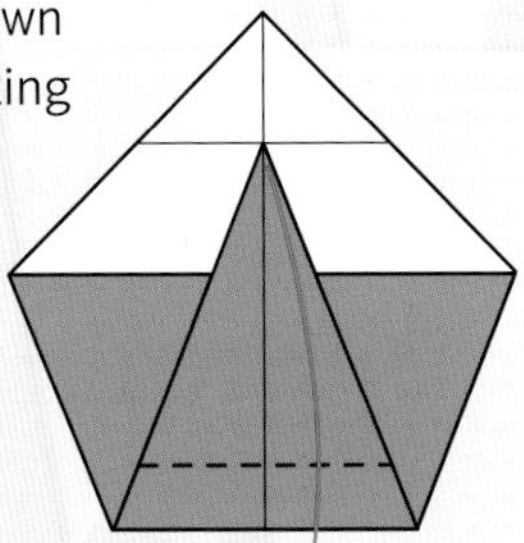

5 Fold the top point of the front layers down using the existing crease.

6 Fold both top corners of the front layers diagonally down using the hidden horizontal edge of the back layers to locate the fold.

7 Fold both sides of the beak into the center and flatten the top of the folds to look like step 8.

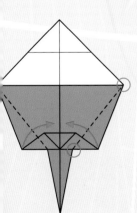

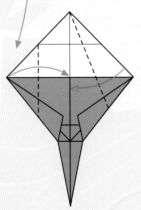

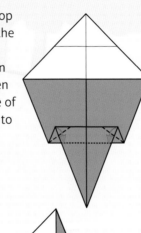

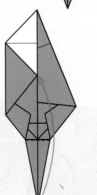

8 Fold both bottom corners of the head in as shown.

9 Fold the left corner into the center. Also fold the top right sloping edge onto the vertical center crease.

10 Fold the bottom point upward along the line of the bottom of the layers behind it.

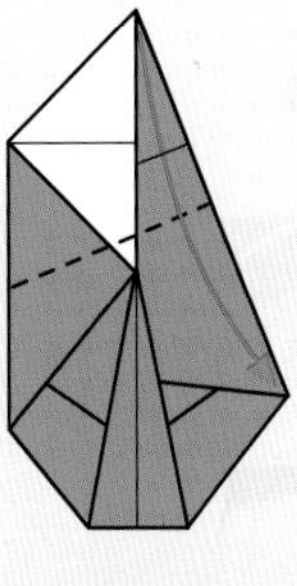

11 Fold the top right sloping edge in half down.

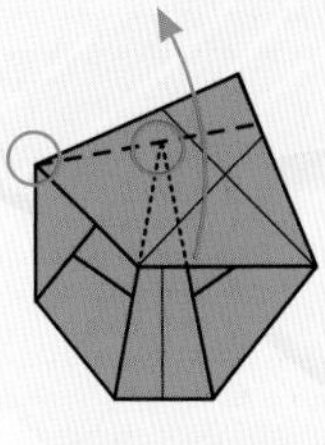

12 Fold the front flap up in the way shown here.

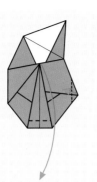

13 Fold the beak down. Also fold the right corner in as shown to round off the top of the head. Step 14 shows what the result should look like.

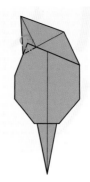

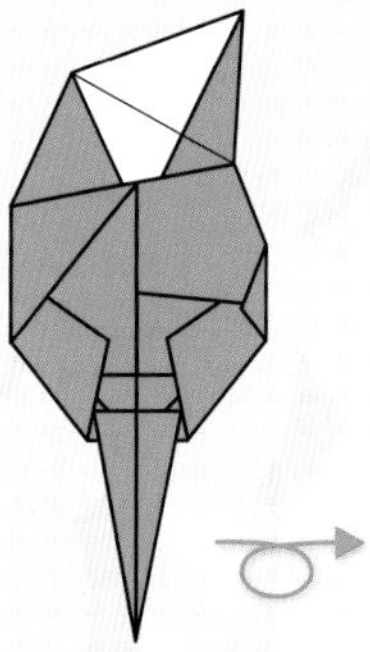

14 Turn over sideways.

15 Fold this triangular flap back as far as it will go to lock the layers together.

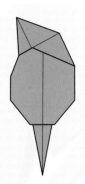

16 Pikipek's head is finished.

Folding the body

Make sure you start folding with the template arranged so that the asterisk is at the top.

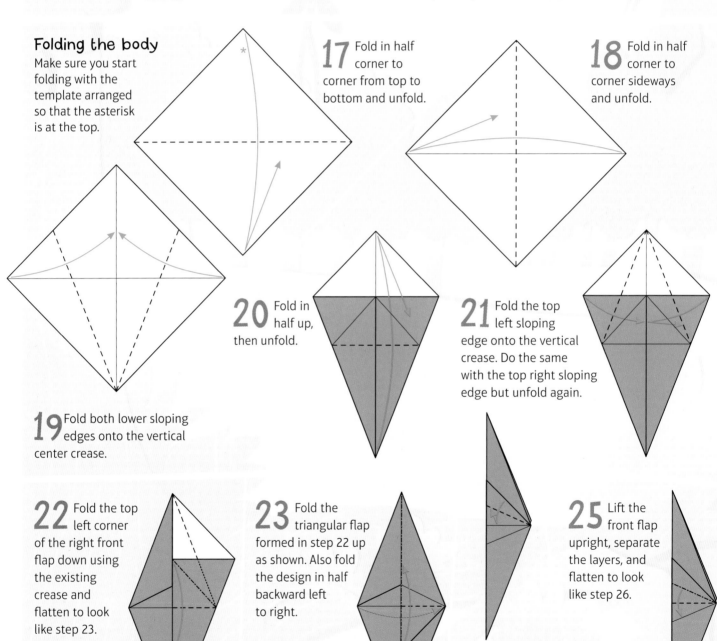

17 Fold in half corner to corner from top to bottom and unfold.

18 Fold in half corner to corner sideways and unfold.

19 Fold both lower sloping edges onto the vertical center crease.

20 Fold in half up, then unfold.

21 Fold the top left sloping edge onto the vertical crease. Do the same with the top right sloping edge but unfold again.

22 Fold the top left corner of the right front flap down using the existing crease and flatten to look like step 23.

23 Fold the triangular flap formed in step 22 up as shown. Also fold the design in half backward left to right.

24 Fold the front flap in half down, then unfold.

25 Lift the front flap upright, separate the layers, and flatten to look like step 26.

26 Turn over sideways.

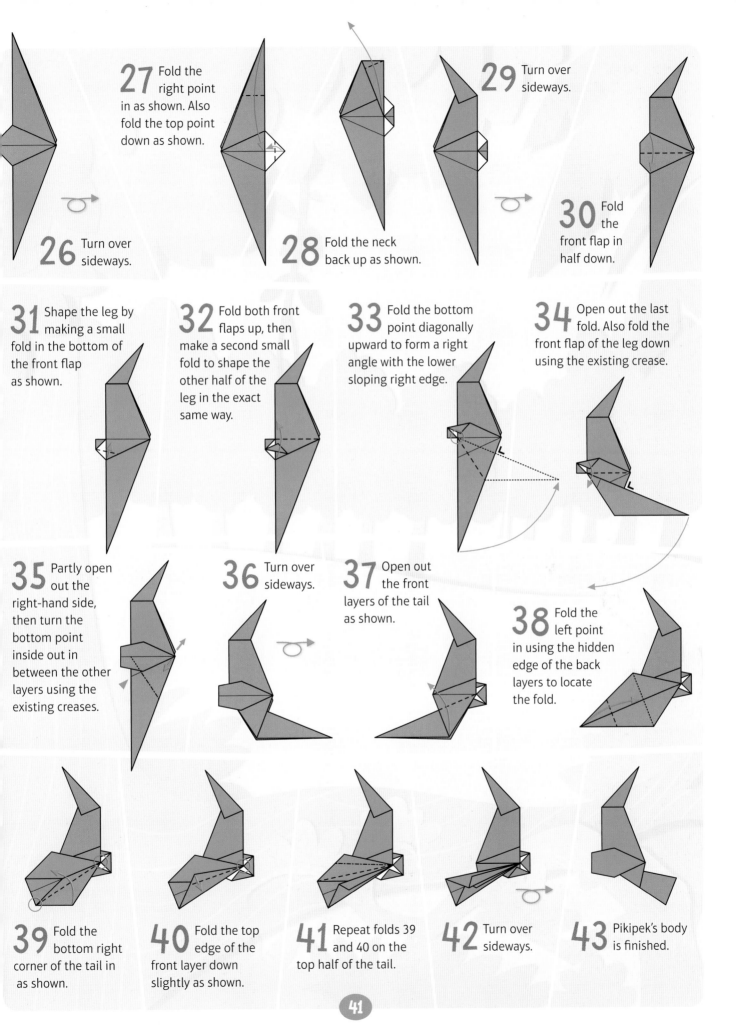

27 Fold the right point in as shown. Also fold the top point down as shown.

28 Fold the neck back up as shown.

29 Turn over sideways.

30 Fold the front flap in half down.

31 Shape the leg by making a small fold in the bottom of the front flap as shown.

32 Fold both front flaps up, then make a second small fold to shape the other half of the leg in the exact same way.

33 Fold the bottom point diagonally upward to form a right angle with the lower sloping right edge.

34 Open out the last fold. Also fold the front flap of the leg down using the existing crease.

35 Partly open out the right-hand side, then turn the bottom point inside out in between the other layers using the existing creases.

36 Turn over sideways.

37 Open out the front layers of the tail as shown.

38 Fold the left point in using the hidden edge of the back layers to locate the fold.

39 Fold the bottom right corner of the tail in as shown.

40 Fold the top edge of the front layer down slightly as shown.

41 Repeat folds 39 and 40 on the top half of the tail.

42 Turn over sideways.

43 Pikipek's body is finished.

Folding the wing

Start folding with the plain side of the template face up.

44 Follow steps 1 and 2 of "Folding the head."

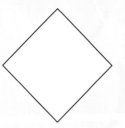

45 Fold the top corner down as shown.

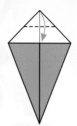

46 Fold the right corner in as shown.

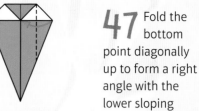

47 Fold the bottom point diagonally up to form a right angle with the lower sloping left edge.

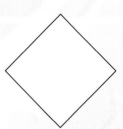

48 Make three tiny folds to round off the corners of the wing in the way shown in step 50.

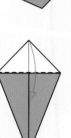

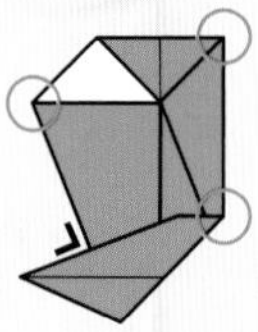

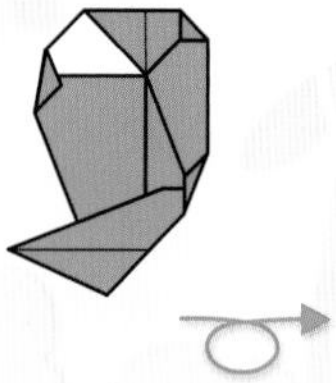

49 Turn over sideways.

50 Pikipek's wing is finished.

Folding the foot

Start folding with the plain side of the template face up. Because Pikipek's foot is so tiny, these diagrams have been drawn on a larger scale than usual.

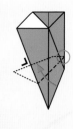

51 Follow steps 1 and 2 of "Folding the head."

52 Fold the top corner down along the line of the top edge of the front layers.

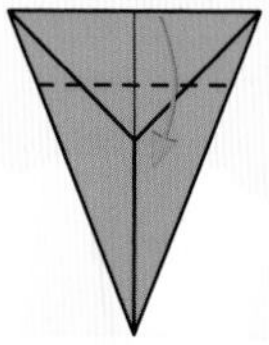

53 Fold the top edge down. There is no location point for this fold. Just make it look as much like step 55 as you can.

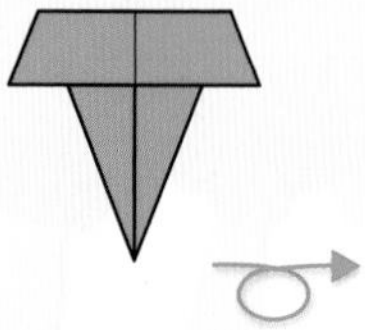

54 Turn over sideways.

55 Fold the bottom point up at a slight angle as shown.

56 Fold both sides of the leg into the center and flatten the paper to look like step 58.

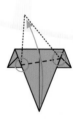

57 Fold both top corners of the foot diagonally in as shown.

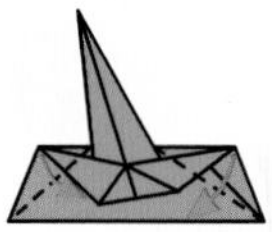

58 Turn over sideways.

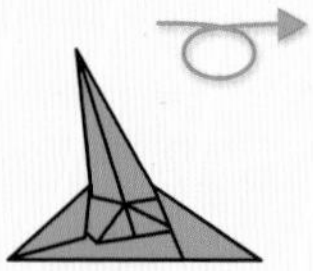

59 Pikipek's foot is finished.

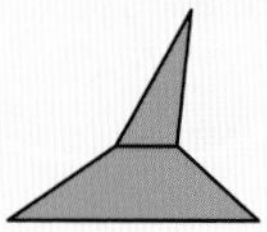

Assembling Pikipek

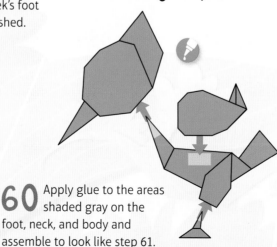

60 Apply glue to the areas shaded gray on the foot, neck, and body and assemble to look like step 61.

61 Pikipek is finished.

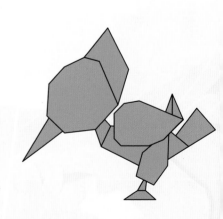

Alolan Exeggutor

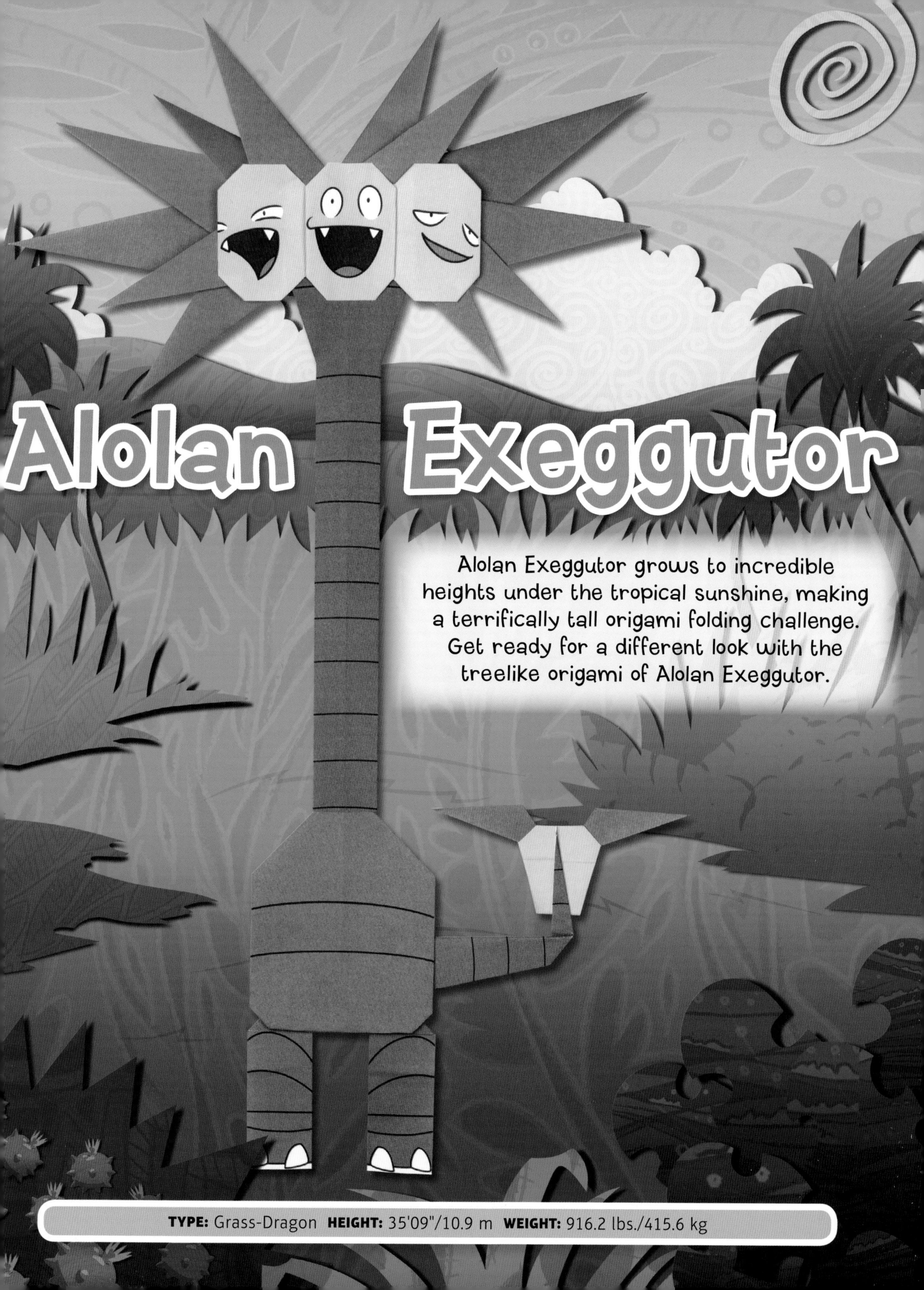

Alolan Exeggutor grows to incredible heights under the tropical sunshine, making a terrifically tall origami folding challenge. Get ready for a different look with the treelike origami of Alolan Exeggutor.

TYPE: Grass-Dragon **HEIGHT:** 35'09"/10.9 m **WEIGHT:** 916.2 lbs./415.6 kg

How To Make
Alolan Exeggutor

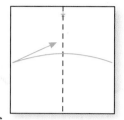

 Alolan Exeggutor is folded from twelve pieces of paper. You can find the templates on pages 71, 73, 75, and 79. Cut out all the pieces carefully.

Folding the body
Make sure you start folding with the template arranged so that the asterisk is at the top.

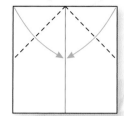

1 Fold in half sideways, then unfold.

2 Fold both top corners into the center.

3 Fold both outside edges in by about one-third, as shown.

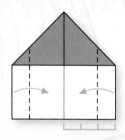

4 Fold both bottom corners in as shown.

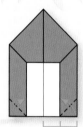

5 Fold the bottom edge up slightly.

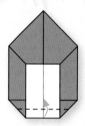

6 Turn over sideways.

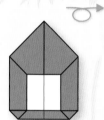

7 Alolan Exeggutor's body is finished.

Folding the neck
Make sure you start folding with the template arranged so that the asterisk is at the top.

8 Fold in half sideways, then unfold.

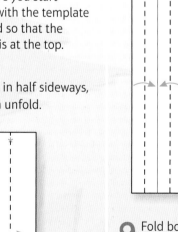

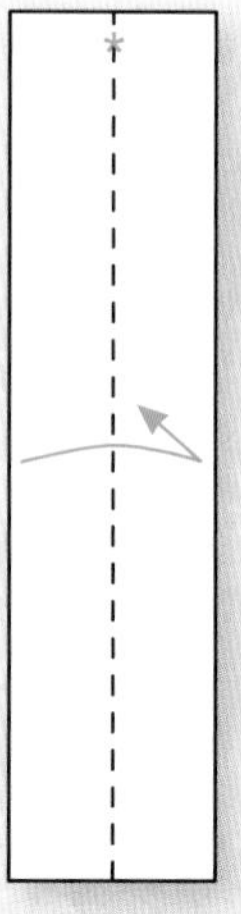

9 Fold both outside edges into the center.

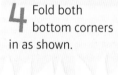

10 Open out the folds made in step 9.

11 Fold in half sideways again.

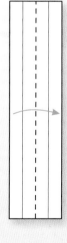

12 Cut along where indicated by the thick black line. This cut should be made in both layers.

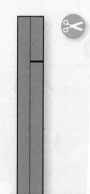

13 Open out.

44

14 Fold both top outside flaps in diagonally as shown.

15 Fold the lower part of both outside edges into the center again using the existing creases, then turn over sideways.

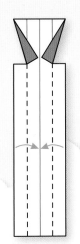

16 Alolan Exeggutor's neck is finished.

Folding the legs

Make sure you start folding with the template arranged so that the asterisk is at the top.

17 Fold in half sideways, then unfold.

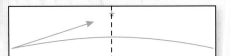

18 Fold both outside edges into the center, then unfold.

19 Fold both outside edges in along the bottom of the printed feet.

20 Fold in half down.

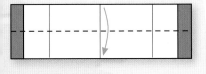

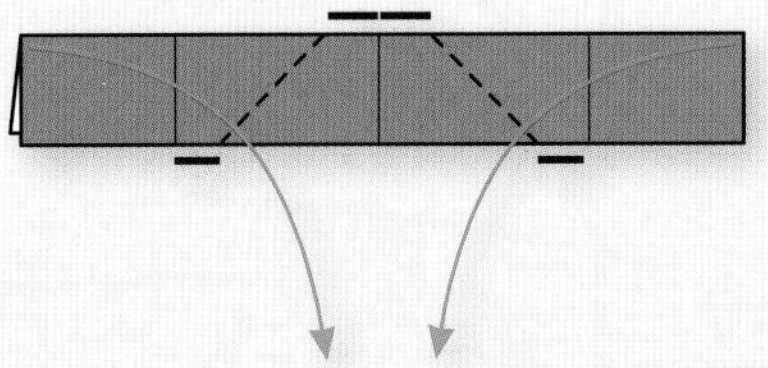

21 Fold both legs diagonally down as shown. The thick black lines show you how the creases are located.

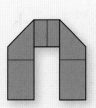

22 When they are finished, Alolan Exeggutor's legs should look as shown.

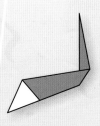

Folding the tail

Make sure you start folding with the template arranged plain side up.

23 Fold the right sloping edge onto the bottom edge.

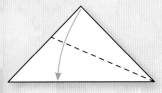

24 Fold the bottom edge onto the top sloping edge.

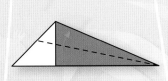

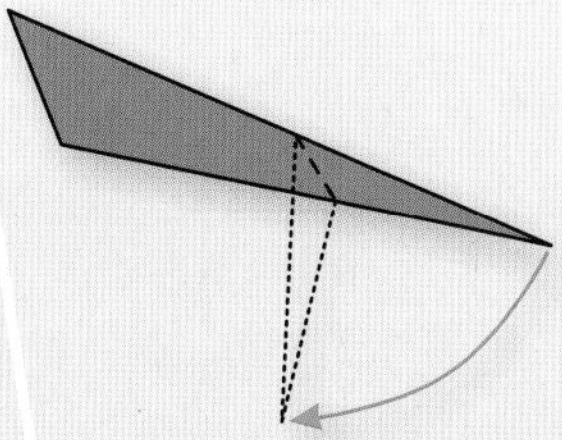

25 Fold the right point down to the position marked by the dotted line.

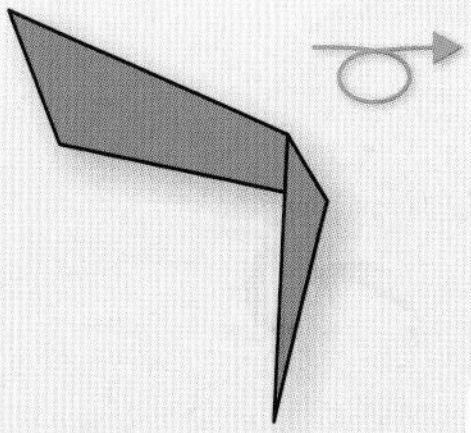

26 Turn over vetically.

27 Alolan Exeggutor's tail is finished.

Folding the triple heads

Make sure you start folding with the template arranged so that the asterisk is at the top.

28 Fold in half sideways, then unfold.

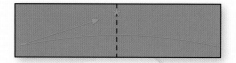

29 Fold both outside edges into the center.

30 Turn over sideways.

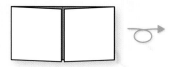

31 Fold both outside edges into the center but only make creases in the front layers, allowing the back layers to flip out. The result should look like step 32.

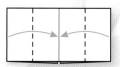

32 Open out the front right flap to the left.

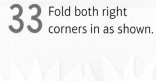

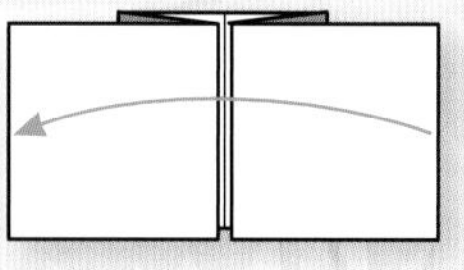

33 Fold both right corners in as shown.

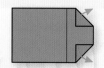

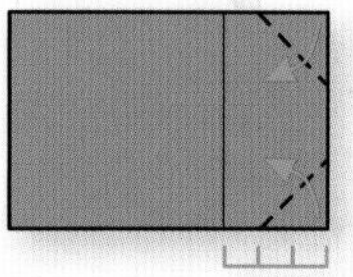

34 Open out the folds made in step 33.

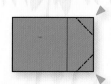

35 Turn both right corners inside out in between the other layers using the creases you made in step 33.

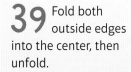

36 Fold the right edge in as shown.

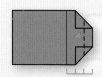

37 Fold the left edge across to the right using the existing crease.

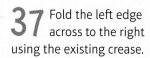

38 Fold the new left edge across to the right using the existing crease, then repeat steps 33 through 37 on the other half of the paper in mirror image.

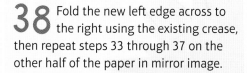

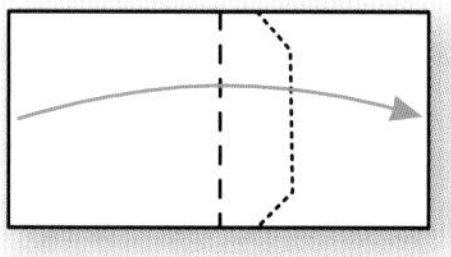

39 Fold both outside edges into the center, then unfold.

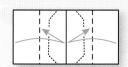

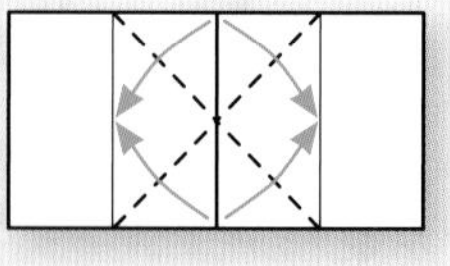

40 Fold all four central corners out diagonally using the creases made in step 39 to locate the folds.

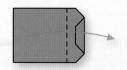

41 Make four tiny folds to shape the four outside corners. The result should look like step 42.

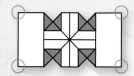

42 Turn over sideways.

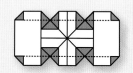

43 Alolan Exeggutor's three heads are finished.

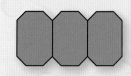

Folding the tail head

Make sure you start folding with the template arranged with the plain side facing up toward you.

44 Fold both top corners onto the bottom corner.

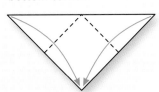

45 Fold both lower sloping edges into the center, then unfold.

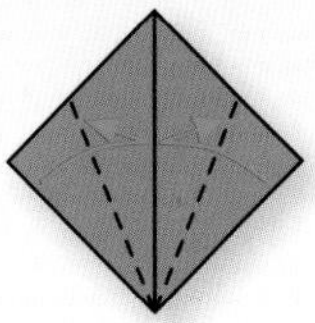

46 Turn both outside corners inside out in between the other layers using the creases made in step 45.

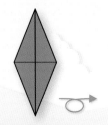

47 Fold both front bottom points up as shown.

48 Turn over sideways.

49 Fold the front flap down as shown.

50 Fold both top points outward to the positions marked by the dotted lines.

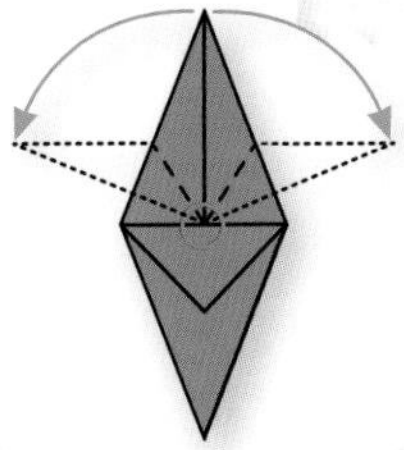

51 Undo the fold you made in step 49.

52 Turn over sideways.

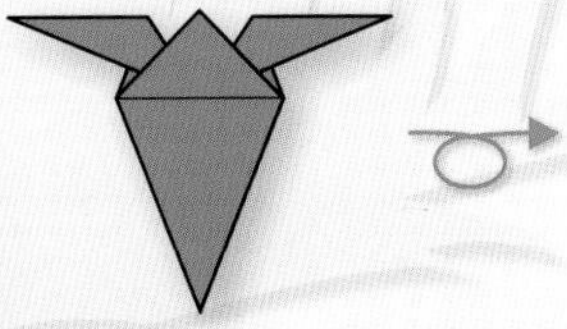

53 Narrow the face by folding both lower sloping edges in as far as they will go. Don't worry if the bottom point becomes untidy.

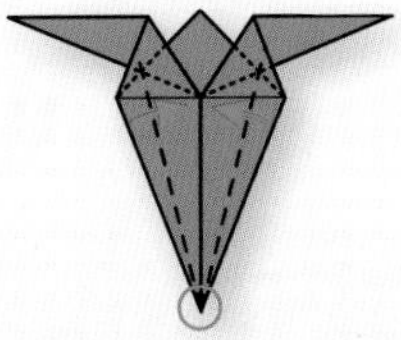

54 Fold the top central corner down as shown.

55 Fold the bottom point up and tuck it underneath the small flap at the top.

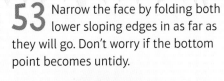

56 Turn over sideways.

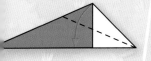

57 The tail head is finished.

Folding the leaves

Make sure you start folding with the template arranged with the plain side facing up toward you. There are six sets of leaves to fold altogether, two from large triangular templates and four from small ones. They are all folded in exactly the same way.

58 Fold the left sloping edge onto the bottom edge.

59 Fold the right sloping edge onto the bottom edge.

60 Fold the left point across to the right into roughly the position marked by the dotted line. It will not matter if some of your leaves are slightly different.

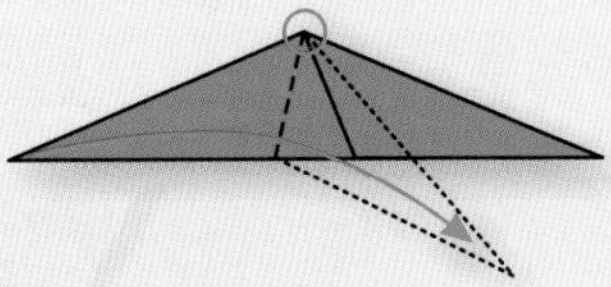

61 You will need four small sets of leaves as shown . . .

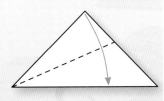

62 . . . and two large sets of leaves as shown.

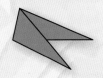

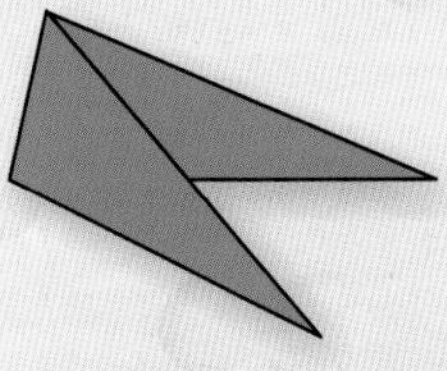

Assembling Alolan Exeggutor

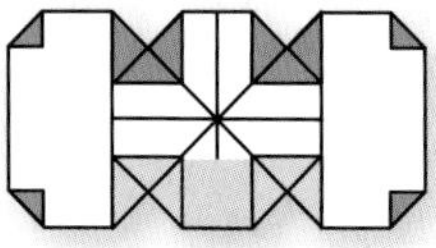

63 Apply glue to the area of the back of Alolan Exeggutor's triple head marked in gray here.

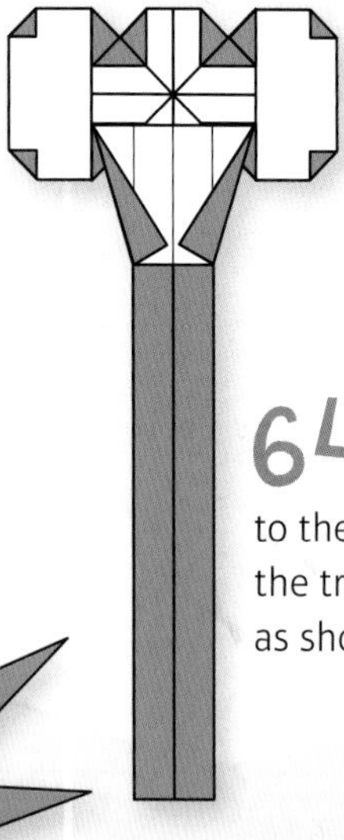

64 Attach the neck to the back of the triple head as shown.

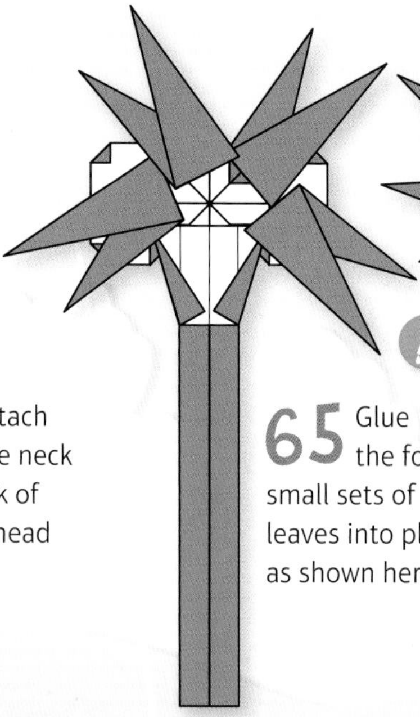

65 Glue the four small sets of leaves into place as shown here.

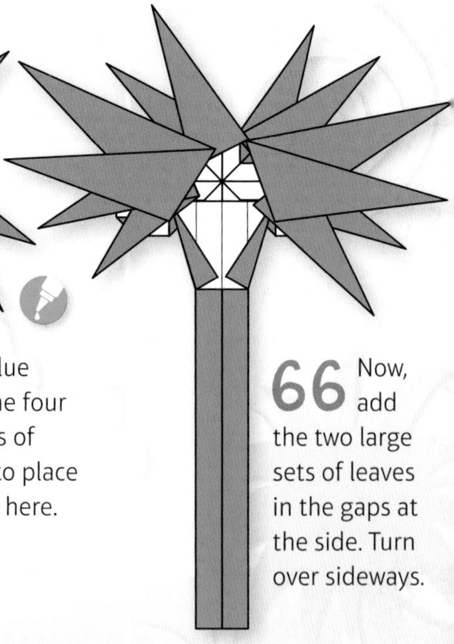

66 Now, add the two large sets of leaves in the gaps at the side. Turn over sideways.

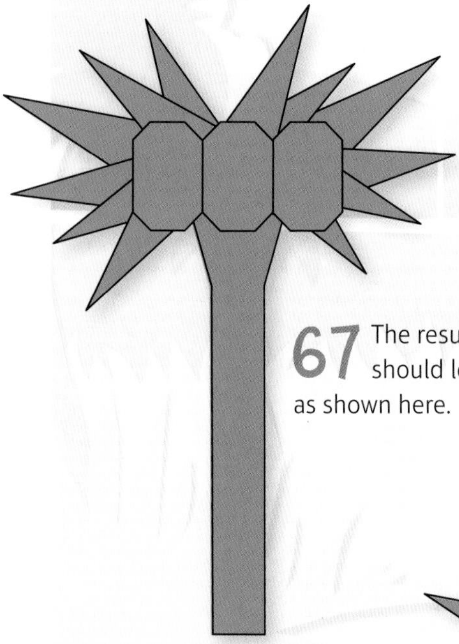

67 The result should look as shown here.

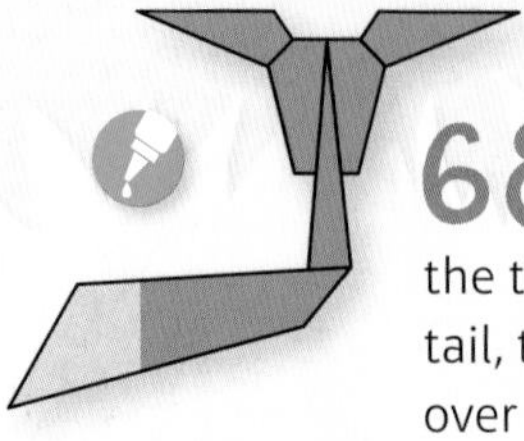

68 Apply glue to the tip of the tail, then turn over and . . .

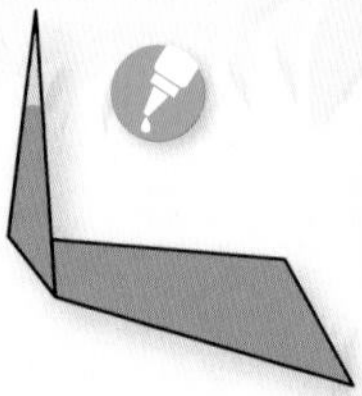

69 . . . attach to the front of the single tail head as shown. Apply glue to the other end of the tail . . .

70 . . . and attach to the back of the body as shown. Apply glue to the top of the legs and also attach them to the back of the body.

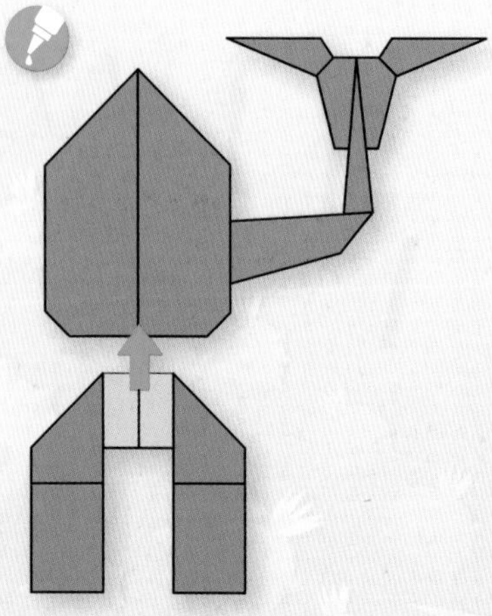

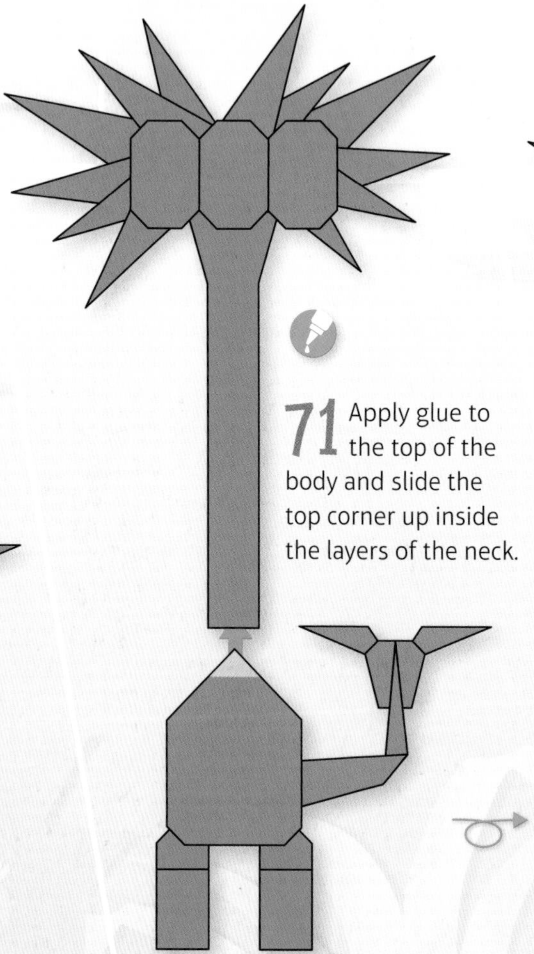

71 Apply glue to the top of the body and slide the top corner up inside the layers of the neck.

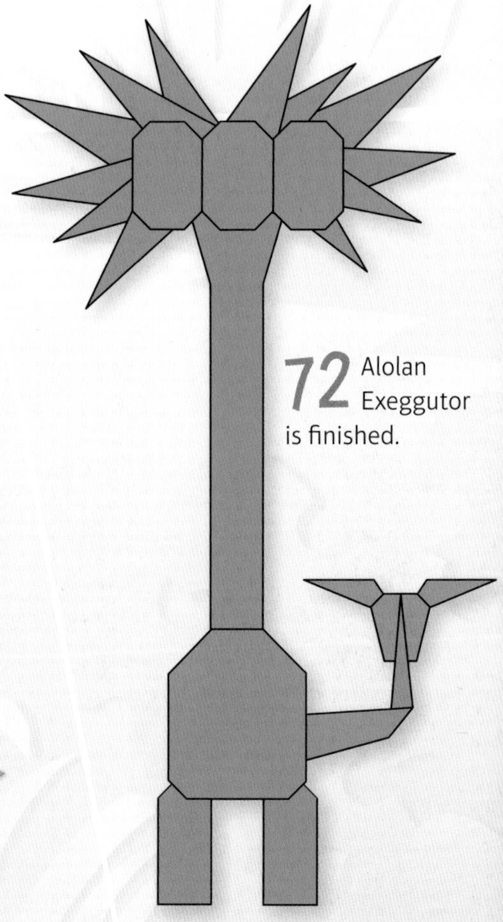

72 Alolan Exeggutor is finished.

Pikachu

Pikachu is folded from four pieces of paper. You'll find the other pieces on page 51.
See instructions on page 4

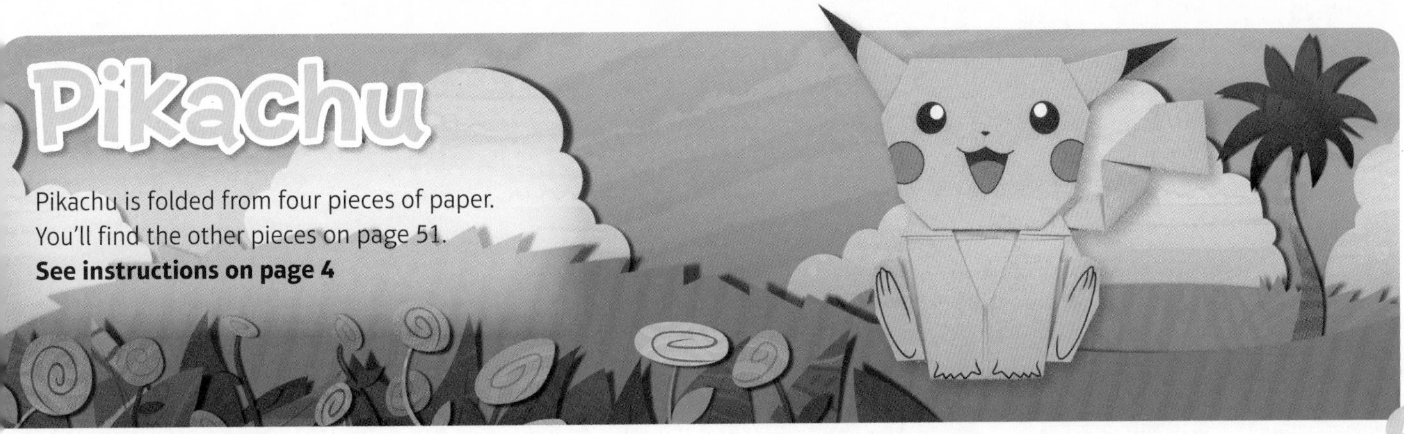

Body

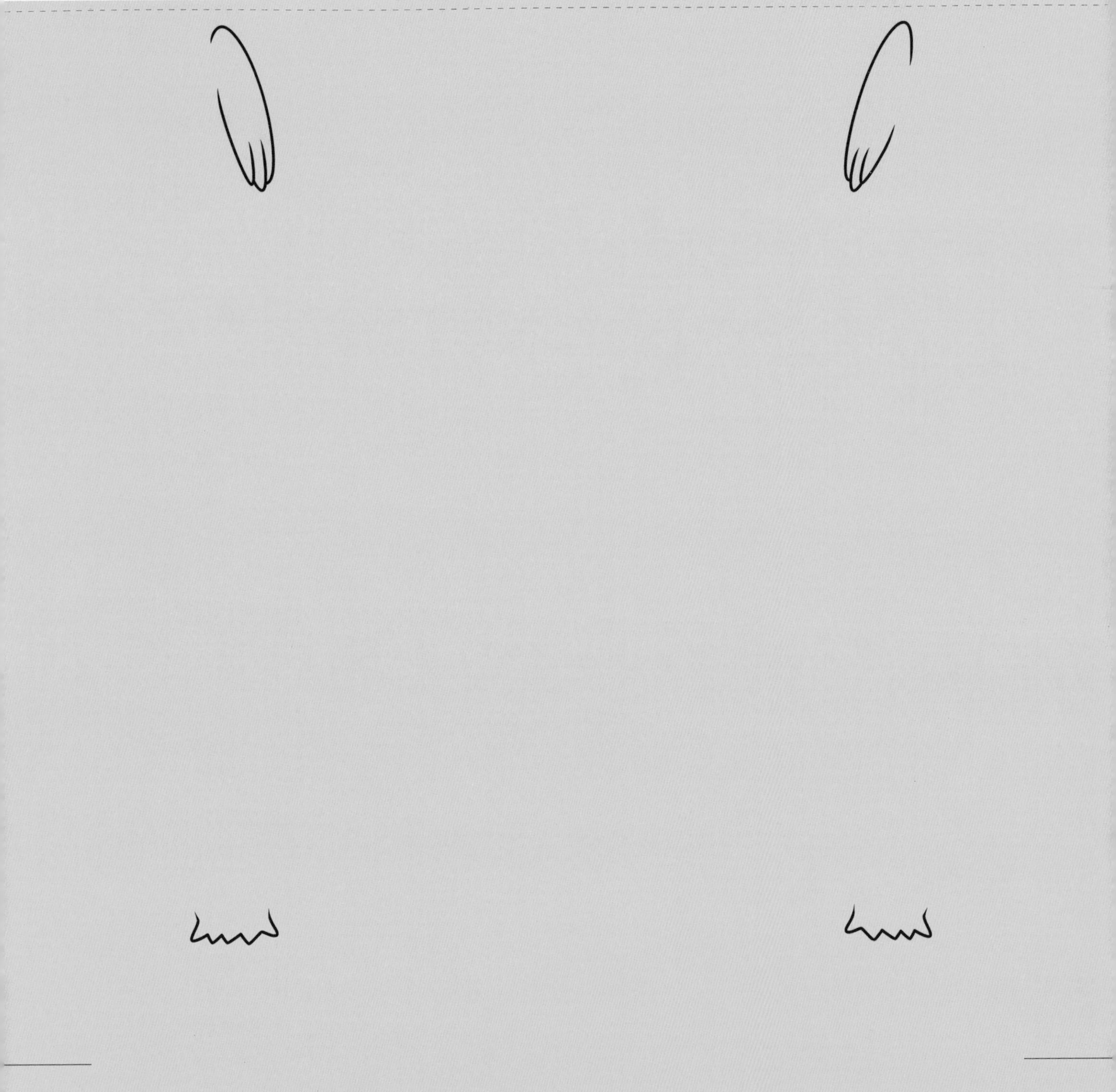

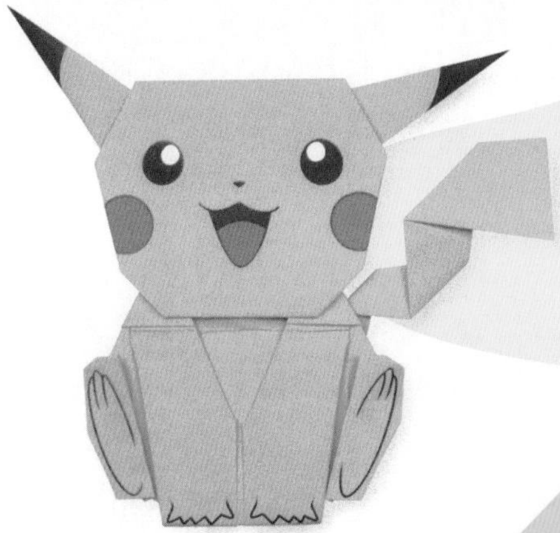

Here are Pikachu's face, ears, and tail.
See instructions on page 4

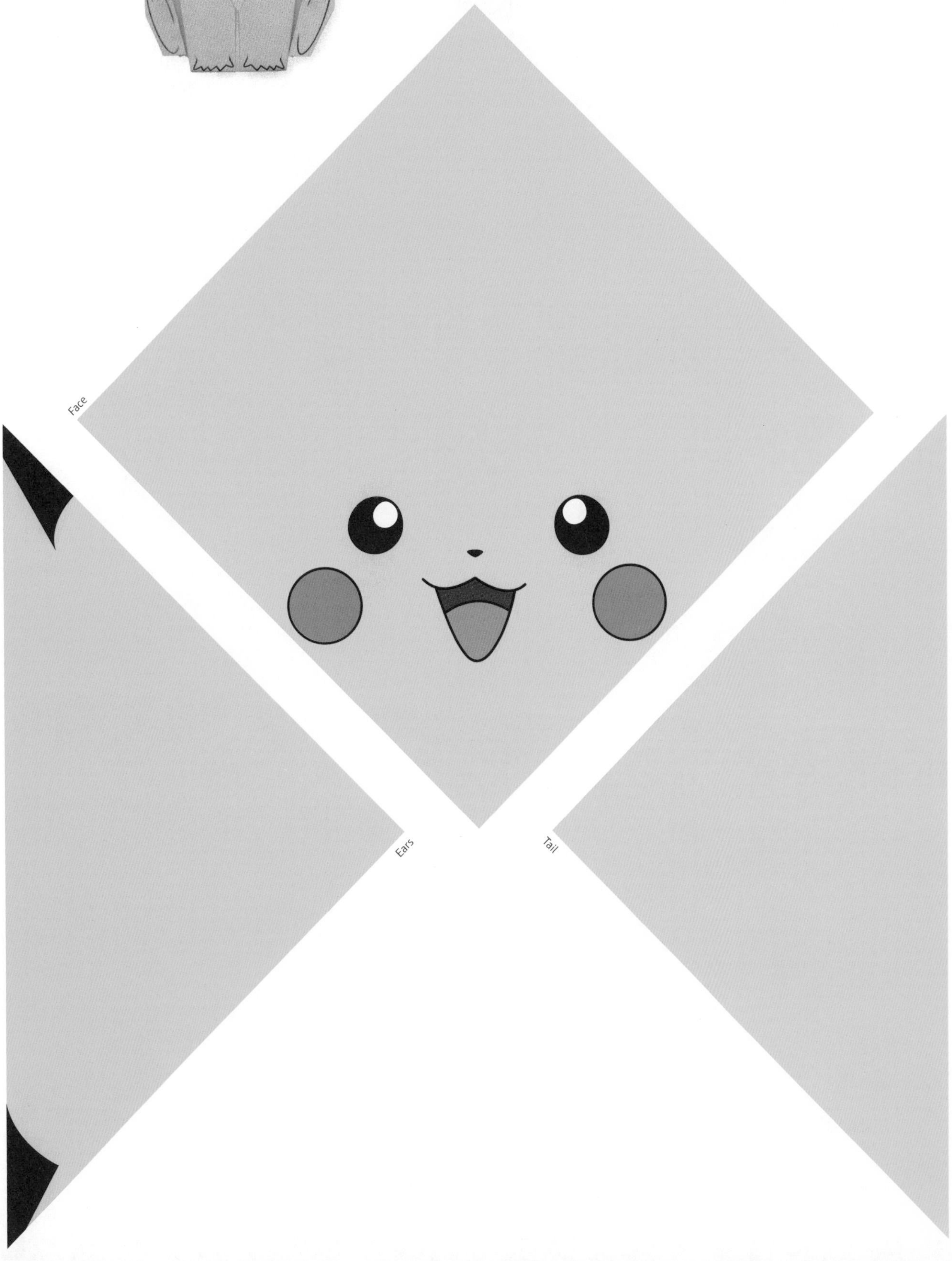
Face
Ears
Tail

*

Rowlet

Rowlet is folded from a single piece of paper.
See instructions on page 9

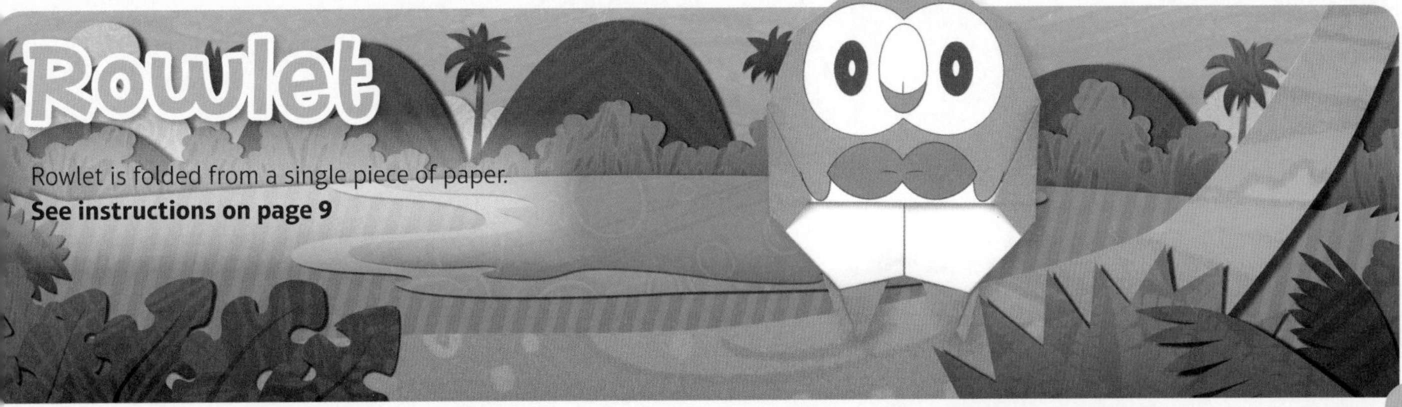

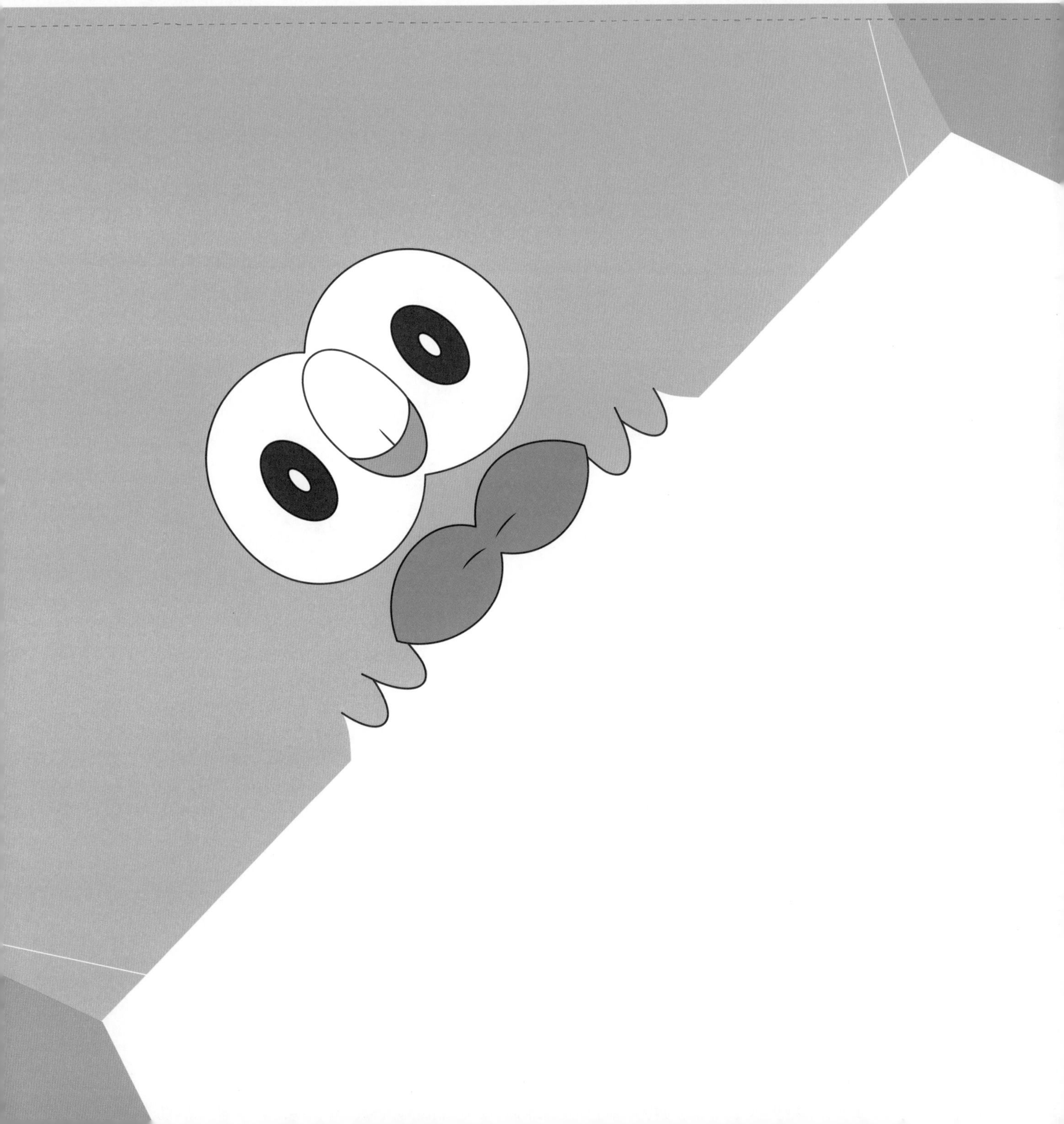

Togedemaru

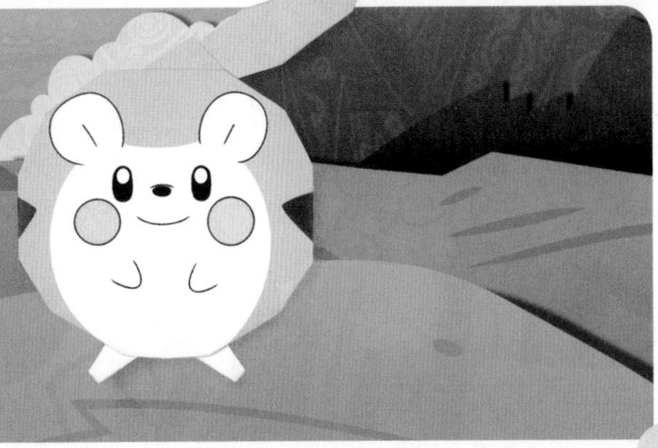

Togedemaru is folded from two pieces of paper.
You'll find the other piece on page 77.
See instructions on page 12

Body

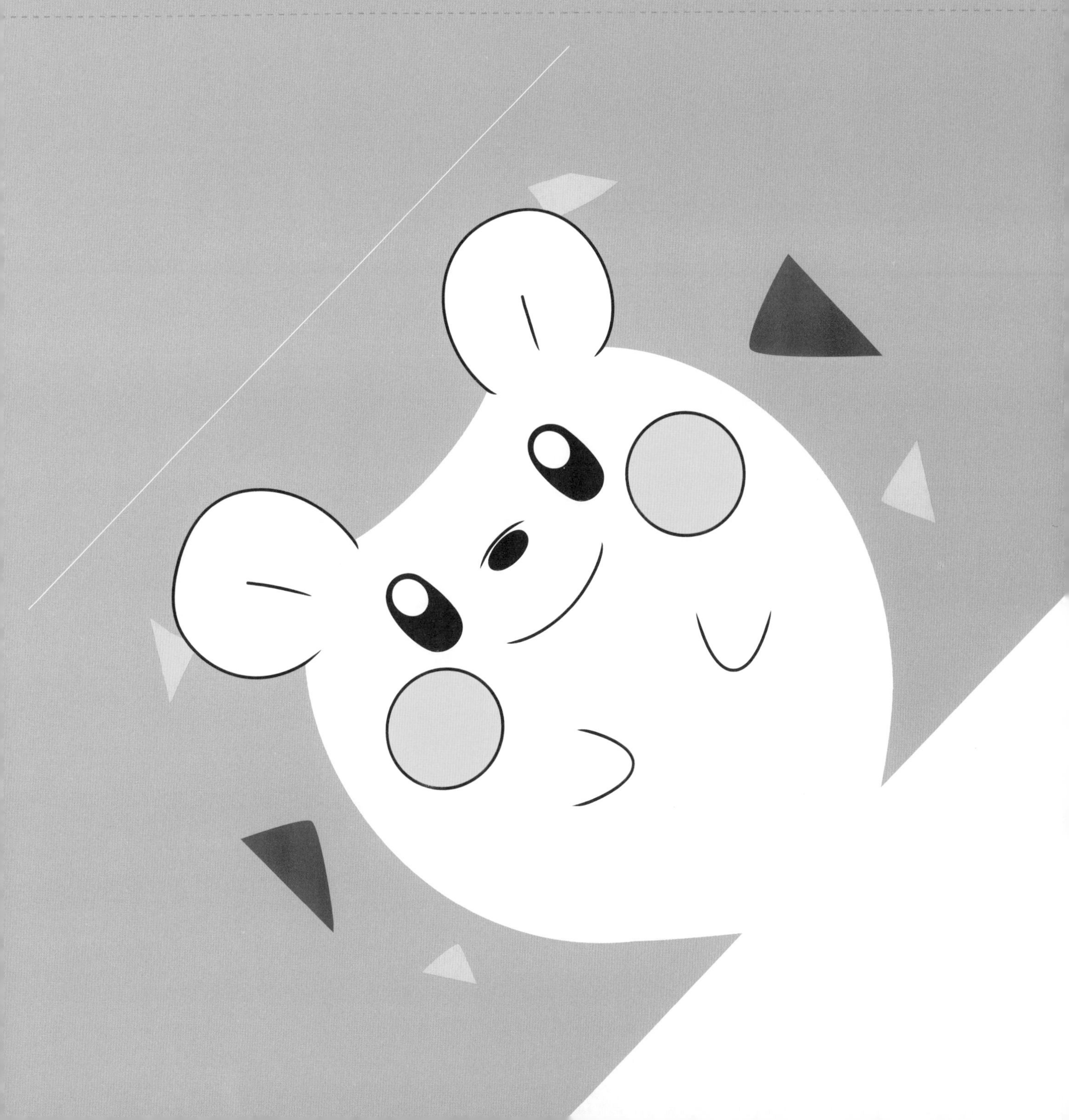

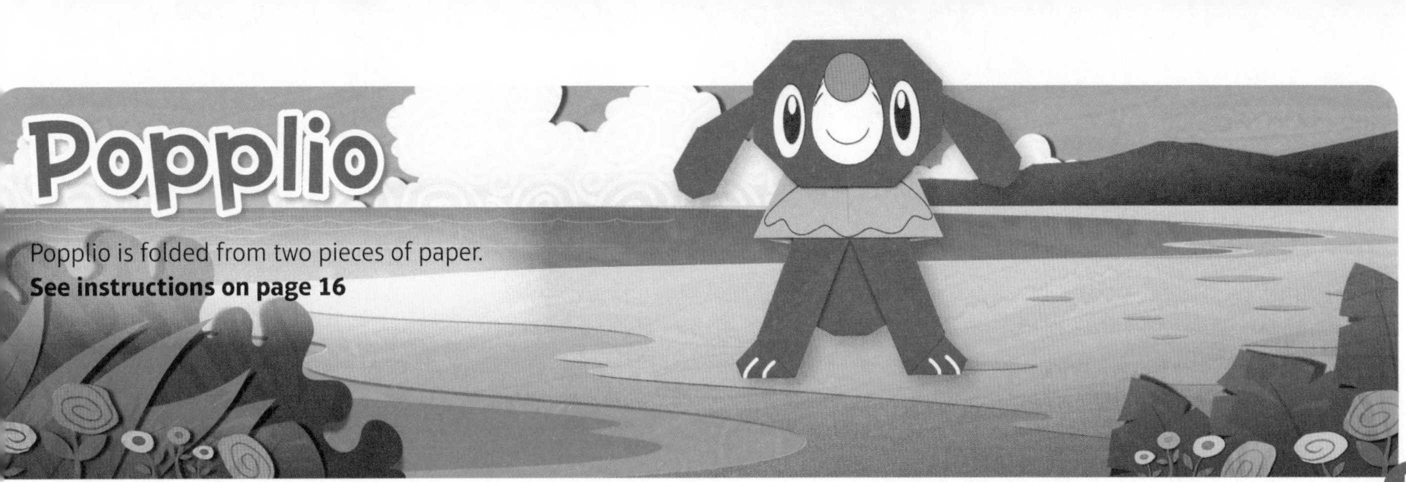
Popplio

Popplio is folded from two pieces of paper.
See instructions on page 16

Head and Body

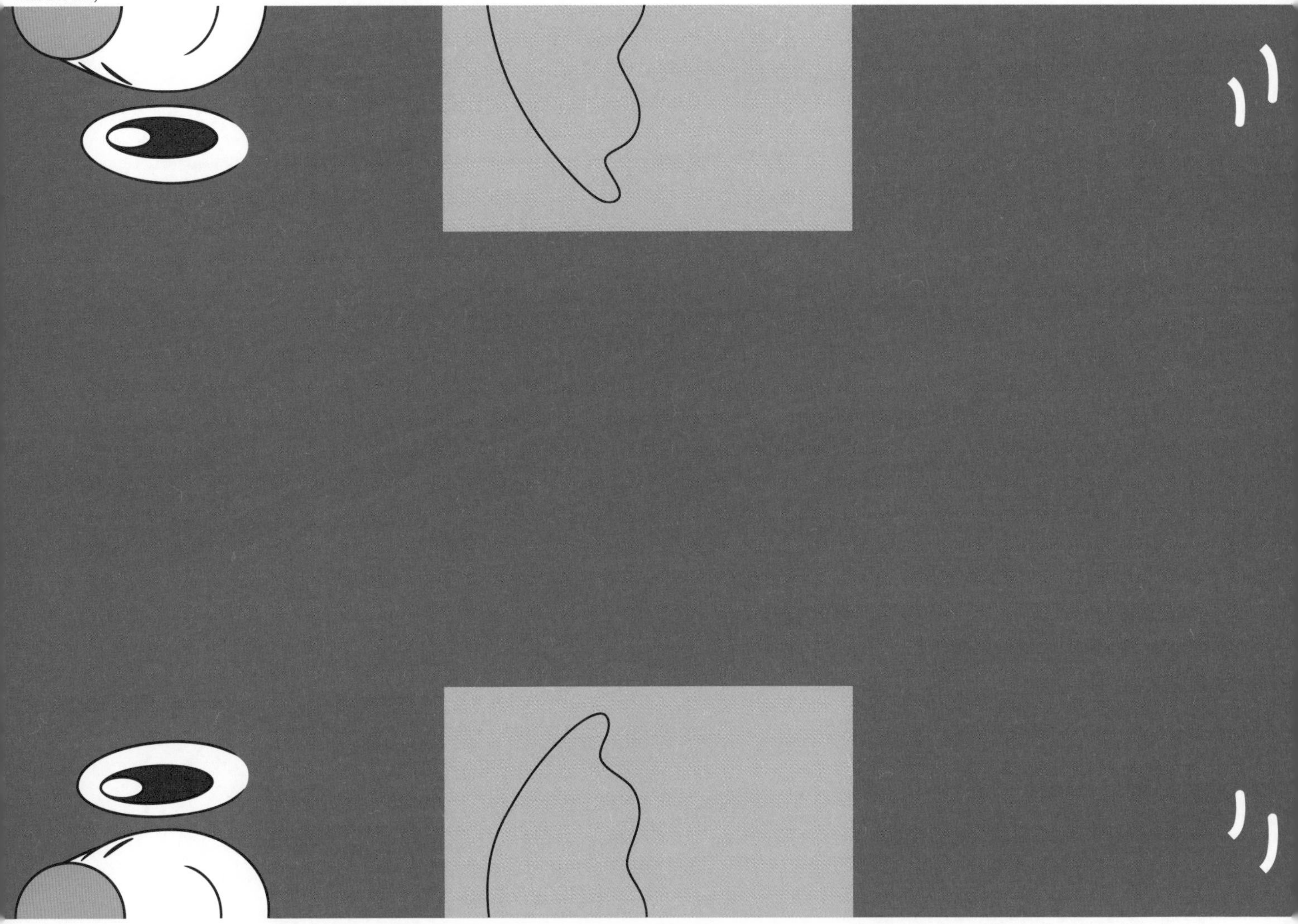

Ears

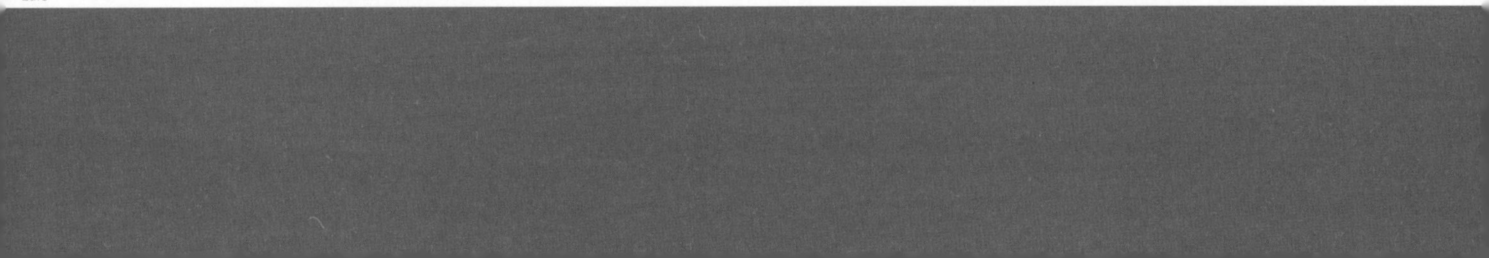

Mimikyu

Mimikyu is folded from two pieces of paper.

See instructions on page 20

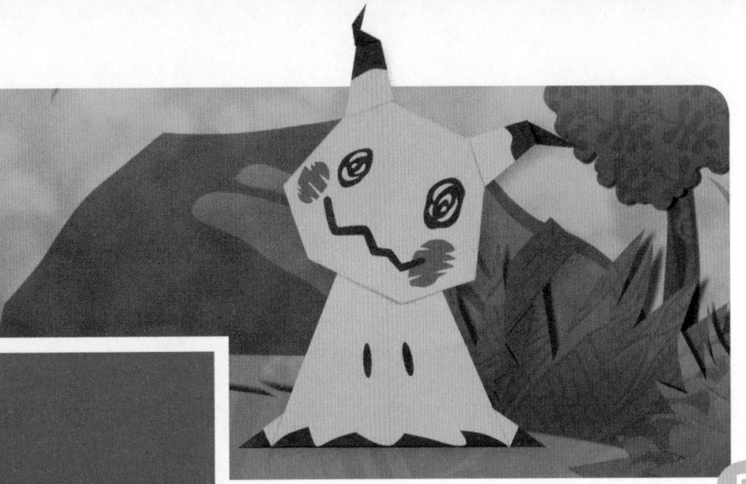

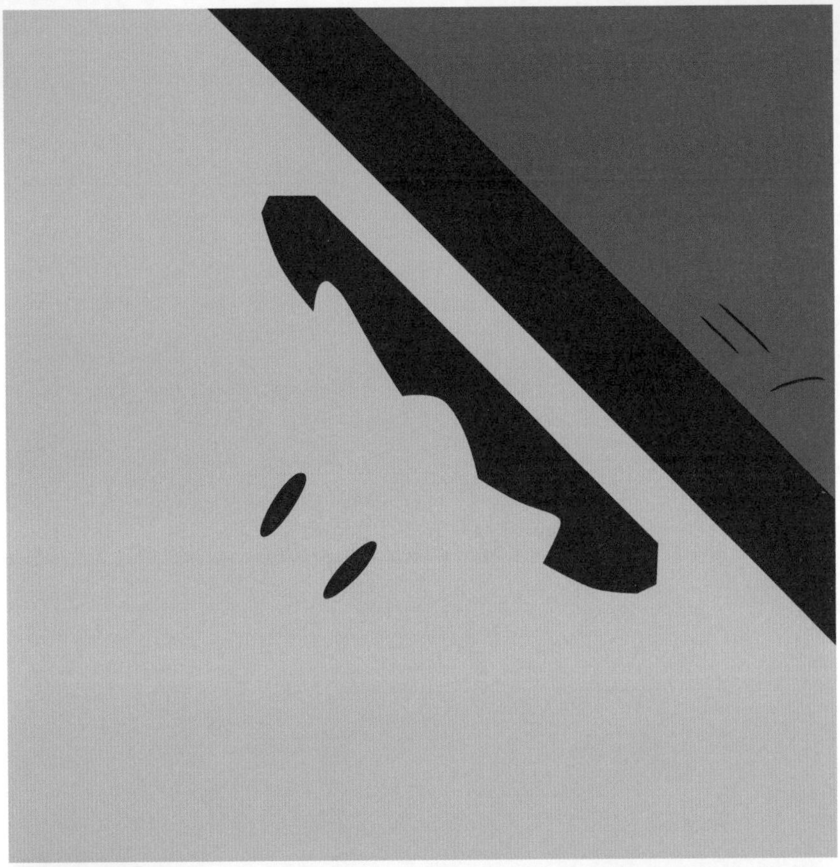

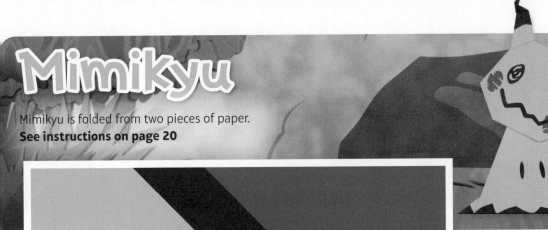

Body and Tail

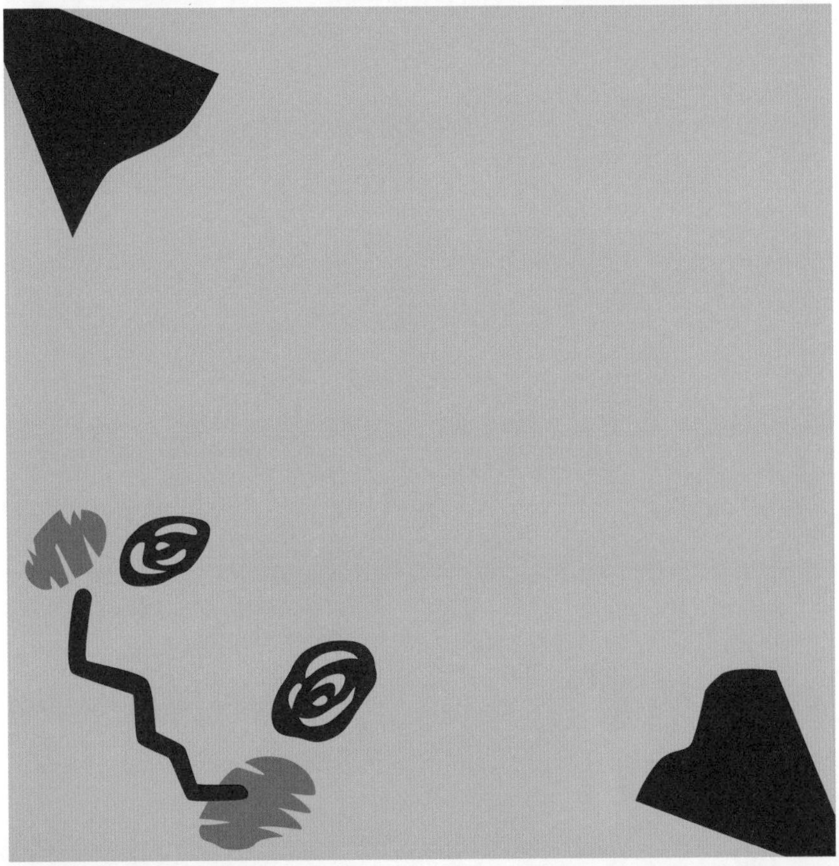

Rag Face and Ears

*

*

Rotom Dex

Rotom Dex is folded from four pieces of paper.
See instructions on page 24

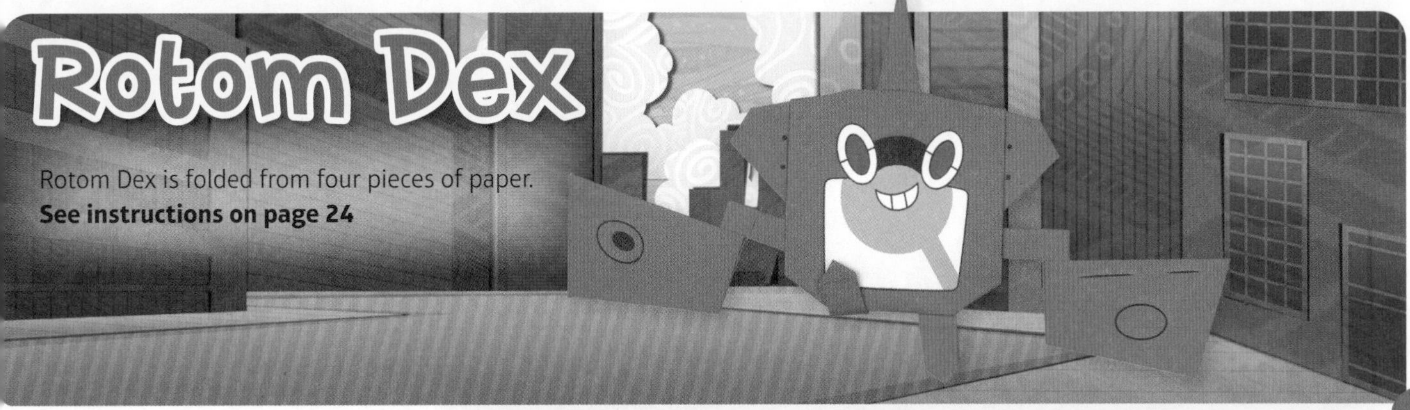

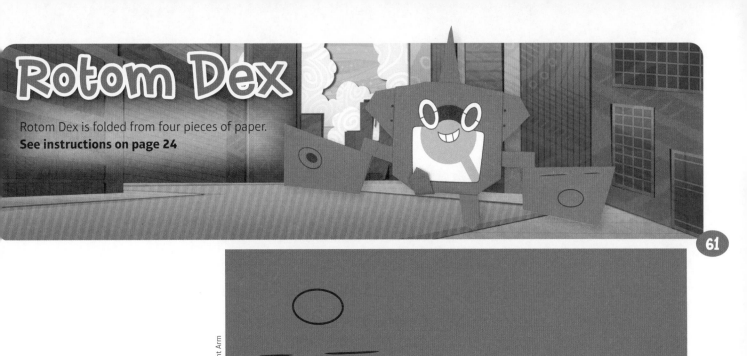

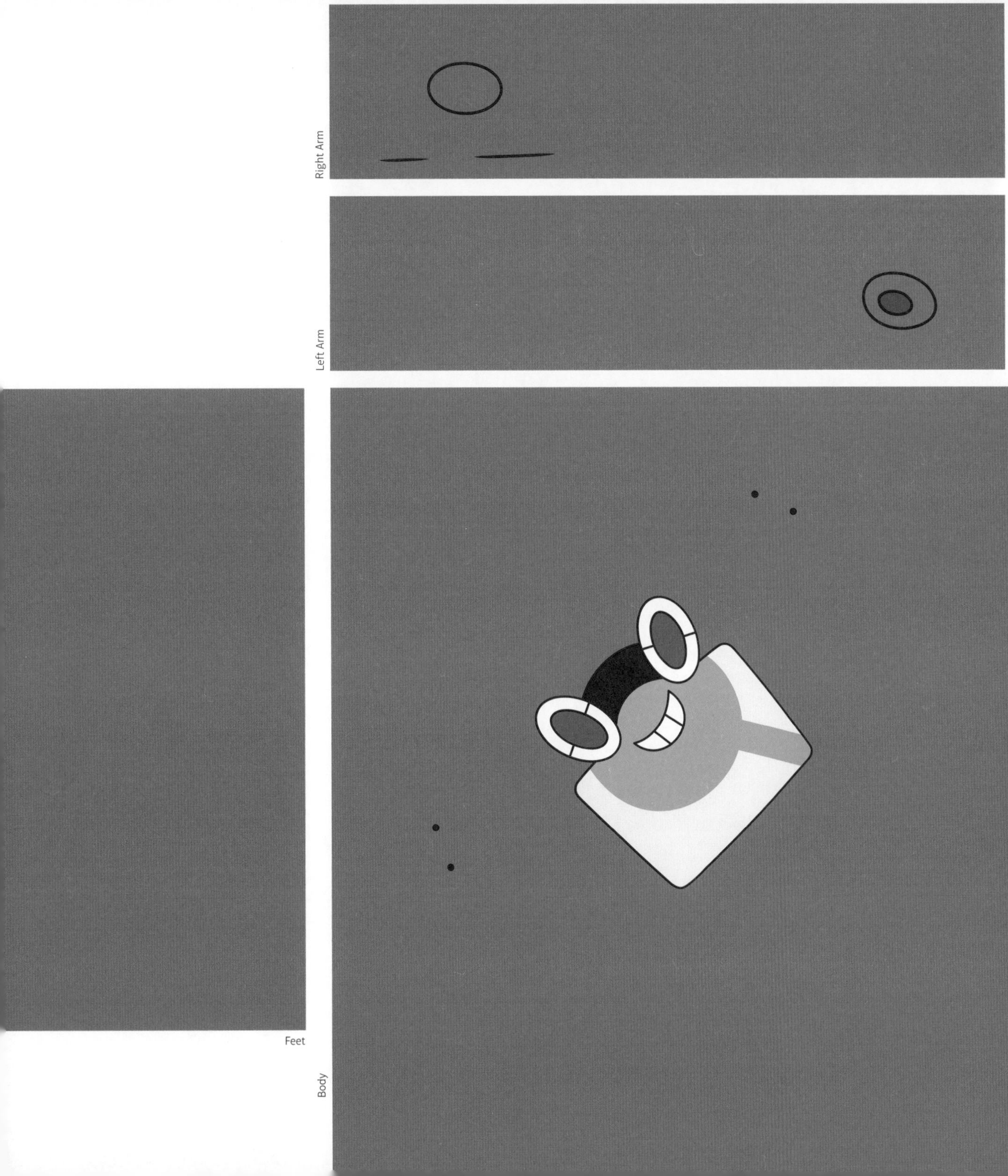
Right Arm
Left Arm
Feet
Body

Litten

Litten is folded from four pieces of paper.
You'll find the other piece on page 77.
See instructions on page 28

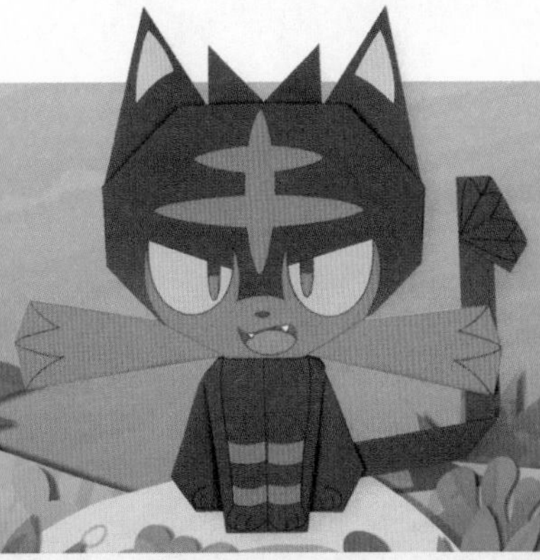

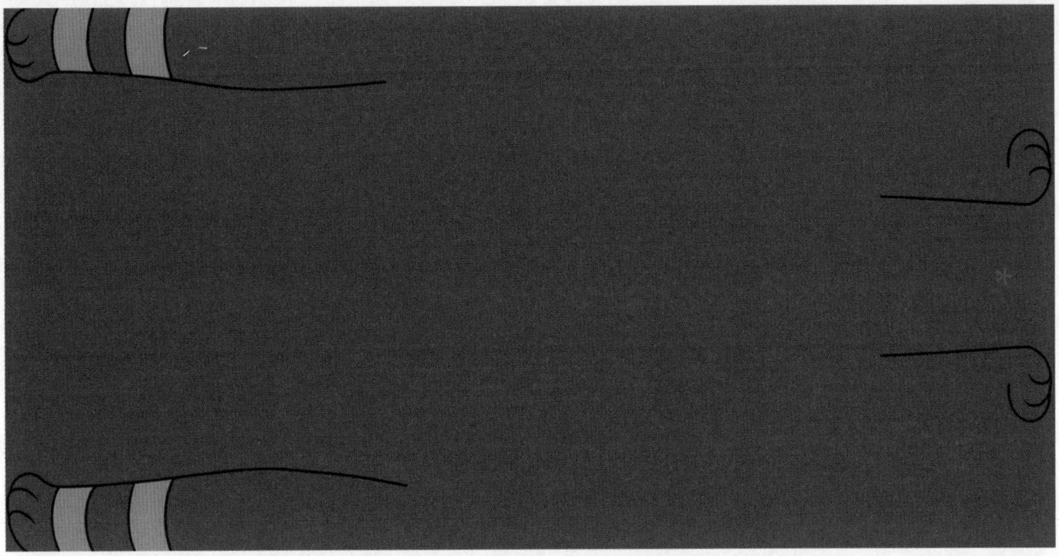

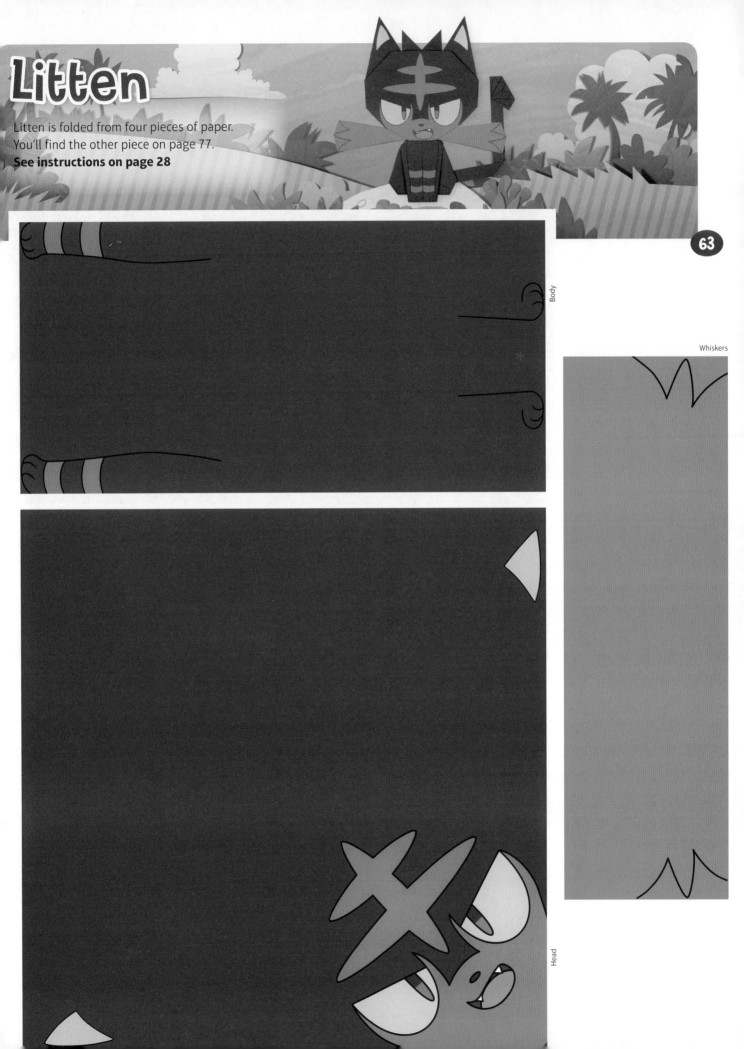

Body

Whiskers

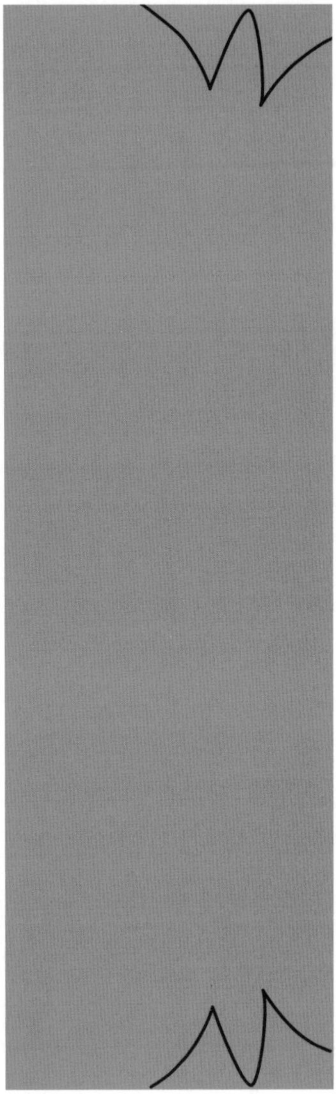

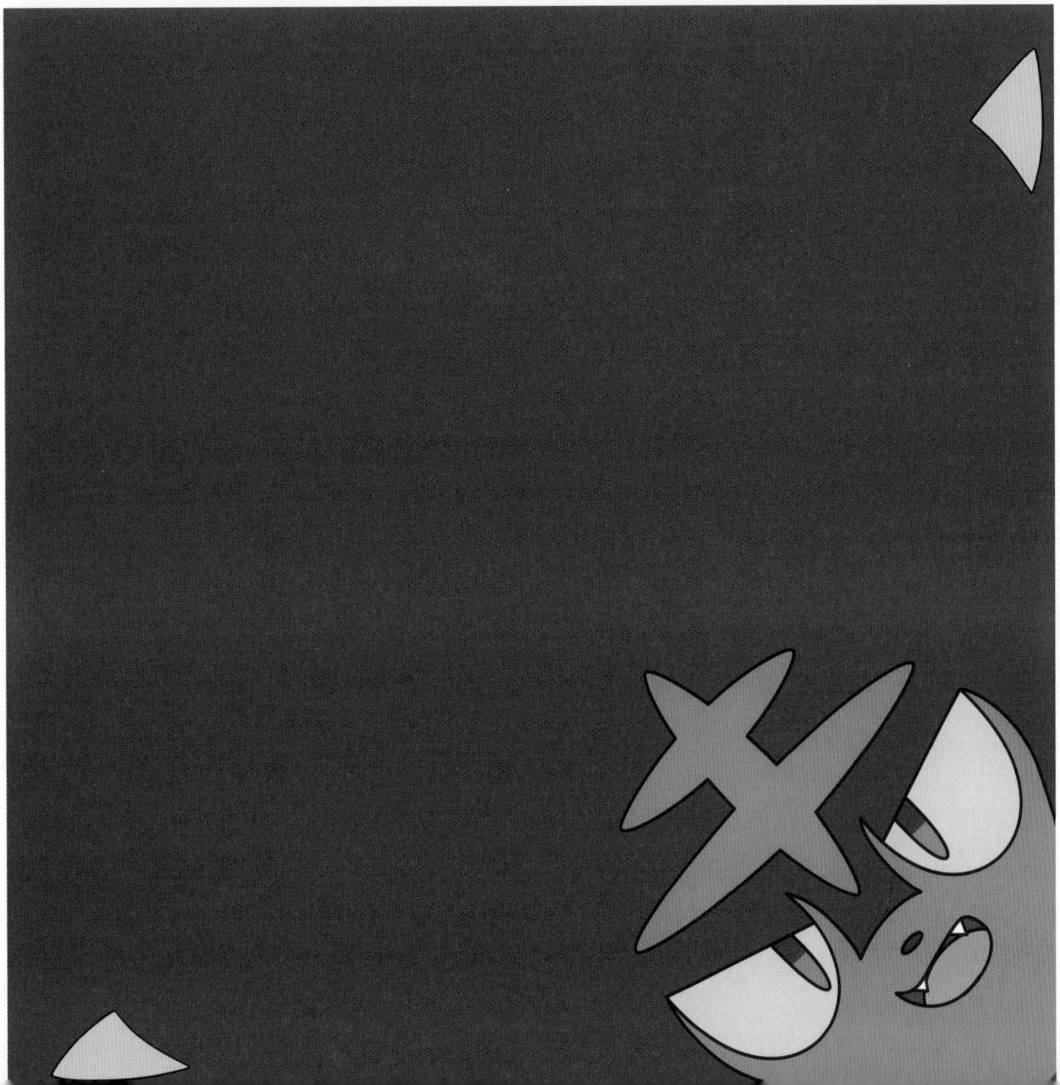

Head

*

*

Alolan Vulpix

Alolan Vulpix is folded from three pieces of paper. You'll find the other pieces on pages 67 and 77.

See instructions on page 33

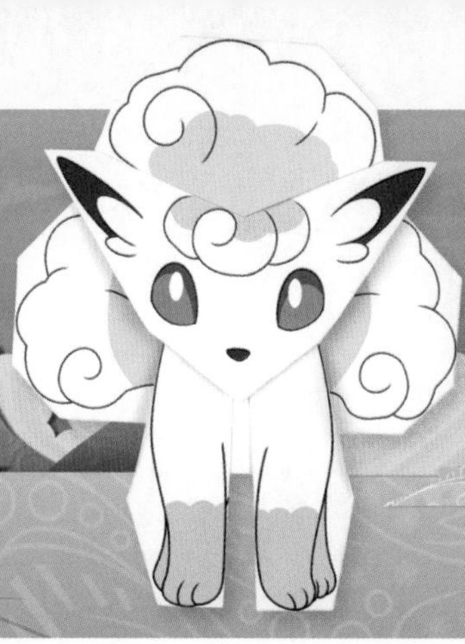

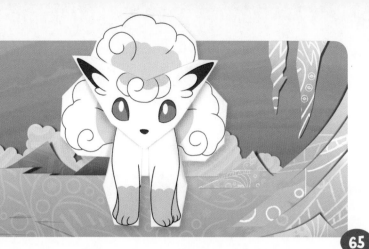

Tuft and Tails

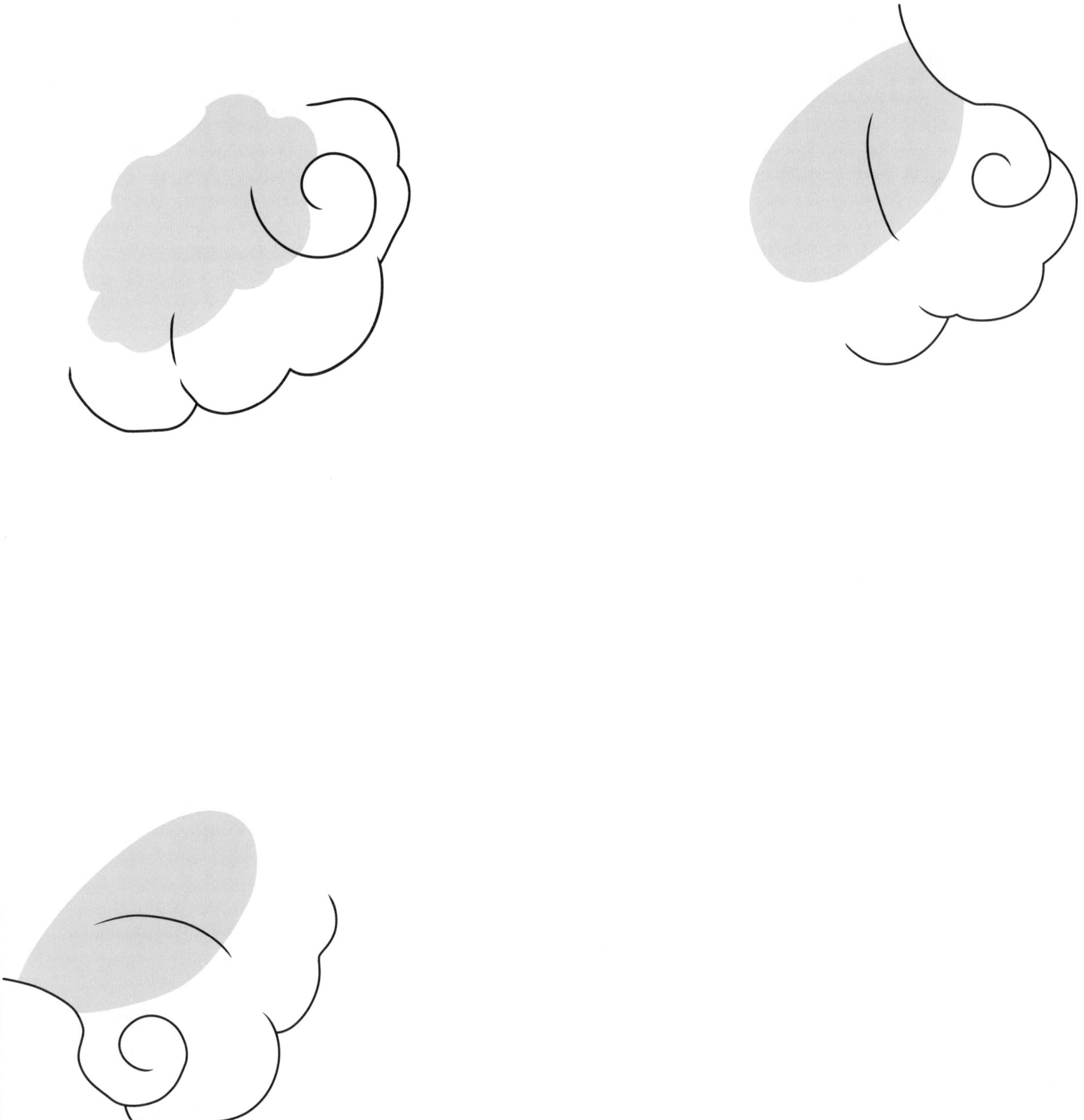

*

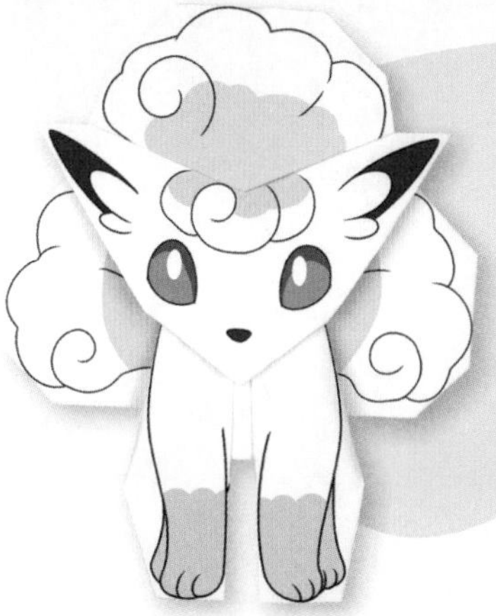

Here are Alolan Vulpix's legs.
See instructions on page 33

Legs

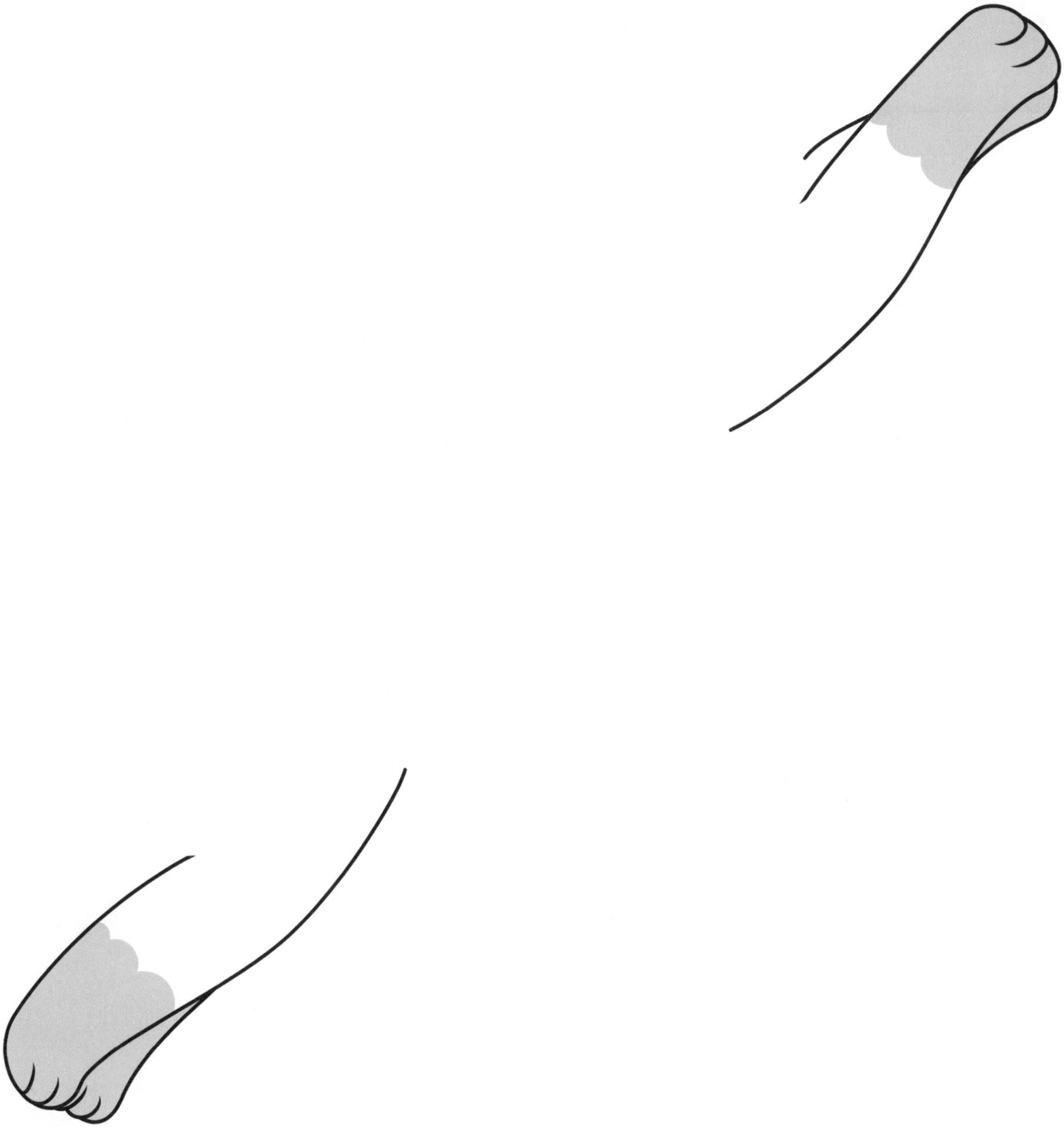

*

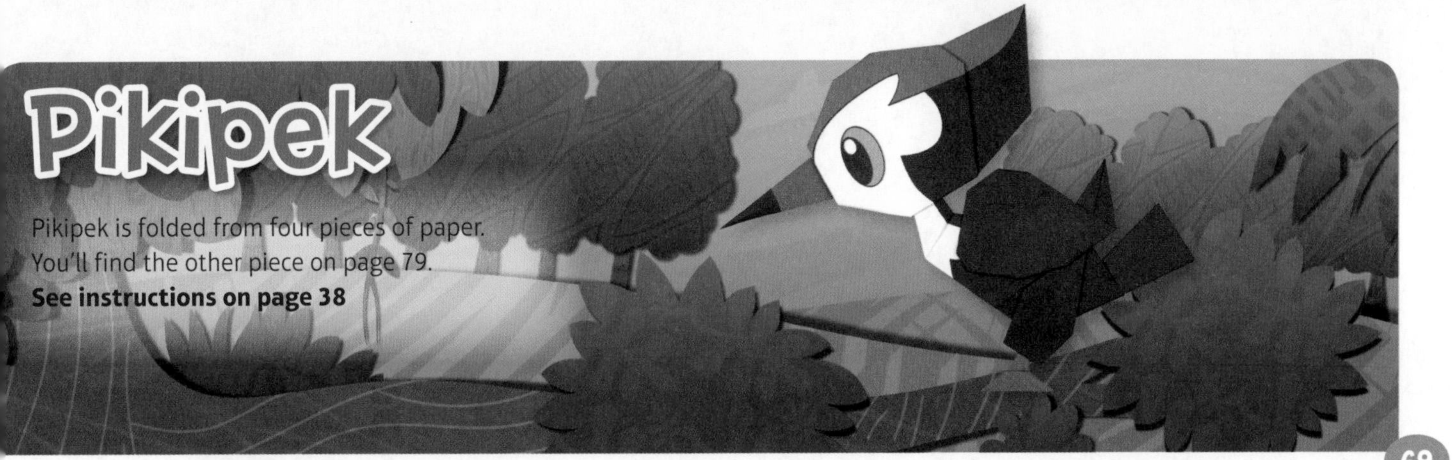

Pikipek

Pikipek is folded from four pieces of paper.
You'll find the other piece on page 79.
See instructions on page 38

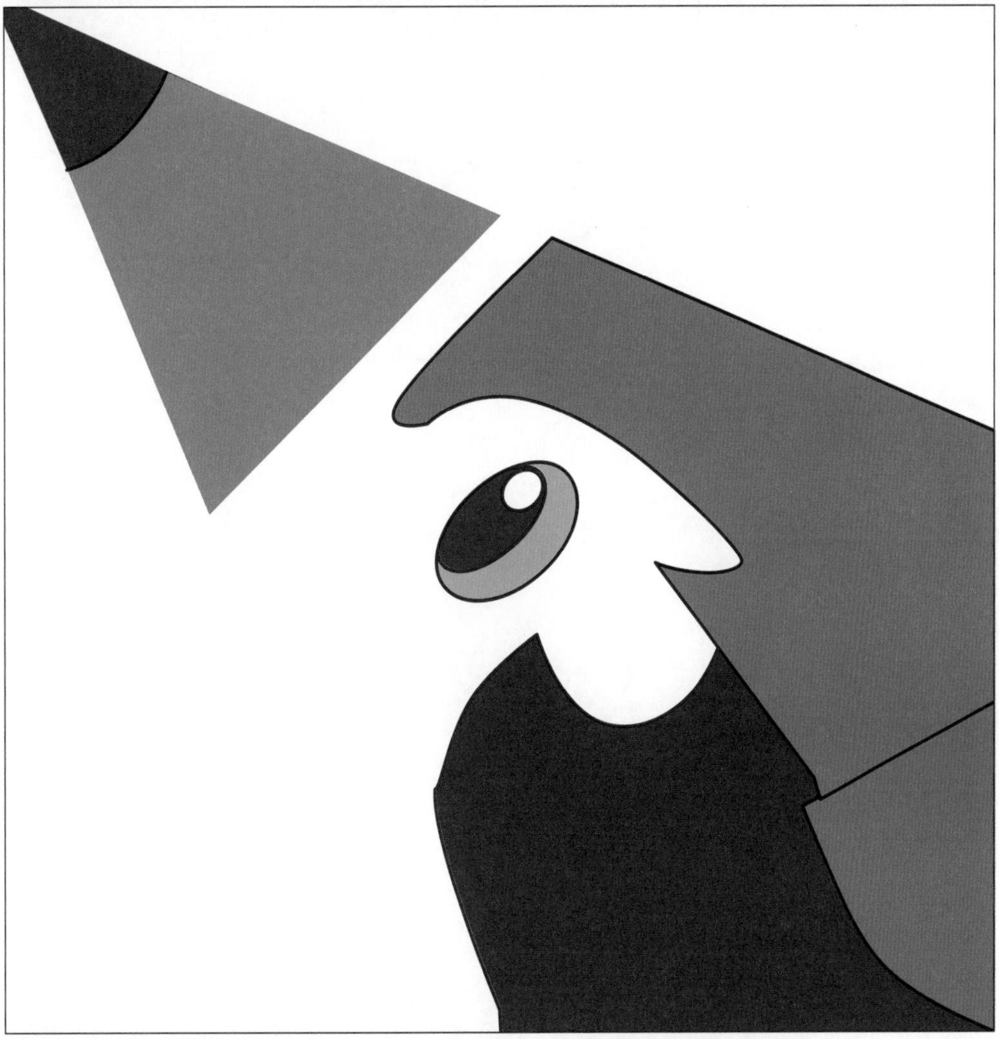

Head

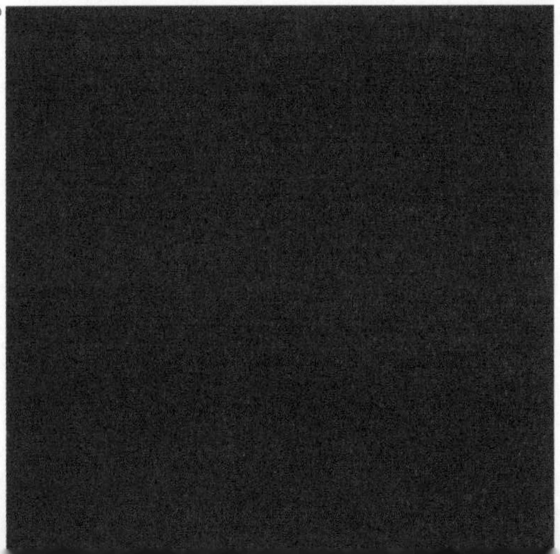

Wing

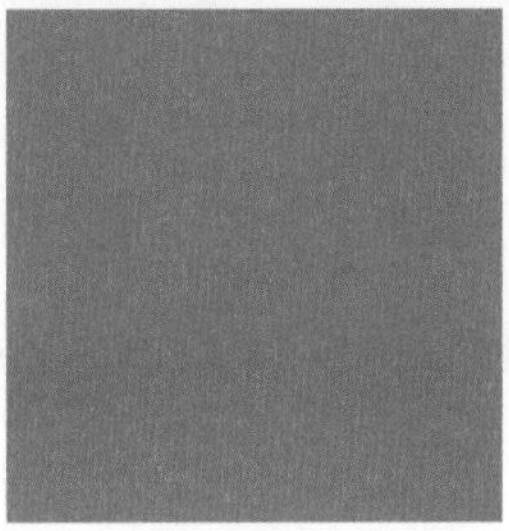

Foot

Alolan Exeggutor

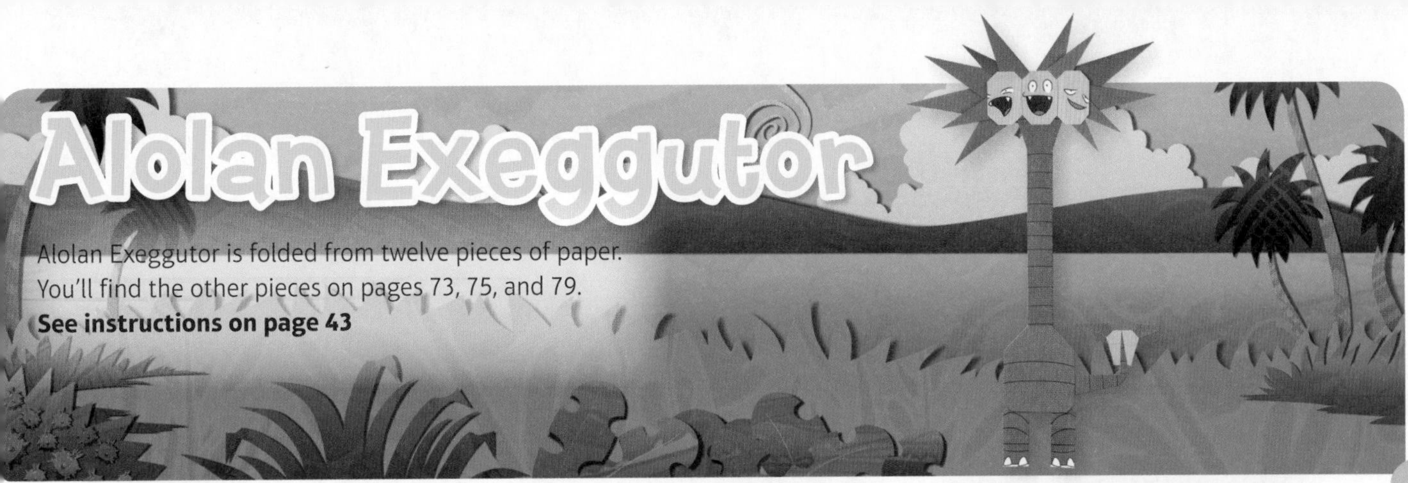

Alolan Exeggutor is folded from twelve pieces of paper. You'll find the other pieces on pages 73, 75, and 79.

See instructions on page 43

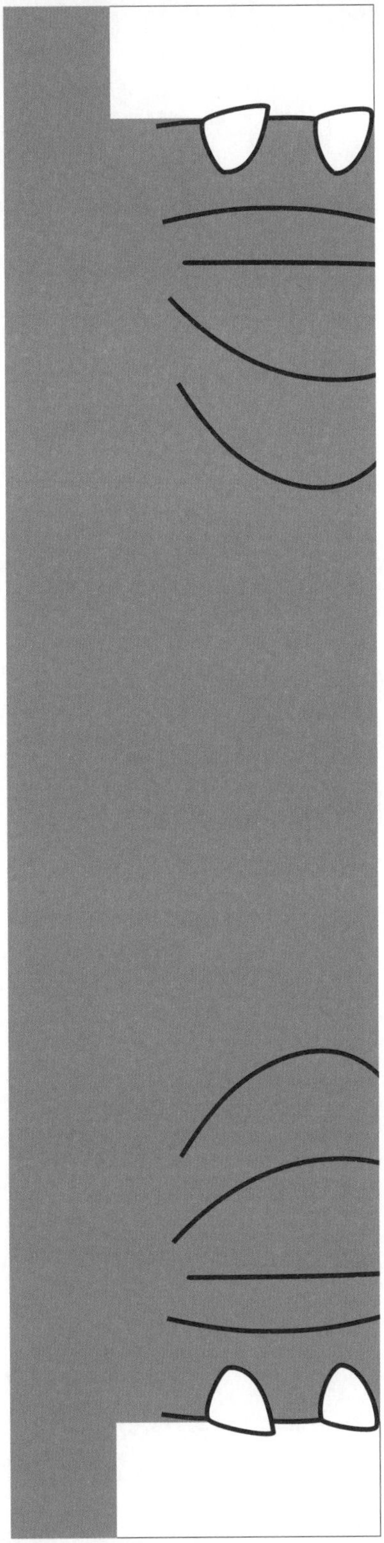

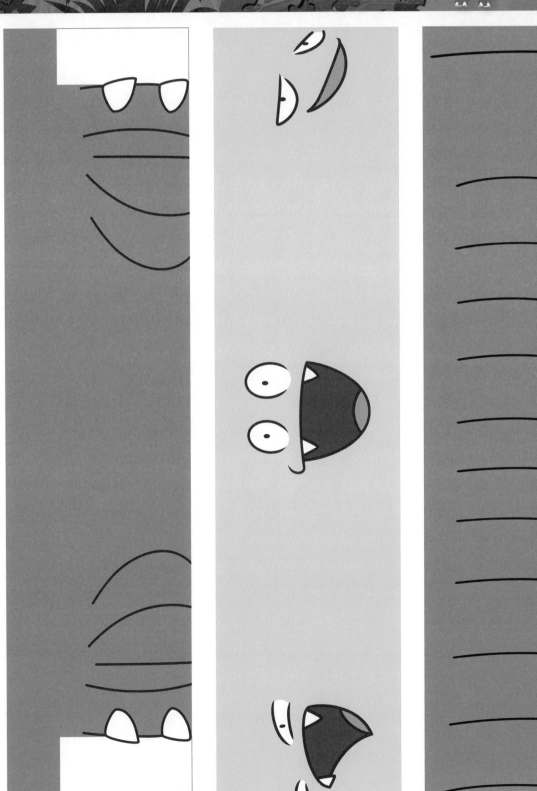

Legs

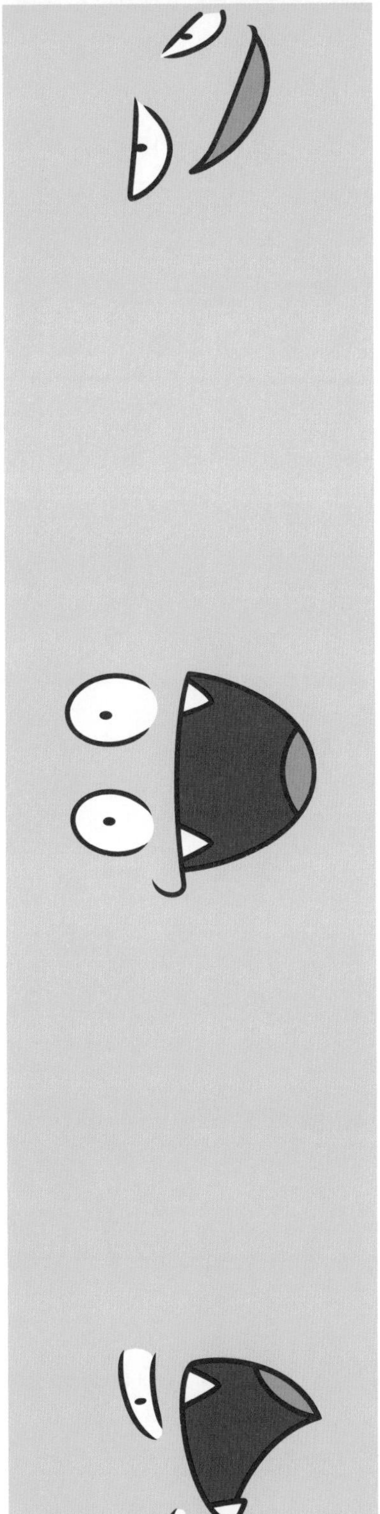

Triple Heads

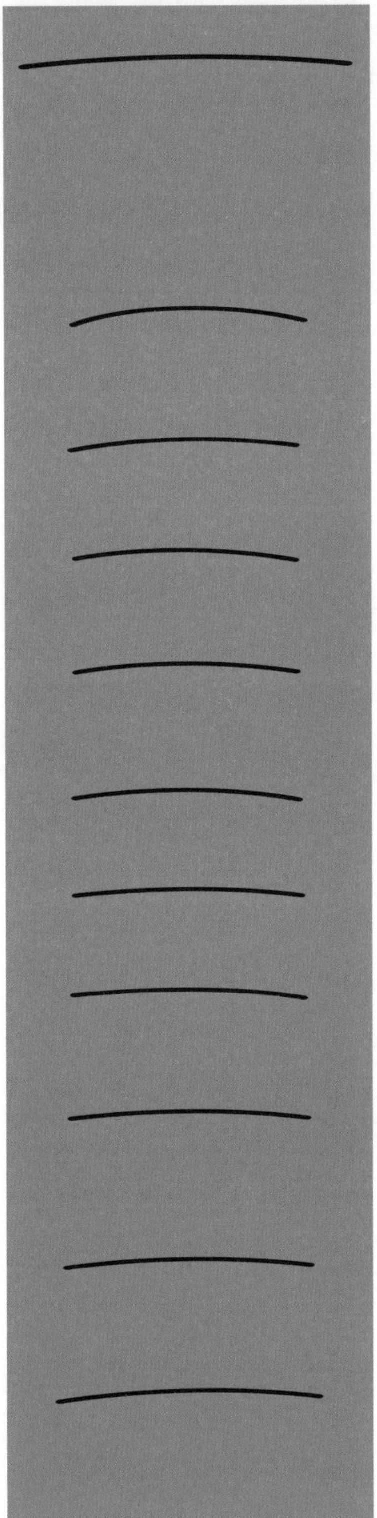

Neck

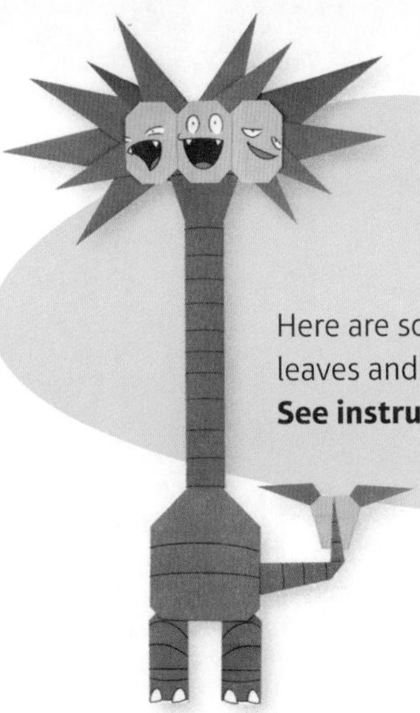

Here are some of Alolan Exeggutor's leaves and the head at the end of the tail.
See instructions on page 43

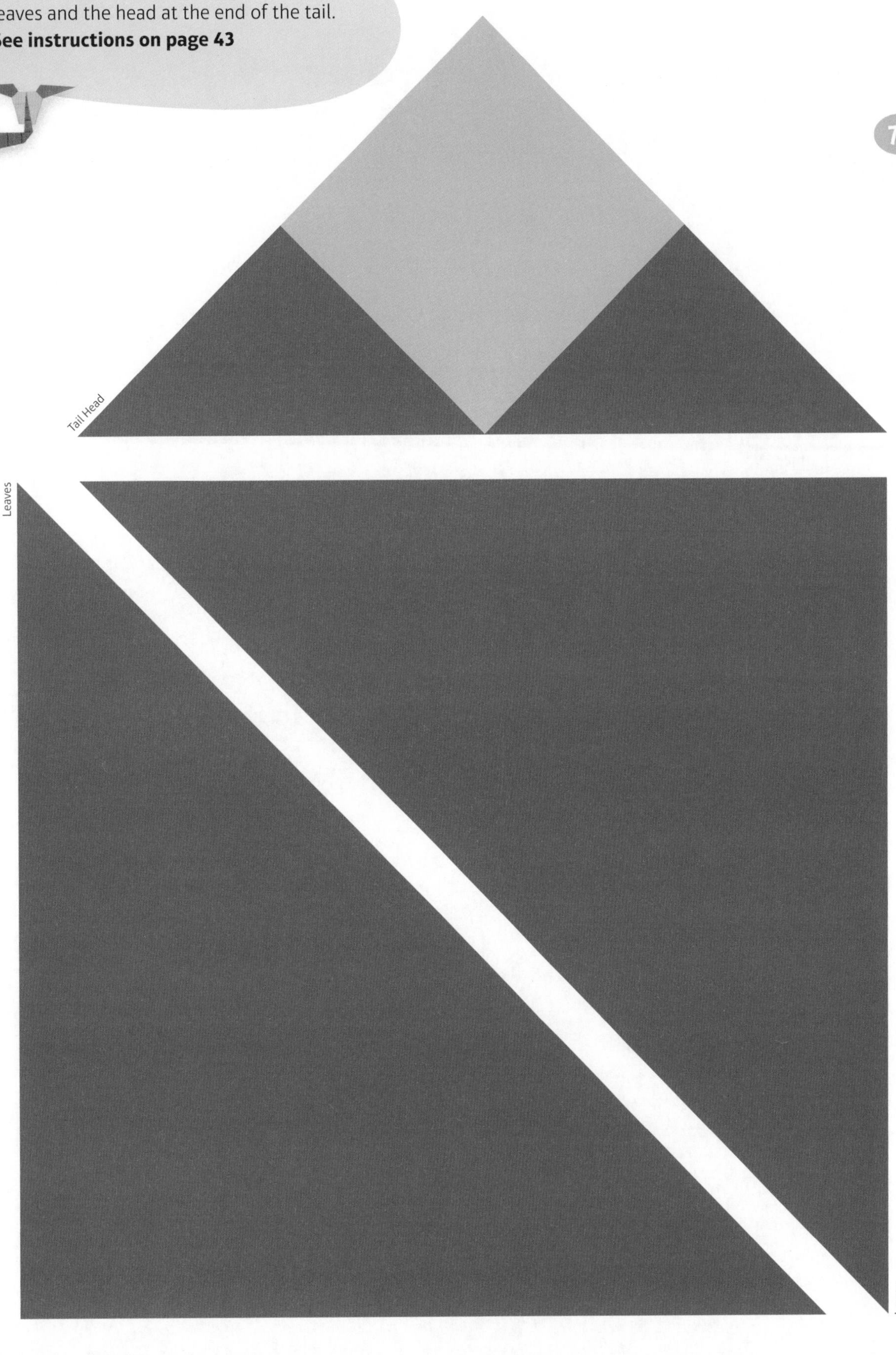
Tail Head
Leaves
Leaves

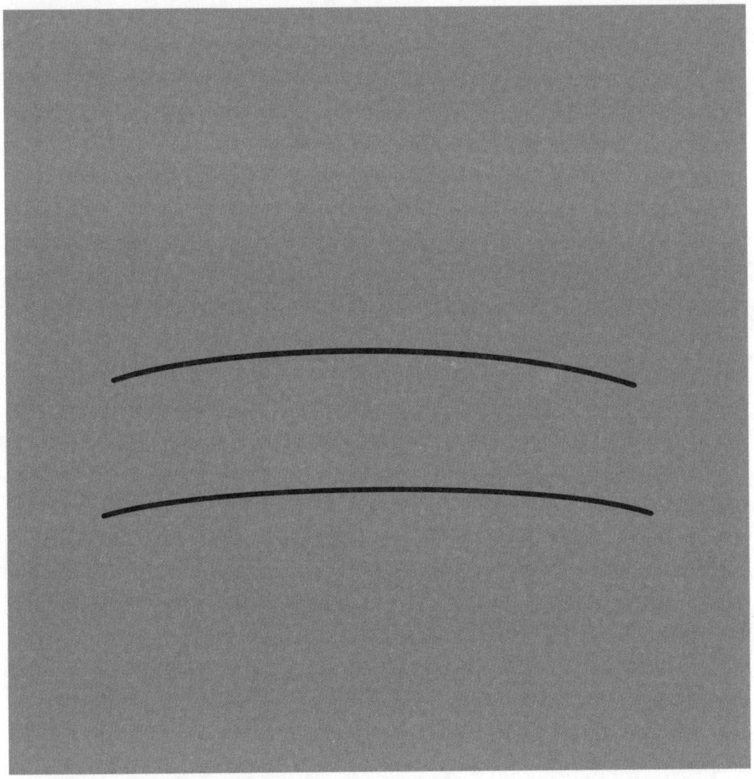

Body

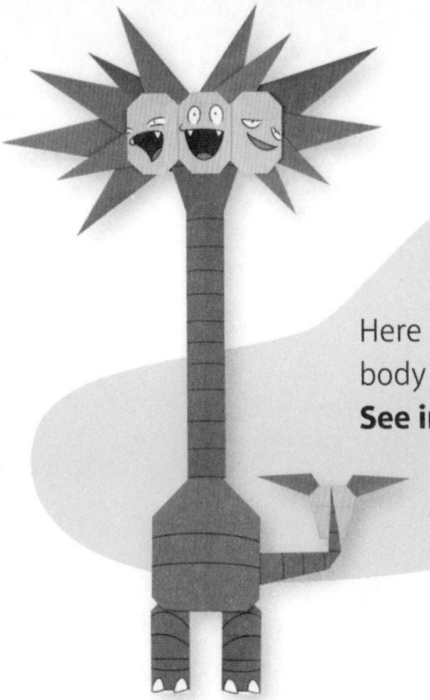

Here are Alolan Exeggutor's body and some of the leaves.
See instructions on page 43

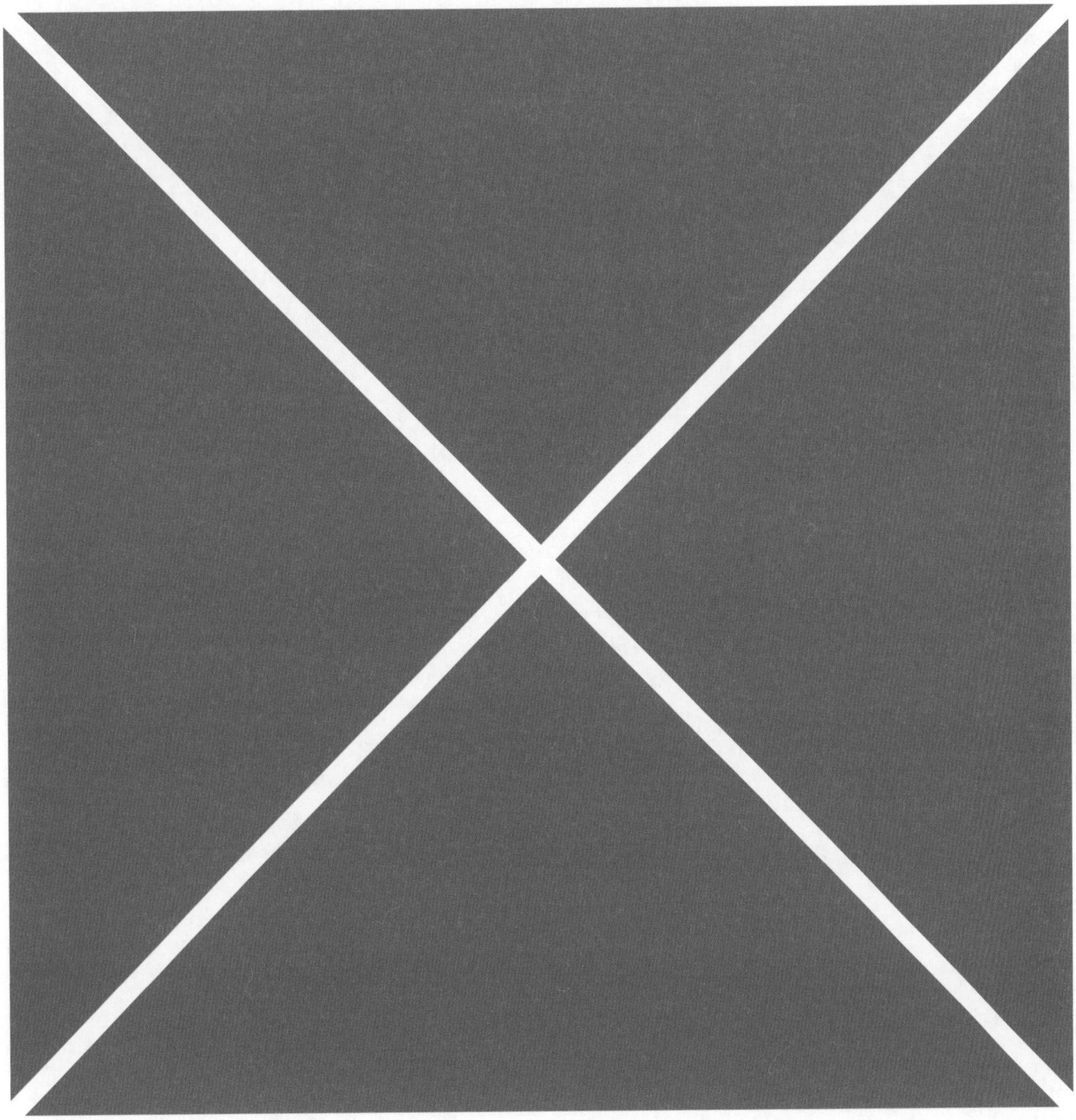

Leaves

*

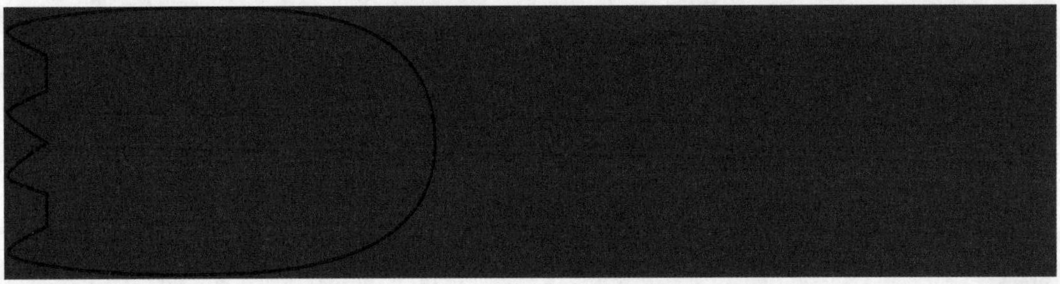

Litten's Tail (cut around the edge on this side of the paper)

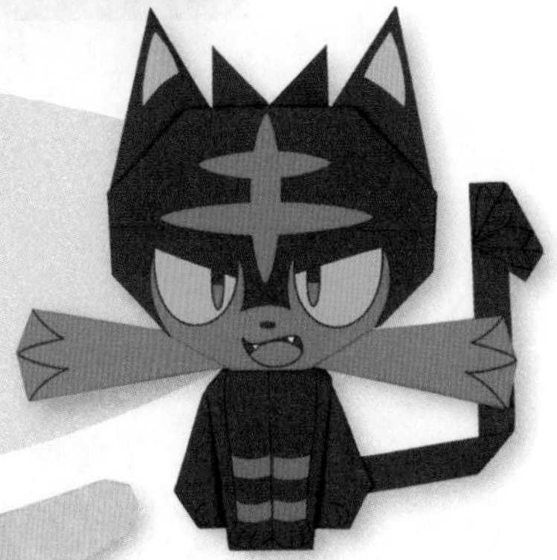

The dark rectangle is Litten's tail.
See instructions on page 28

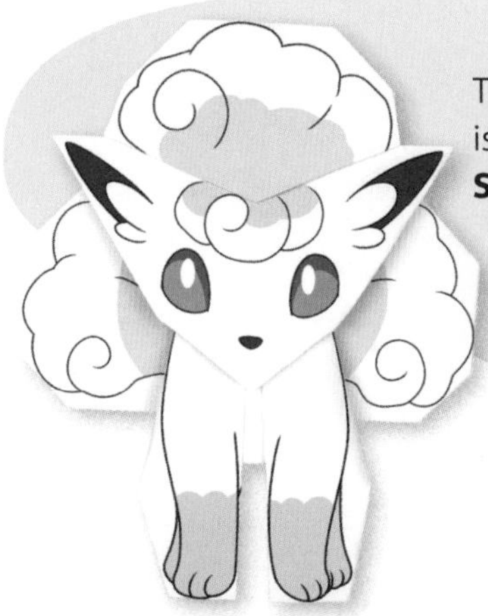

The white square
is Alolan Vulpix's face.
See instructions on page 33

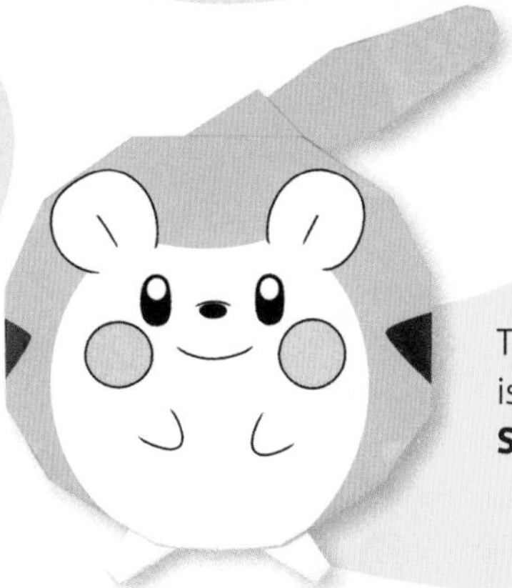

The yellow and gray rectangle
is Togedemaru's antenna.
See instructions on page 12

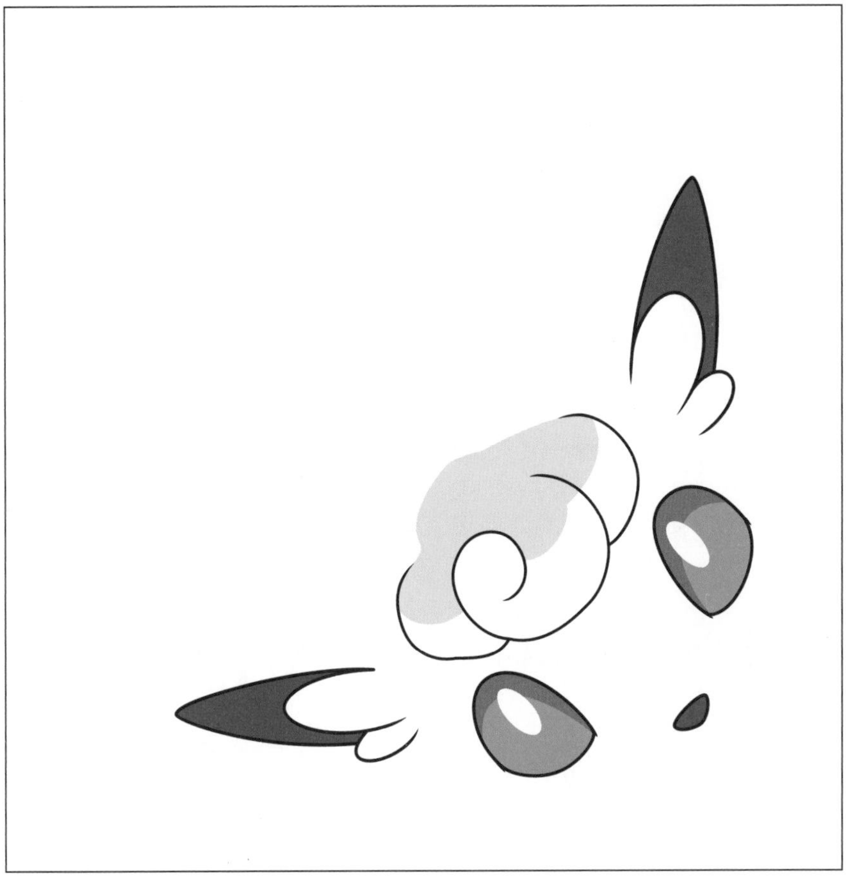

Alolan Vulpix's Face

Togedemaru's Antenna

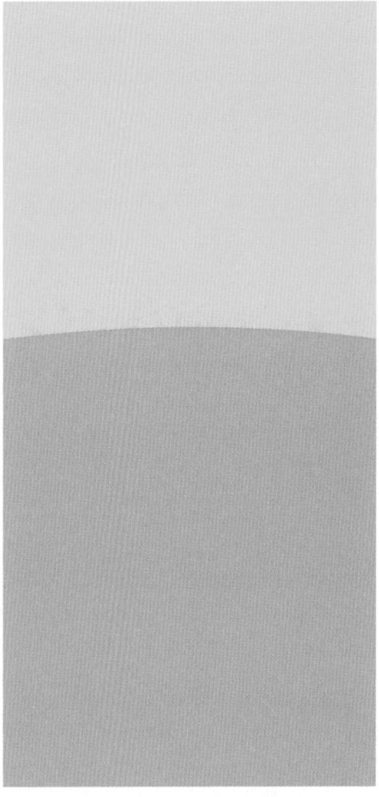

[redacted]

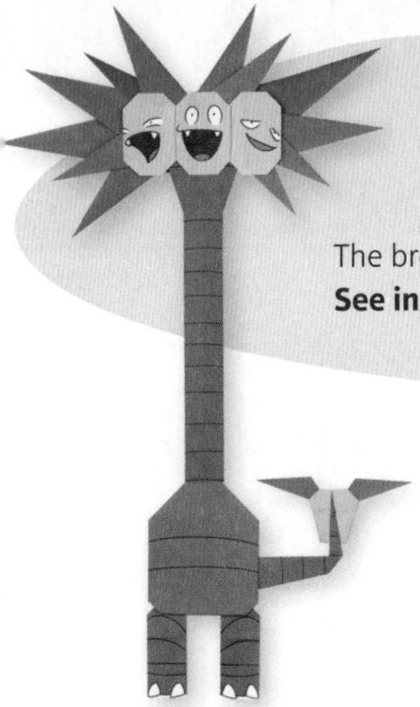

The brown triangle is Alolan Exeggutor's tail.
See instructions on page 43

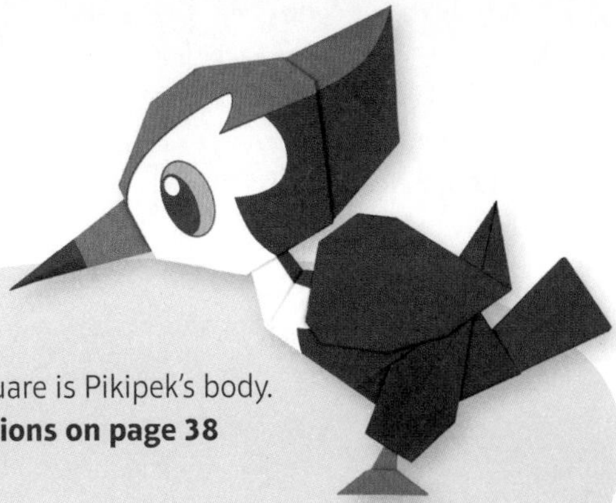

The large square is Pikipek's body.
See instructions on page 38

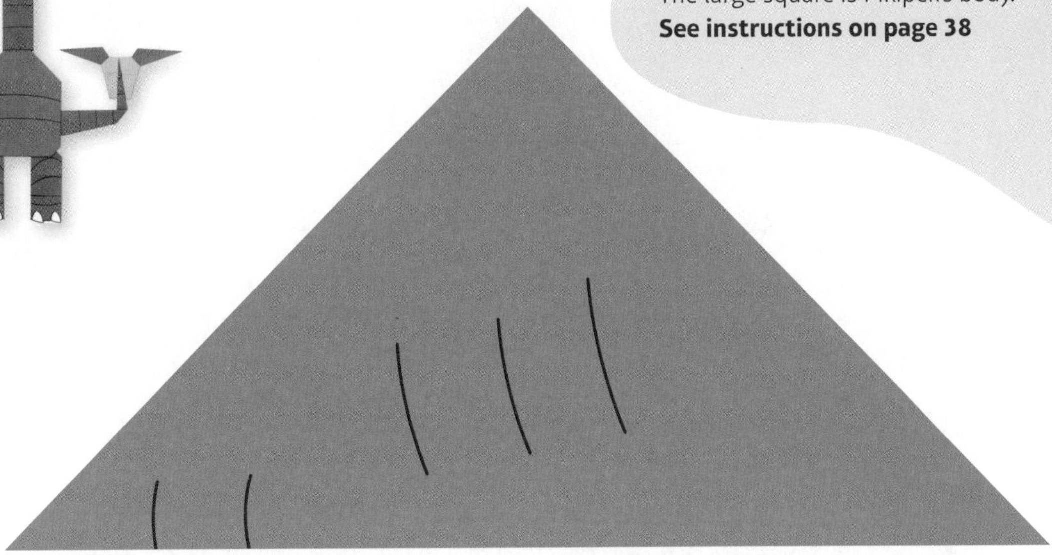

Alolan Exeggutor's Tail

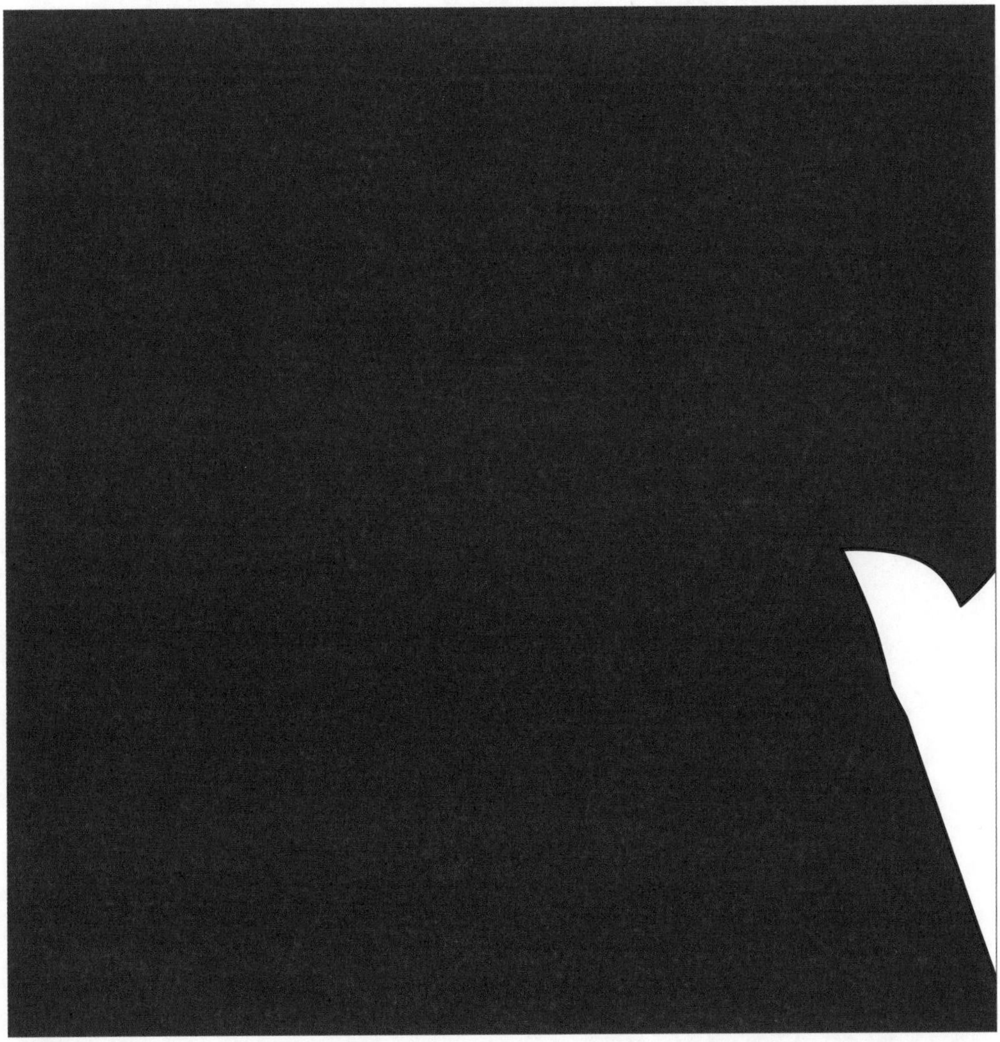

Pikipek's Body

*